The giant held the body of Sharif aloft,
ready to dash it to the ground...

Suddenly, he emitted a low growl. Shaking his head, he paced this way and that like a frustrated beast.

"What do you want from me?" he bellowed at last, foam bursting from his lips.

Erim was astounded. Had he detected a note of fear?

"Put him down," a soft voice answered.

The giant snarled, and lowered Sharif to the steps.

"Now," the voice continued, "come out of that man."

From nowhere came a sound like a titanic whipcrack. The demoniac giant arched backward, a mighty tumult of voices pouring from his throat; something huge and terrible was departing his distended flesh.

Then Erim heard the beating of many wings, and turned to see vultures rising from the ground. Squawking hideously, they circled for a moment before flying directly into the side of the cliff.

The stranger who had spoken stood before him, eating an apple with great calm. He pointed a thumb at Erim's broken arm. "Would you like me to fix that for you?" he asked.

The man reached to touch him near the wound. Consciousness teetering, Erim demanded...

*"Who are you?"*

# MARK E. ROGERS

# THE BLOOD OF THE LAMB

## THE EXPECTED ONE

ACE BOOKS, NEW YORK

This book is an Ace original edition,
and has never been previously published.

THE EXPECTED ONE

An Ace Book / published by arrangement with
the author

PRINTING HISTORY
Ace edition / May 1991

ISBN: 0-441-06826-X

Ace Books are published by The Berkley Publishing Group,
200 Madison Avenue, New York, New York 10016.
The name ''ACE'' and the ''A'' logo
are trademarks belonging to Charter Communications, Inc.

PRINTED IN THE UNITED STATES OF AMERICA

10  9  8  7  6  5  4  3  2  1

**To Sam,**
**who egged me on when I thought of it.**

# ╋

# Chapter 1

Beautifully delivered, the last blow of the padded quarterstaff brought a collective grunt from the spectators surrounding the sparring-pit; practically feeling the jolt beneath his own chin, *Sibi* Iyad Hamchari grimaced and almost looked away.

*Poor Kassim,* he thought as the victim's feet lifted from the packed earth. Master Iyad had been a diver in his youth; Kassim's backward arc reminded him of cuttlefish he had seen shooting through the water. But there was no cloud of ink now, only a few droplets of blood, trailing behind Kassim through his protective wire-mesh mask.

Iyad rubbed his jaw, looking at the other young men sprawled about the floor of the pit. Fifth-Level Adepts, all had studied logic and doctrine under him.

*I hope Sharif hasn't rattled their brains too much,* he thought.

Their conqueror, Sharif Ben Shaqar, was also a student of his, and Iyad loved him dearly. Indeed, as far as he knew, the whole Order loved that valiant, exuberant soul. But so terrible was Sharif's onslaught with sword or quarterstaff that one's heart went out wholly to his prey. Once, in the thick of a battle against the Black Anarites, Sharif had split the skull of a man

1

who had laid Iyad low. The Master had never forgotten the smashed-melon sound, nor the thunderstruck look in the devil-worshipper's eyes; just summoning it to memory made his head ache.

The spectators began to recover from the impact. Eyes shining with delight in his prowess, Sharif lifted his staff on high. The gymnasium rang with cheers. Turning toward Iyad, he leaned the weapon against his chest and held up six fingers, asserting that he had all but attained the Sixth Level. Iyad laughed and nodded.

Sharif repeated the gesture in the direction of his close companions, Erim Sawalha and Nawhar Barak. Erim answered with seven fingers. Dour Nawhar made no response.

The vanquished rose slowly and unsteadily. Healers came forth to inspect them. Sharif removed his helmet and went to thank his antagonists, shaking their hands, coming last of all to Kassim. Kassim laughed dizzily and tousled Sharif's sweaty black hair before a healer led him away.

*Sibi* Akram Hawatma, who had served as the referee, climbed the stairs from the pit. Mounting his platform, he stretched forth his arms, quieted the throng, and cried:

"You've passed the Second Trial, Sharif Ben Shaqar. May God grant you fare as well in the third and last."

Sharif bowed and started for the steps.

Akram rejoined Iyad and the other Masters. Skin a dark leathery red, white hair close-cropped, Akram was the Order's Master of the Martial Arts. He was in his mid-sixties, but his compact body was still a model of conditioning, the great muscles of his chest clearly defined beneath his robes. Iyad wished he was so well preserved.

"Our pupil is a force to be reckoned with," Akram said.

"We knew that already," said *Sibi* Khaddam Al-Ramnal, the Master of Sorcery. "He certainly profited by your instruction, if that display was any indication."

"To be honest," Akram said, "I suspect that I've played the least part in his development."

"His aptitudes *are* extraordinary," Khaddam agreed. "It's the same with the magic. Sometimes I'm tempted to stand back and let him teach for me." He looked at Iyad. "But his intellectual gifts aren't quite so remarkable. Does that mean we have to credit you for his performance in the First Trial?"

"Not entirely," Iyad replied. "Erim and Nawhar worked with him day and night."

"He's fortunate to have such friends," Khaddam said.

"God loves him. He'll make Master someday, and earlier than most."

"We are, after all, a wizard's order, first and foremost," Khaddam agreed. "Will you be coming to the Third Trial?"

Iyad shook his head. "The outcome's hardly in doubt. And besides, this is an ideal day for planting."

"You and your garden," Khaddam said.

"Need I remind you that labor was not always so despised in this Order?" Iyad replied. "Consider the Grand Master Ghaznavi. He set great store by horticulture."

"Ghaznavi, Ghaznavi," Akram said thoughtfully, putting a hand to his brow. "Wasn't he the one who raised up Mancdaman Zorachus?"

"What does Zorachus have to do with my private plot?" Iyad asked.

"Indeed, what does Ghaznavi?" Khaddam responded. "Times change, Iyad. We felt the need to impress others with our humility."

"Whereas now, in our newfound wisdom, we no longer regard humility as a virtue at all?"

"*False* humility *is* no virtue. What's gained by grubbing in the earth alongside our tenants?"

"Melons," Iyad answered stoutly.

"He *does* grow the best melons," Akram told Khaddam.

"Admit it, Khaddam," said Iyad.

Khaddam weighed the point. Massive, broad-shouldered, he loomed over the other Masters, rubbing his thick but carefully trimmed beard. Only on his chin did it retain any vestiges of its original red—the rest had gone the color of old ivory. His face showed numerous scars, fine silvery lines. Akram and Iyad watched him with bated breath, wondering what he would say. It was a rare thing when he admitted defeat in an argument. Then again, he was rarely defeated, even when pitted against the Master of Logic and Doctrine.

"Go forth and grub," he said at last.

"Make a note of this, Akram," Iyad said.

"I will," Akram replied. "Now off with you, before he starts up again."

As Iyad headed away, he heard Khaddam sigh: "Ah, logic."

But before making for the fields, the Doctrine Master decided to stop at Sharif's armoring-chamber. A crowd of lower-level Adepts clustered around the door, all adoring admirers of Sharif; Iyad shooed them away, then went in.

Lying on his cot, Sharif was still in his armor. Erim sat next to him, passing him a wine-skin. Nawhar was standing against a wall, looking on disapprovingly. Sharif and Erim jumped up as Iyad entered.

"Wine?" the Master asked. "Before the Third Trial?"

Erim took the skin back from Sharif, as though this might spare his friend some embarrassment.

"Would you care for some, *Sibi*?" Sharif asked.

Iyad shook his head.

"I only had a bit," Sharif said.

"There was a time, Sharif," Iyad began, "when the span between Trials was spent in contemplation. In composing the soul, not drinking wine and receiving well-wishers."

"And why did *you* come by, *Sibi*?" Erim asked politely.

Iyad eyed Erim. Erim had a look of absolute innocence on his round face, as though to show he could not have meant anything by the question. But Iyad knew better. Erim was a master at turning arguments back upon themselves; and Iyad was too much a logician to be annoyed by Erim's slight insubordination.

"I came by . . ." Iyad said, turning his eyes to Sharif, "to tell you that I won't be at the Third Trial, and . . . to wish you luck. My prayers will go with you."

"Thank you, *Sibi*," Sharif said. "But where will you be?"

"My presence isn't required. I wish to do some gardening."

"Are you so certain I'll win, *Sibi*?" Sharif said.

"Aren't you the greatest wizard since Zorachus?" Iyad asked. "Even greater, perhaps?"

"There *are* rumors to that effect, yes," Sharif replied. Erim nudged him with an elbow. Sharif was not known for modesty about his sorcerous abilities.

"Furthermore," Iyad continued, "I don't need to watch you destroy anyone else today. The last Trial was quite enough for me. You really should cultivate more restraint. Hasn't Akram ever talked to you about it?"

"Master Akram encourages him," Nawhar put in sourly. "He says the padding's enough protection, and that the Trials should approximate real combat as closely as possible."

Iyad considered this. In a deceptively pleasant way, he always insisted on the utmost rigor from his own students; then again, he had never heard of anyone losing their teeth to a syllogism.

"I'd prefer to err on the side of caution," he said.

"You are a man of reason, *Sibi*," replied Nawhar.

"So is Master Akram."

"That's what he always tells us," Nawhar answered. "He contends that the Martial Arts are a form of logic. *Practical Dialectics,* as he puts it."

Iyad laughed. But Nawhar did not. That was totally in character. He seemed to have no sense of humor; moreover, the idea of practicality was genuinely distasteful to him. A born ascetic, he preferred his words abstract, never made flesh. But he had a fine mind, and possessed specialized talents which made it possible for his superiors to ignore certain aspects of his thought that seemed to verge on the heterodox. His appearance was perfectly in keeping with such an earnest, otherworldly personality. He was small and slender, extremely pale, with wide dark eyes; his nose was long and very sharp.

What a contrast with Erim! Everything about him said that here was a man who loved life and the physical world. He was tall but ran to fat, and Iyad guessed that in later life that handsome but double-chinned face would become a classic winebibber's countenance, the very image of the jolly, slightly tipsy Sharajnaghi who often figured in peasant tales.

Sharif, on the other hand, was cut wholly from the heroic

mold, rawboned, almost lanky, with a chiselled face that would have been too handsome but for the expansive spirit that informed it. A single look at him, and one thought instantly: *If it comes to blows, I want this man at my side*. In Sharif, the pure joy of combat did not seem the vice it clearly was in other men; he was like a warhorse scenting battle from afar, and saying "Ha!," a wonder of creation.

Even so, Iyad didn't want to watch him at work in the Third Trial. The two Sixth-Level wizards Sharif was about to lay low had been Iyad's students too. And Iyad was already smarting for them.

"In any case, Sharif," he said, "it's time you began your devotions. Erim, Nawhar, come."

"May God stand behind you," Erim called to Sharif over his shoulder.

"Out," said *Sibi* Iyad.

He kept a sharp eye on Erim and Nawhar until they quit the gymnasium; once he was sure they were going to leave their friend in peace, he proceeded along the spacious whitewashed corridors to his quarters. There he changed out of his master's robes into the plain gray habit he wore while gardening, took up his tools and seeds, and went out through the east gate into the fields.

It was a gray spring morning; earlier a fine drizzle had dampened the ground. He guessed there would be a good amount of rain for several weeks; then the Order would have to pay its yearly fee to the New Khan, who had taken control of the immense irrigation system the Sharajnaghim had constructed along the Gura River.

*The New Khan,* Iyad thought bitterly as he strode along towards his plot. In fact, the Mirkut invader Batu had controlled the Kadjafi lands for twenty years; but few Kadjafim had fully accustomed themselves to the fact. The Old Khans had descended from Urguz tribesmen out of the far east; the founders of the dynasty had been little less bestial than their Mirkut cousins were today. But the Urguz had eventually adopted the customs and religion of the people they had conquered, and so had become just another ruling class.

Batu Khan's Silver Horde, however, was still on the road

to civilization—and the Khan himself was setting a deliberate pace. Indeed, he was constantly bringing new horsemen in from the wasteland to replace followers he thought were growing too much like Kadjafim.

*If only we'd won,* Iyad thought.

At first, the Sharajnaghim had joined the Old Khan in resisting the invasion. Ultimately, they had been overwhelmed. But Batu Khan, while a cruel man and a savage, was too shrewd to try to destroy them. He had no interest in suppressing the Kadjafi religion. Knowing the Sharajnaghim were held in great esteem by the people, and having painful experience of their prowess in war, he allowed them to surrender and retain many of their holdings. Soon afterwards, when he found his newly won power challenged by the Black Anarites, he had solicited aid from the *Comahi Irakhoum.* And once the Anarites were defeated (but also allowed to surrender), he tried to draw the Sharajnaghim more closely into his embrace.

He offered free water; he offered more lands, and high posts in his government and army. Not a year went by when these bribes were not repeated and embellished. But the Sharajnaghim had not become his servants.

*Yet,* thought Master Iyad. *Perhaps the Expected One will Deliver us . . .*

He shook his head, dismissing the hope. Someday the Anointed would surely liberate the oppressed of Thorgon Karrelssa. Still, Iyad knew in his heart that he would never live to see it. He had seen so many false Messiahs. *Condemned* so many. . . .

He reached his plot. It was marked off by a low wall of small stones; no matter how many he unearthed, there never seemed to be an end to them. Scanning the fields, he saw scores of the Order's tenant farmers, but there were none within a quarter-mile. Pity; he enjoyed talking to them. They were so refreshingly different from his colleagues. Or his students, for that matter.

The melon-patch he had planted was coming along nicely. There were creepers everywhere. He inspected the leaves. It came as no surprise that the rain beetles had arrived.

Putting down his equipment, he assumed a Griffin Stance

and loosed several bolts into the air, siphoning off repellent force and releasing his binding-powers. Removing a pouch from his belt, he took out a handful of small round eggs, uttered a brief spell, and hurled them into the air. Instantly they hatched, freeing a squadron of little black birds. Within moments every melon-leaf in the patch was scoured free of beetles.

The birds sped back towards Master Iyad. He lifted the pouch, spreading its mouth wide. The birds darted upwards. He craned his neck back, watching them gather overhead. Tucking in their wings, they curled up and plummeted. He caught high, thin cries, like the shouts of children sliding down wet rocks on a riverbank; the falling black balls whitened as the birds resheathed themselves in leathery shells, raining past his face into the pouch. Looking down, he saw the last egg bounce and settle atop the rest, and pulled the drawstring taut.

He considered what to do with the empty patch beyond the creepers. It was either cucumbers or *more* melons—he had seeds for both.

Ultimately he decided on the latter. His last few melon-crops, raised according to new principles of his own devising, had totally ruined his peers for melons grown by the tenants; he wanted to make sure he kept the Seventh Level well supplied. The teasing about his gardening had already decreased considerably.

He was about to pick up his tools when his attention was drawn to several blanched leaves among the creepers. As he watched, more and more leaves began to pale. A large leprous discoloration spread outward through the green, the plants in the center of it curling and withering.

Furious, he stamped and swore, immediately repented the blasphemy. This was some lower-level Adept's work, he was sure of it. He was regarded as a figure of fun in some of the younger circles, where the disdain for physical labor had gone well beyond anything to be found among the Masters. His crops had suffered from other such pranks.

He rose and resumed his Griffin Stance, plucked a counterspell from memory. But the blight was no longer spreading so quickly. He elected to let it run its course—a counterspell would damage the evidence. This time he intended to uncover the culprits.

The withered spot was perhaps ten feet in circumference when it ceased expanding. He went in among the vines, reaching the edge of the affected area. The plants there were still shrinking, knotting upon themselves with a dry crackling noise. Out in the middle, they were already crumbling into powder.

As the residue settled, Iyad noticed something lying on the ground, dusted white. He entered the blighted circle, squinting. *Some sort of mask,* he decided. A finely crafted one at that. Almost on top of it now, he reached to pick it up—

And paused at the last moment. He had assumed the object was lying flat on the surface, but saw now that it protruded from the earth—could it be that it was not a mask after all?

*Impossible,* he thought. Yet the longer he stared, the more his horrible certainty grew.

*A corpse? Buried in my garden?*

A burst of wind spilled the powder from the face onto the moist ground, where it stuck. A shock of recognition struck him.

Mirrors were a vanity frowned upon at Qanar-Sharaj. The concubines and wives in the Women's Quarters had them, but Iyad, following the ancient tradition, was celibate. He had not peered into a looking-glass in years.

Still, he knew. With its heavy-lidded eyes, high cheekbones, and thick moustache, the face was identical to his.

*Trap,* he thought—

Just as the ground erupted in black, jointed legs. Hooking over his back, they knocked him to his hands and knees.

He tried to slip out from under them, not knowing that the legs were armed with spurs, and that his flesh was already deeply snagged. Jerking to an agonized halt, he realized his mistake. He attempted to drop to the earth, but the spurs were cruelly barbed, and held him fast.

He looked down at the face, tears dripping from his eyes onto its cheeks. Slowly its mouth opened. He could see no palate or tongue. It was like staring into a burrow.

Something appeared in the blackness. Orange and ovoid, it rose steadily, a second face, leering at him vilely with slitted

eyes and a thin-lipped smile. Bulging up out of the mouth, it
opened its own. Twin blood-red tongues roiled like eels. A
name leaped to Iyad's mind, a fearsome legend out of the
grimoires and the dim dead past:

*Morkulg.*

He searched his mind for spells, but the Influences were
against him. He could do little without assuming a stance.
Mumbling a formula, he felt the magic instantly dispelled by
the presence below him. He attempted another spell; the limbs
holding him jerked in response, spurs twisting, digging. He
coughed, the rusty taste of blood spreading down his tongue
from the back of his throat. His lungs had been pierced. He
was going to die.

He gasped out the first few words of a prayer. As if they
angered the thing in the earth, the jerking intensified murder-
ously. Falling silent, he continued in his mind:

*Please, Oh Lord, have mercy on the soul of this thy serv-
ant. . . .*

Beneath him, the tongues squirmed and lifted. After caress-
ing Iyad's chin, depositing a film of burning saliva, they
dropped back into Morkulg's mouth.

*Grant me Your Grace in the hour of my death. . . .*

The orange face began to sink between the other's distended
lips. Eyes widening, the demon grinned up at Iyad. Then, with
a burst of laughter, Morkulg plunged from sight, straight down
into the darkness.

Four huge mandibles thrust up on either side of Iyad's gaping
likeness. They threshed inward, crushing, rending. Iyad closed
his eyes, refusing to terrify himself with that grisly foreshad-
owing of his own fate. He would not play the demon's game.

Warm fluid splashed his face. His ears were full of a moist,
hateful, pulping sound. If only to block it out, he coughed his
prayers aloud once again.

In retaliation, more legs locked over his back. Spurs pried
and dredged, working between his ribs. Inexorable pressure
forced him downwards.

Into the splattering blood.

Into the churning fury of the jaws.

✝

# Chapter 2

Sharif stepped out into the duelling-hall. He could see the spectators in the gallery high up on the right, but could not hear them through the thick crystal panes that served as protection from stray bolts. Erim and Nawhar were there; the former showed Sharif seven fingers.

On the left was the Masters' gallery. Nine members of the Council had gathered, Khaddam and Akram among them. Yet there was no sign of Grand Master Ahwaz. The old saint had promised he would attend this Trial at least; it would have been his first official appearance since the stroke. Sharif felt a keen pang of disappointment, but quickly overcame it. There was nothing to be done.

*Heal him, Lord,* he asked. *Let him stay with us a little longer yet.*

He began to whistle, watching the doorway at the far end of the hall. Where were his opponents? He guessed they were in no hurry.

Eventually they showed themselves, two Sixth-Level Adepts, Ezzedin Moukarbal and Gamal Salameh. For Sharif to secure his elevation, it was not enough to prove himself equal

11

to one Sixth-Level wizard. Given luck and a proper configuration of the Influences, a mage of inferior rank (or even ability) might be able to defeat a single superior. Defeating two was quite another matter—in fact, Sharif had merely to achieve a stalemate.

But he was not about to settle for that. As the pair came nearer, he studied their demeanor. Ezzedin was trying to look confident, but was not very convincing; there was a bit too much strut in his stride. Gamal trailed behind, his attitude slightly hangdog, as befitted his situation. Sharif appreciated Gamal's realism, although he also thought there was something to be said for Ezzedin's approach. At least Ezzedin was trying to put a brave face on things.

They halted thirty feet from Sharif, standing almost shoulder to shoulder. That was strange; two wizards facing one generally tried to keep well away from each other, in order to divide their antagonist's attention.

*Do we have a plan, my lambs?* Sharif wondered.

Up in the Masters' gallery, Khaddam swung one of the protective plates aside.

"Sharif Ben Shaqar," he cried. "Would you elevate yourself to the Sixth Level?"

"I would, *Sibi*," Sharif replied.

"There are lions in your path. Can you best them?"

"If the Almighty Wills it."

"Very well." Khaddam swung the pane shut and raised his hand.

Sharif stared straight ahead, perfectly at ease. Ezzedin and Gamal appeared to be whispering to each other.

*The lambs are definitely up to something,* Sharif thought.

Out of the corner of his eye, he saw Khaddam lower his arm. Immediately Sharif entered a Dragon Stance, without shields.

Gamal leaped in front of Ezzedin, dropping to one knee in the Penitent's Gambit, both force-bucklers raised; Ezzedin assumed a Chimera Stance, overlapping Gamal's shields with his own.

*That's a new one,* Sharif thought approvingly. At the very least they had contrived a temporary standoff; clearly they had learned from the mistakes of others. Attacking him with force-bolts was quite useless—his fearsome reputation derived primarily from his freakish capacity to absorb repellent energy and fling it back doubled at whoever had loosed it. Even without additional repellent force, his strikes were awesome; he could shatter a shield with a single blast. He had been victorious in every wizard's duel he had ever fought, and none had lasted longer than the initial exchanges. Never had he been forced to resort to the simplest spell—although his conjuring powers were terrible indeed, as training exercises had made abundantly clear.

Still, he had never dealt with four overlapping bucklers before, and began tentatively. A mere probe, the cataract-bolt had little effect. He winced; looking at Gamal and Ezzedin made his head hurt slightly—their images rippled as through a curtain of falling water. Plainly they hoped he was going to try and batter through their shields—simply maintaining the screens drained off their repellent forces.

*Want to free your binding-powers, do you?*

True, loosing strikes would accomplish the same for him. But the Influences were not with him. And Ezzedin and Gamal could pool their energies, starting with spells before he could reply in kind.

He pondered his situation for a few more moments, then started forward at a run. The solution was so obvious. All he needed to do was touch their shields. The energy-barriers were repellent force themselves, stationary bolts. He would simply absorb them and strike.

He was halfway to his antagonists before they seemed to fathom his intention. Ezzedin dropped one of his shields and launched a blast of yellow energy; as it sped towards Sharif, it assumed the shape of a charging bull.

*A fine touch,* Sharif admitted to himself. He tried to stop, but the bull's head struck him before he could resume his stance. Unable to give the force immediate outlet, he took the full brunt. It was like being smashed full in the chest by a breaking wave.

*Good blow,* he thought, shaking his head, expecting Ezzedin to hurl another. To encourage him, Sharif staggered as if he had been stunned.

Ezzedin took the bait. Another yellow blast hurtled from his fist, taking the form of a leaping tiger.

Sharif snapped back into his Dragon Stance. The tiger sank into him with a puff of flame, but there was no shock this time; a surge of wonderful warmth rose through his chest and flooded up into his arm. His fist recoiled slightly as the energy, doubled now, flew out of him like a quarrel from a crossbow. *Two* glowing tigers, one beneath the other, coalesced out of the strike.

Ezzedin was trying to reform his second shield, but without success. The tigers crashed into the three remaining overlapping bucklers. The flash completely obscured Ezzedin and Gamal. When it faded, Ezzedin was kneeling behind his partner, the latter warding them both with a single feeble shield. Sharif demolished it with a cataract-bolt.

"Surrender?" Sharif called.

"Yes!" cried Gamal.

"No!" Ezzedin shouted.

The two of them exchanged words.

"Well?" Sharif demanded.

They leaped up, entering stances. What they intended to accomplish, Sharif had no idea, although he had to admire their spirit.

Crimson force exploded from his hands. Ezzedin and Gamal went over with their feet high in the air, like players in a farce.

Nonetheless, they had not done too badly. Masters had fared worse against Sharif. He strode to his antagonists and helped them up.

"I hope I haven't caused you too much discomfort, sirs," he said.

Swaying, Ezzedin looked at Gamal as though he saw several of him. "*Sirs*," he said. "As if he's still Fifth Level."

"I haven't been ordained," Sharif replied.

"Please," Ezzedin groaned. It was a mere technicality; unlike a Master's initiation, the Sixth-Level ordination was pure ceremony—no sacramental power was passed. "You're one of us now. So tell us, man to man. How did we do?"

"Very well, actually," Sharif said.

"I *thought* we had," Ezzedin said, clearly relieved. "I told Gamal here I had a good feeling. Before the Trial, that is."

"It's true," Gamal acknowledged.

"Who thought of overlapping the shields?" Sharif asked.

"I did," Gamal answered.

Sharif clapped him on the back. Gamal coughed.

"Took me aback for a moment there," Sharif said. "Good work. Good work all around."

Gamal's hangdog look immediately left him; he beamed.

Ezzedin pointed. Up in the Masters' gallery, *Sibi* Khaddam had opened the crystal plate once more. Gamal and Ezzedin retired in the company of two healers, who had been waiting patiently for some moments.

"A splendid performance, Sharif," Khaddam called. "You've certainly earned a place upon the Sixth Level. Go to your chamber. We'll send word when all is ready."

Hardly had Sharif bowed when Erim rushed out of the stair-well from the Adepts' gallery, followed at some distance by Nawhar, who apparently saw no need to hurry.

"Where's the rest of the crowd?" Sharif asked Erim, some-what disappointed.

"All your admirers?" Erim said. "*Sibi* Akram collared me and Nawhar before he went over to the Masters' gallery. Said we should tell everyone to leave you in peace—something about adulation being bad for your soul."

"Sounds like he's been listening to Iyad."

"Maybe so. But he didn't tell *us* to stay away." As though expecting a possible rebuke, Erim looked up at the Masters' gallery; but it was already deserted.

"Do you still have that wine?" Sharif asked.

"Drank it," Erim said.

"What shall we do until the ceremony, then?"

"Drink the other wine."

"And what about Nawhar?" Sharif asked, just as Nawhar came up.

"I'll watch you and disapprove," said Nawhar, quite mirth-lessly.

"Of course," Sharif said. "How else would we know it was you?"

"By the borderline orthodoxy of the opinions he's sure to express," Erim answered. "Which reminds me—he never explained why I'm wrong about Instantiation of the Divine Ideas."

"It's simple," Nawhar answered, scratching himself on the shoulder. "You seem to think that matter is so receptive to forms that God, following an original intervention in the natural world, would not have needed subsequent miracles in order to create human beings. That He could have planted seminal ideas into the archaic prime matter, and that all life as we know it would then have developed.

"But prime matter is by definition devoid of form or quality. Which makes it difficult for me to see why it would react at all, even *if* forms were introduced. At the very least, you must maintain that it contains the *capacity* for organization, even if the *pattern* of that organization is introduced from outside. But would not such a capacity be a kind of form? Is not receptivity a quality?"

"That sounds simple to me," Sharif said.

"It is," Erim replied. "Too simple."

"Then speak on," Sharif said. "I do love to listen to you two."

He made for the exit, Erim and Nawhar going at it hammer and tongs just behind him.

Once the preparations for Sharif's elevation were complete, *Sibi* Khaddam sent an acolyte named Kebir to fetch Iyad. The young brown-robe had been told that Iyad would probably be tending his private plot; but on the way to the main gate, he noticed that the Master's door was open, and went up to the threshold.

"*Sibi?*" he called. Beyond was a study, walls lined with books; to the left was a huge desk, covered with leatherbound tomes, scrolls, and official clutter. Papers were scattered about it for some distance.

An acolyte with a broom emerged from an adjoining chamber.

"Master Iyad won't let me touch anything near his desk," he announced. "Won't even let me pick the papers off the floor. Says he has a system."

"Is he in?" Kebir asked.

"Out gardening. Although I expected him back before now. He didn't take his lunch."

Kebir grunted, not thinking much of it. Going to the east gate, he went out into the fields. Off in the distance by Iyad's plot, coal-black ravens wheeled in the grey sky, some even now beginning to land. A lone vulture circled high above them, obviously drawn by whatever had piqued the rooks' interest, but unwilling to face their wrath.

Kebir saw no sign of *Sibi* Iyad, but that did not trouble him. He guessed the Master must be down on all fours, obscured by the wall surrounding his plot.

More ravens descended. Kebir grew puzzled—if Iyad *were* in the enclosure, would they have landed? Indeed, as Kebir drew closer, he saw that the wall was simply not high enough to conceal anyone, unless they were lying prone; nor, for that matter, were the plants growing within.

Yet where, then, was the Master? And what was attracting the rav—?

A frightful possibility occurred to Kebir. Without realizing it, he began to trot, then to run. As he approached, the ravens cawed angrily; in twos and threes they fluttered from that pale, bare circle in the midst of the melon-plants. . . .

Kebir leaped over the stone wall. "*Sibi!*" he cried, dashing for the denuded spot. "*Sibi* Iyad!" He kept shouting, waving his arms. The remaining ravens burst skyward. Black feathers drifted lazily to the ground.

One floated into the oblong depression in the direct center of the white circle. A human figure lay in the concavity, almost sunken from view.

Arriving at the side of the hole, Kebir had his first clear look at the body, and clapped a palm over his mouth. Turning, he stumbled a few steps, doubled over, and vomited.

* * *

Despite Akram's orders, a crowd of Sharif's young hangers-on came to his room to bask in the glow of his victory. They had the door blocked, and more than a few sat inside on the floor. Yet they had quickly forgotten Sharif, absorbed by the disputation in progress between Erim and Nawhar. Sharif might have been a demi-god when it came to sorcery, but his two friends were almost as famous for their murderous performances on the battlefield of logic.

"I believe matter is an illusion," Nawhar was saying, "because the concept is radically unsatisfactory. Compare it with the concept of Form. Is the idea of Form coherent? Manifestly. Can *triangle,* considered as an abstraction, be said to be incoherent? Of course not. Moreover, the very notion of *coherence* is predicated on the notion of Form.

"But coherence aside, can Form be observed? We observe it simply by abstracting the meaning of that question. Meaning resides in organization, after all.

"But can Form be observed apart from Matter, as a thing extant in itself? Certainly. A poem may exist, and be perceived, even before it is written down, indeed, even before it is spoken aloud. The laws of logic would be true even if nothing else existed. A or not-A? In such a situation, not-A, clearly.

"Now consider the idea of matter. Is it coherent? We've already been over my objections to the concept of Prime Matter. Can Matter be observed apart from Form? If so, I've never had such an experience. All physical objects are organized in some way. Indeed, it is the *organization* of matter that we perceive, not some underlying substrate. Matter proper must consist in such a substrate, if it exists at all. But its existence cannot be demonstrated in any way that I'm aware of. And something believed in which does not exist is an illusion."

"I was wondering when you were going to take a breath," Erim said with a smile. Nawhar remained impassive, though most of the listeners laughed. Erim went on:

"Some of your contentions have merit. But why go so far to cast aspersions on God's physical creation? Given your arguments, why couldn't we simply view Matter as a variety of Form and leave it at that?"

"Because that would do great violence to the meaning of both words," Nawhar replied. "When men speak of Matter as a thing in itself, they *mean* the substrate. And it is precisely that concept which should be relentlessly attacked. It is as perverse as believing that the sun literally rises and sets, or that the world is flat."

"Perverse?" Erim asked. "Are we talking about morality, or a mere error in interpretation?"

"Given the darkening of Human Intellect and Will," Nawhar answered, "is it really possible to draw such a distinction?"

"What exactly are you saying?" Erim inquired. "That our belief in matter is purely an outcome of the Fall? That the physical universe did not even exist *as an illusion* before our ancestors transgressed?"

"Precisely," Nawhar said. "And that the world we think we see is the creation of our own sinful imaginations. A phantasm willfully imposed on a spiritual reality that is fundamentally different."

Erim immediately objected: "It clearly implies in the Scriptures that the physical universe predated men, and therefore the Fall."

"I am not wedded to a literalistic interpretation of the Scriptures," Nawhar responded. "Nor does Orthodoxy require it. The Scriptures may be divinely inspired, but they were also inspired for the benefit of Fallen Man, who is convinced of the literal reality of matter. Would it serve God's purpose to leave men totally confused? Could they possibly digest the unalloyed truth from God's own point of view? Again and again the Masters of Doctrine have insisted that the Scriptures, particularly the earliest strands, were written after the fashion of folk-tales—divine parables, true in their essence, nonhistorical in their particulars. You yourself, Erim, in your promulgation of the idea of Evolution from Seminal Causes, are at odds with any literalistic interpretation of the Creation Parables."

Erim nodded. "That's true. But aren't *you* plainly at odds with many of the essential lessons that the Creation Parables teach?"

"And what are they?" Nawhar demanded. "I accept that Man was created by God, in His own image. And that Man fell from grace in the second generation, cursing us to a life of pain and disease.''

"But the parables also teach that *God* created the physical universe," Erim countered. "And that He saw that it was good."

"I accept the essence of that statement," Nawhar said, "though I am not entirely sure what that essence is."

"How can you accept a truth you do not understand?"

"There are things that I—and you, though you might not care to admit it at this moment—take on faith as mysteries; such as the fact that God could look at the heavens and the earth and decide they were good, even though he obviously would have known that they were good beforehand. In the same way, I can accept the notion that God, in some sense, 'created' the earth. But I am not sure that the Scriptures mean what we mean by the word earth. Perhaps nothing more is meant than the *illusion* of matter. In which case I would allow that the physical universe is good—but only inasmuch as it is part of the divine plan. God can bring goodness *out* of anything. Even our own feverish delusions."

Erim folded his arms on his chest, shaking his head. "Your reading of Scripture seems thoroughly perverse, to say the least. It is one thing to insist that the creation stories are divine parables. It is quite another to ignore the plain essence of the tales. It has long been an article of our Faith that God created the universe, and that matter is *fundamentally* good. This principle is explicitly stated in the tales itself, placed on the lips of God. Perhaps He did not speak the words aloud on the Third Day. But He inspired the authors of the Scriptures to write them down in His Name.

"There are those, Nawhar, who wish to deny that the Fall of Man ever took place. Citing their own difficulties with the story, they insist it *has* to mean such and so, no matter what it appears to mean; ultimately, they arrive at interpretations radically different from ours. But are they justified in this? Simply because parts of the story are confusing, does this mean we can rewrite the intelligible parts to suit any theological fantasy we wish to promulgate?''

"Certainly not," Nawhar answered. "But it all comes down to which parts are intelligible, doesn't it?"

"Please," Erim said. "Would you simply admit, just for once, that the Orthodox teaching makes you terribly uncomfortable?"

"The physical universe makes me uncomfortable," Nawhar replied. "I have suffered greatly from it." He raked his nails under his arm. "My skin rarely gives me a moment's peace, and there is no cure. My joints ache; Master Shoua has told me that I will certainly be a cripple before I reach my fortieth year. You and Sharif will probably become Masters; I will not pass the tests. My whole family died of plague. . . ."

"We know," said Erim, suddenly sure that he was going to lose this skirmish, and in front of all these youngsters too. Nawhar was not trying to play on their sympathies; he was too single-minded when it came to argument. But Erim sensed how they were reacting—because he felt the same. Nawhar *was* pitiable, and that fact was not irrelevant at all. Especially when Erim had asked him so personal a question to begin with.

"Moreover," Nawhar went on, "I refuse to believe that God is the author of my misery. I wish to locate its source *anywhere* but in Him. My foremost desire is to retain my faith in God. Is that not in total accord with Orthodoxy?"

"Well spoken, sir!" cried several of the listeners in high, callow voices. They seemed to break Nawhar's concentration.

"Where were we?" he asked Erim.

"You were admitting total defeat," Erim replied.

Just then there were more cries, faint at first, but swelling quickly. Erim began to make out the words echoing down the hall.

"Master Iyad is *what?*" Sharif asked.

Erim cocked his head. "Slain," he said.

"What?"

"Come on," said Erim. With Sharif and Nawhar he followed the acolytes towards the tumult. A large crowd had already gathered in a juncture up ahead; Adepts and brown-robes were pouring from their rooms.

"Where was he found?" Erim demanded.

"His plot," a voice shouted back.

The throng pressed towards the main gate. Erim and his companions managed to slip out in front, breaking into a run. As they raced out into the fields, Erim saw figures some distance ahead, already nearing the garden. Three were white-robes; Erim picked out Khaddam by build and gait, as well as Akram and Khaddam's lieutenant Samadhi Maruf, the Order's intelligence chief. A brown-robe had Khaddam by the hand and was leading him over the garden wall, gesticulating wildly. Ravens flapped aloft; a ring of men formed around something in the middle of the plot.

Within moments several staggered away. Erim, Nawhar and Sharif stepped into the gaps.

"God in Heaven," Sharif breathed. Nawhar went down on one knee. Dimly Erim heard Akram ask:

"*Is* that Iyad?"

The corpse's head was gone; the remains of the neck trailed into the bloodsoaked dirt in blackening rags, as though whatever had eaten through it had vanished into the earth, pulling strings and fragments down after it. From the waist up, there was barely an inch of habit that remained its original gray; stained purple with blood, the garment had been stripped away from the dead man's back, which in turn had been shredded down to the ribcage.

Samadhi bent and reached into the hole, taking the corpse's right arm and easing it out from under the body. There was no hand at the end; the stump was cleanly sheared.

Erim wondered dizzily what Samadhi was looking for, then remembered Iyad's ring. Each Master wore one, a silver circlet with the wearer's name engraved.

Samadhi gently lowered the mutilated arm, beardless face unreadable. He was the Order's youngest master; forty-five years old, he looked barely out of his twenties, his hair a lustrous jet black, swept straight back from his forehead.

"We may never identify him positively," he said, rising. "Still, given the location, I think it's safe to assume this was Iyad."

"Shall we move him now?" Akram asked. "Those ravens . . ."

"No," said Samadhi. "I must examine the site further. In

fact, we'd do well to keep the onlookers back. At least beyond the wall—"

"It was a sending, wasn't it?" Sharif demanded, almost choking with rage.

The Masters ignored him.

"Do you think we'll find the hand?" Akram asked.

"No," Khaddam replied.

"Who could have done this, My Lords?" Sharif cried.

"Silence!" Khaddam roared.

"Come, Sharif," said Erim, taking his arm. Rising, Nawhar took the other. They pulled him away from the brink.

"All of you, back!" Khaddam cried.

Sharif shook free of his friends after a few paces. The three turned.

Before them, Adepts and acolytes making for the hole had stopped in their tracks, stung by Khaddam's voice.

"What did you see?" the newcomers asked.

Sharif seemed not to hear them. "Who could have done such a thing?" he sobbed.

✜

# Chapter 3

Sharif's elevation to the Sixth Level was postponed; once Samadhi and Shoua Abu Anseh, who held the Chair of Medicine, had made a full examination of the corpse, preparations for Iyad's funeral proceeded apace. On the third day following the discovery of the body, the rite was held in the great rotunda at the heart of Qanar-Sharaj.

The beauty of the dome had recently been marred by a mysterious disease that laid waste to much of the ivy and flowering growths that lined the interior. With his interest in horticulture, Iyad had led the effort to check the blight; as if to mock his failure, one of the greyish withered areas directly overarched his bier.

Grand Master Ahwaz was in attendance, but still too ill to preside. Khaddam acted in his stead, sprinkling the shroud with blessed water, reading passages from scripture concerning the immortality of the soul. Then he enjoined his fellow Masters to speak. One by one, in their own way, they eulogized Iyad; Khaddam himself spoke last of all.

"I am in pain," he said, "so I will be brief. Nothing I say can express my sorrow. I have been pierced; I cannot come to grips with this loss. Even though I believe that there is life eternal, and that I will once again experience his friendship, that knowledge cannot dull my torment. For I must live out the long years without him, and his absence will be cruel.

"I was frequently at odds with him, I am the first to admit. But we never let our disagreements spoil our friendship. And always, even when I believed he was wrong, I acknowledged that his reasoning sprang from traditions, great and virtuous traditions, deeply rooted in our Order. He was the guardian of doctrine, dedicated to ensuring that the integrity of our beliefs was never compromised; and he faithfully upheld that charge. He was unswerving. He was tireless. He was formidable. The *Comahi Irakhoum* has lost one of its great sons. And have no doubt, we will seek out and punish the author—or authors— of his death."

A murmur rose from the assembly; this was the first official confirmation that Iyad had been murdered, although there had never been any real question.

Khaddam continued: "This day the Council of Masters will be gather to hear the preliminary conclusions of Master Samadhi; he has uncovered many clues. While we do not yet know the truth, we are well on the way to uncovering it. And when that day comes, let the guilty tremble."

Heads nodded in the crowd; eyes were sullen.

"But in the meanwhile," Khaddam went on, "let us remember: earthly justice serves only the living. If we would demonstrate the love we bore, and still bear, Iyad, we must help him in another way.

"A Sharajnaghi Master has died. Let us now ask mercy for the soul of Iyad Hamchari."

Lifting his arms, he led the assembly in prayer.

Later that day, once Iyad was interred in the Crypt of the Masters, deep beneath Qanar-Sharaj, the Council assembled in their chamber, seating themselves at the great semicircular table. Grand Master Ahwaz lay on a cot between the table's wings, propped almost into a sitting position on pillows, his paralyzed right hand resting across his once-ample belly. On his little finger shone his silver Seventh Level ring, on his ring finger the gold Grand Master's circlet with its blue diamond. Until the stroke, his hair had remained miraculously dark, even though he was well into his seventies; now it had gone white at the roots. He spoke with some difficulty, his pronunciation slurred; he sounded quite drunk.

"I think," he began, "that before we turn our thoughts to Samadhi's investigation, we should consider the elevation of a new Master, to replace Iyad."

Iyad's position as Master of Logic and Doctrine had already been filled by his subordinate Massoud Namtar, the Order's finest scientist and mathematician. But that still left a vacancy in the Council.

"I can think of several candidates," Khaddam said.

On the other side of the table, Akram laughed. "Undoubtedly, all members of the Knot," he said, referring to a group of Sixth-Level Adepts whose progress through the Order had been carefully overseen by Khaddam; they were known jokingly as "The Knot of Serpents" because they were so close. But they were extremely able and for the most part well liked; all had distinguished themselves in combat, and their leader, Mufkadi Umar, was an expert in the formulation of new spells.

"Would anyone deny the achievements of my apprentices?" Khaddam asked. "Mufkadi, Karaz and Arghun Khan have certainly earned the opportunity."

"I couldn't agree more," said Akram. There was general assent from the other Masters.

"Arrange the Trials," said Ahwaz. "Mufkadi first, I should think." He shifted his weary gaze to Samadhi. "Very well, then. What have you learned?"

"Iyad was killed by a sending," Samadhi answered.

"You're certain?" the Grand Master asked.

"Yes," Samadhi replied. "First there's the matter of the withered patch among the vines. We examined the dust. The destruction of the plants was caused by the presence of a demon, perhaps more than one."

Akram interjected: "And you have complete confidence in these new techniques of yours?"

Samadhi sighed; he had been over this ground too many times. "It's been known for years that some spells release a burst of energy—a wave, if you will—that can alter the chemical composition of materials within a certain radius. The nearness of a supernatural entity can effect similar transformations.''

"Yes, yes," Akram said. "But—"

Khaddam rose to his lieutenant's defense. "Samadhi's methods are extremely reliable. Iyad and I oversaw his experiments ourselves. The tests have been brought to a very high degree of perfection."

Akram subsided. Khaddam's guarantee was very persuasive; the more so because he and Samadhi were frequently at loggerheads. The two were well known for their antagonism—an extremely ambitious man, Samadhi was a difficult if highly talented underling. It was common wisdom that he and Khaddam were simply too similiar.

"Proceed, Samadhi," said Ahwaz—and Khaddam, both at once.

Samadhi nodded. "Leaving aside the question of chemical evidence, there's the matter of the depression where we discovered the corpse. It seems to have been created by the collapse of a cavity in the ground under Iyad. Given the evisceration of the victim, and the fact that portions of the neck were buried in the earth, I conclude that an entity was lying in wait just under the surface; and that the hollow it occupied gave way beneath the corpse once the demon returned to its own plane."

"But you suspect that more than one demon was involved?" asked *Sibi* Massoud, a Numalian black. He was diminutive, but his head was very large, the lofty brow rendered still more imposing by a receding hairline; if ever a man looked as though his skull was simply about to burst with ideas, it was Massoud.

"Possibly," Samadhi replied. "Not in the actual killing, perhaps; but the essences we discovered in the white dust seemed to indicate the presence of a second being. Also, there's the matter of the missing hand. The severed wrist was not consistent with the other mutilations. The hand was removed in an almost surgical manner, with a straight-edged blade of exceptional sharpness."

"For ritual purposes?" Akram asked.

"It would be a repository of considerable power," Samadhi said. "Particularly with the ring. But we can't be certain."

"And who do you think is responsible?" Massoud asked.

"Impossible to say at this point," Samadhi answered.

"But whoever conjured the sending, the spell was cast within seven miles of Qanar-Sharaj. It could have been done as far away as Thangura. Or inside these walls."

"You're saying that a *Sharajnaghi* might be the killer?"

Samadhi shrugged. "Membership in the Order doesn't cleanse us of the effects of the Fall. Must I remind you that there have been evil Sharajnaghim? Consider Zorachus. The most murderous evildoer who ever lived."

Massoud weighed Samadhi's points—and chose not to answer.

"But certainly," Samadhi continued, "we have no *good* reason to suspect that the conjurer is one of ours. There is, after all, the matter of motive. What could it be? For a Sharajnaghi, that is? Revenge of some sort? Against Iyad? Possible—but highly doubtful, to say the least. A less offensive man never existed. He was more sinned against than anything else—all those pranks, the mockery he had to endure because of his so-called 'eccentricities' . . ."

"Perhaps a disgruntled student was responsible," suggested Master Ghazal, a thin, distinguished-looking man with a sharp spade-beard; he supervised dealings with the Khanate and foreign states.

Samadhi dismissed the suggestion with a wave of his hand. Ghazal looked at him resentfully. Now that he had reached the seventh level, Samadhi frequently revealed a lack of respect for the old Masters.

"Well, then," said Ghazal, "Maybe we've been penetrated."

That was a deliberate barb; as Chief of Intelligence, Samadhi was charged with weeding out enemy agents. "I'm only human," he conceded. "Perhaps my efforts have failed. But it's not necessary to postulate that. Not yet. Our enemies had no need to enter Qanar-Sharaj. As I said, the spell could have been cast as far away as Thangura. The Khan's hedge-wizards and shamans might be more powerful than we've been led to believe. . . ."

"Nonsense," said Khaddam. "If that sending was conjured in Thangura, you know perfectly well who did it. You yourself discovered their outpost."

"Patience," Samadhi said. "I was coming to the Black Anarites. The attack certainly had all the earmarks. During the Almohad War, a hundred years ago, the Master Ibrahim Ben Shafiq died in virtually the same fashion as Iyad. The Anarites boasted openly that they were responsible.

"But that came in the midst of a protracted struggle. We've been at peace with the Anarites for some time. Once again we must raise the question of motive. Why would they attack us? Why now?"

"Has their behavior ever been dictated by rationality?" Khaddam asked. "They're worshippers of Athtar the Fallen, evildoers by definition. They no longer make even the pretense that Athtar is other than Tchernobog the Black Lord, rebel angel and prisoner of Hell. They acknowledge that God is God, then spit on His name and follow one whom He has damned. What insanity are they *not* capable of?"

"You won't catch me putting any particular insanity *past* them," Samadhi said, with the slight smile that had infuriated virtually every member of the Council at one time or another. "But before I'd attribute any particular insanity *to* them, I'd ask for somewhat more proof than we presently have."

"You yourself said the attack had all the earmarks."

"I did," Samadhi admitted.

Khaddam pounced. "Then we agree on the essentials, don't we? If we're struck, what does it matter if the blow was launched for—how shall I put it—*insufficient* reasons? Certainly blood has already been spilled."

"What then do you propose?" Samadhi asked, with a trace of sarcasm.

"Nothing precipitous," Khaddam answered. "You should by all means continue your investigation. But we should begin preliminary preparations for war."

Akram shook his head. A soldier to the core, he nonetheless detested bloodshed; he had seen far too much of it. When hostilities threatened, he was the Council's chief advocate of moderation.

"There's far too little justification," he said, Massoud and Ghazal seconding him with nods.

"One of us has already been murdered," Khaddam replied. "If the killing continues, we must be ready to strike back— and strike hard. We should settle our dispute with the Anarites once and for all."

With that, Ahwaz entered the argument. "Nothing in excess of the law," he said.

"With all due respect, *Sibi*," Khaddam said, "whose law? The Khan's? He wouldn't lift a finger to stop us. He fears the Anarites too."

"God's Law," said Ahwaz quietly.

"God created this Order *expressly* to fight men such as the Anarites, Grand Master. Was it his intention to deny us final victory?"

"Certainly not. But . . ." Ahwaz's voice faltered.

Khaddam waited several moments; when Ahwaz remained silent, the Sorcery Master resumed: " 'War is an evil. And when we must fight, we should try to conclude the slaughter as quickly, as decisively, as possible. Precisely *because* war is an evil.' "

Ahwaz nodded. It was a quote from one of his own dissertations. Khaddam's favorite method of dealing with him was to demonstrate that whatever line of action he wished to pursue was inspired by Ahwaz himself. Luckily for Khaddam, Ahwaz had lived so long, and had faced so many crises, that support for virtually any position could be found in his work. Between the implicit flattery, and the fact that Ahwaz no longer had any relish for decision-making, Khaddam had been very successful; even before the Grand Master's illness, Khaddam had begun to function as the Order's actual head.

But this was hardly usurpation. Khaddam was generally acknowledged to be the greatest sorcerer and most powerful intellect among the Masters. Moreover, he was Ahwaz's hand-picked successor.

Ahwaz closed his eyes, as though he were in pain. "And what . . . 'preliminary preparations' . . . would you recommend?"

"Increased surveillance of the Anarites and their allies," Khaddam answered. "And the drafting of a plan to attack Khaur-Al-Jaffar."

Located high in the Andohar mountains, well to the north of Qanar-Sharaj, Khaur-Al-Jaffar was a mighty fortress, the Anarites' chief stronghold and center of their slave-trading enterprises.

"Akram," said Ahwaz, "have you ever given thought . . . to such an assault?"

"As an intellectual exercise," Akram replied. "But I never convinced myself that we could succeed."

Khaddam said: "You told me once that there were weaknesses—"

"And it *might* be possible to exploit them," Akram acknowledged. "Still—"

"Look into it further," said Ahwaz.

Akram shifted in his seat.

"What do you require?" Khaddam asked. "A full vote by the Council?"

"Do it for me, Akram," said Ahwaz.

Akram cast his gaze tableward. "Very well," he answered.

"And Samadhi," Ahwaz continued, "double your efforts against the Anarites."

"It shall be done," Samadhi said, and looked at Khaddam. "It seems you have what you want."

Khaddam shrugged. " 'It is our destiny to destroy the Anarites,' " he said, once again quoting Ahwaz.

"Are you truly so eager for the final confrontation?" Akram said.

"I prefer consummation, yes," Khaddam replied. "Are you one of those who would rather travel hopefully than arrive?"

"No," said Master Akram. "God founded the *Comahi Irakhoum* to defeat the Black Orders. But who, besides the Anarites, are left? If they were destroyed, what would become of us?"

"The same old question," Khaddam said. "Why do you keep raising it?"

"Because it troubles me."

"Just as it troubled Iyad," Khaddam answered, nodding. "But why should we even consider it now?"

"Because we're contemplating the final moves in the game we were created to play."

"The Order has changed in many ways," Khaddam said. "I expect it will continue to change. We have numerous concerns now. We're the foremost religious authorities in the Kadjafi lands. We foster learning. We have the finest library in the world. Through our trading ventures, we employ tens of thousands. Surely all those things are sufficient to justify the continued existence of the *Comahi Irakhoum*. Even if the last Black Order were gone."

"But could we still justify our military strength?" asked Akram. "Our sorcerous power?"

"They guarantee the rest," said Khaddam.

"But their original purpose was not to safeguard our greatness. It was to combat evildoers."

Khaddam laughed. "There will still be plenty of evil for us to confront. Disease is an evil. Drought is an evil. Heresy is an evil. A greater evil than black magic, as I think even you would agree."

"I would. But is it best combatted with force?"

"You are so full of doubts today," Khaddam said. "Are you still aching for all the false Messiahs that have been put to death?"

"They were wicked men and deserved their fate," Akram admitted. "Nonetheless, as you know well, I wish we would get out of this business of investigating them. The Khan should do his own dirty work."

"You act as if we execute them ourselves."

"The Khan should do *all* of his dirty work. When we condemn these men for heresy, we might as well be wielding the axe."

"But you said they deserved death," Khaddam said.

"They have so far. But do we have the authority to sentence

them? When God spoke to Washallah Irakhoum, did He give
him leave to pass judgement on heretics?''

"No. But is there anyone better suited to the task than us?''

"That's not the issue.''

"I'm not sure you know what the issue is," Khaddam said.
"You seem to think it's the fact that we've been soiling our
hands. I see it quite another way. For me, the question is
whether these madmen should be allowed to inflame the people.
What if one of these imposters ignites a rebellion? You're the
Master of the Martial Arts. You fought alongside the rest of
us when Batu invaded. You, of all people, should know what
he's capable of. The Silver Horde numbers in the millions.
There were great cities in the East of which no trace whatsoever
can now be found; some of them were taken by assault ramps
made from Batu's own living troops. He said, ''Make a ramp,
there.'' And his men scrambled to obey. That is what we
Kadjafim face. And putting blasphemers to death is a small
price to pay to keep the Khan content.''

For some time, Akram did not speak. "But what if the *true*
Expected One arrives? What if we have to investigate *him*?''

"Are you saying we wouldn't give him a fair hearing?''

"Are you saying we couldn't make a mistake? Suppose we
condemned God's own Anointed?''

"I think God will know His own," Khaddam answered.
"And that we will not be able to thwart the Almighty, no
matter how obstinate and stupid we are. Furthermore, I believe
that when and if the Expected One arrives, I for one will have
no difficulty recognizing him.

"Which brings us—coincidentally—to yet another of these
Messiahs. A new one has appeared. Samadhi?''

Samadhi laid a scroll on the table. "We have this day received a request from the Khanate to investigate a certain Essaj
Ben Yussef.''

# ╬

# Chapter 4

Shortly after his elevation to the Sixth Level, Sharif was summoned, along with Erim and Nawhar, to the laboratory of *Sibi* Massoud. It was a large chamber filled with all manner of peculiar apparatus—special scales constructed to meet Massoud's arcane needs, complicated lens-assemblies for concentrating and redirecting sunlight, pumps for withdrawing the vapors from glassed-in furnace-ant colonies, treadmills for weasels; as Sharif and his companions entered, Massoud was in the process of loading a crossbow with a bolt whose tip was enclosed in a small leather pouch.

"What's in the bag?" Sharif asked Massoud's assistant, Farouk.

"Explosive," Farouk replied.

"It's not an explosive *yet*," Massoud corrected, somewhat irritably; he was well known for an irascible streak. "There's a treated capsule inside the sack. A spell will disintegrate it. When the contents are absorbed by the surrounding material, a radically unstable compound forms."

"Percussion detonated, *Sibi*?" Erim asked.

"And extremely temperamental," Massoud replied.

Erim surmised: "Hence the need to keep the components separate until the last moment."

Massoud nodded. "Otherwise it would be quite impractical in combat." He led the newcomers and Farouk into an adjoining chamber. It was long and low, its walls lined with sacks full of sand; at one end was a crude wooden figure.

Massoud spoke the spell, then said: "Cover your ears."

The others complied. Massoud levelled the crossbow at the figure; but just then he seemed to realize that this left him unable to cover *his* ears. He gave the weapon to Farouk, shouted, "Just a moment," and rushed back out into the laboratory, reappearing with wads of moist cotton. Shoving them into his ears, he took the crossbow again.

"Farewell, Cedarhead," he told the figure at the end of the chamber, and launched the bolt. The missile exploded on impact, tearing Cedarhead apart in a wild flurry of splinters.

Sharif and his friends lowered their hands. Massoud pried loose his cotton plugs.

"Splendid, *Sibi*," said Farouk. "Just as you said."

"What are the ingredients, Master?" asked Erim.

"Wouldn't you like to know?" Massoud replied. "If I told you, you'd be destroying things all over Qanar-Sharaj."

Back in his teens, Erim had been infamous for his passion for blowing things up. He maintained that he had outgrown this propensity; but no one else in the Order quite believed him.

Hearing footsteps, Sharif turned to see that Samadhi had entered the laboratory. They went out to meet him, Massoud laying his crossbow on the table.

"Farouk, you may leave us," the Doctrine Master said. The assistant made for the door.

"Did you hear the blast?" Massoud asked Samadhi smugly.

"I take it your experiment worked," Samadhi answered.

"Perfectly," Massoud answered.

"Live and learn," Samadhi replied, his nettlesome smile flickering briefly over his lips.

The exchange seemed innocent enough, but Sharif sensed genuine tension between the two. Though Samadhi was re-

spected by his Seventh-Level colleagues, it was widely known
that he was not well liked, and his relations with Massoud were
particularly chilly. To some extent, Samadhi had achieved his
position as Intelligence Chief at Massoud's expense; secrets
had been reaching the Khan through one of Massoud's men,
and Samadhi had revealed the culprit. The fellow had not been
a spy, merely incautious; nonetheless, it had been a major
embarrassment for Massoud, who had been the ultimate source
of the information. The Numalian had never really forgiven
Samadhi.

"So, Masters," Sharif said, "why have you called us here?"

Massoud started to answer, but noticed Farouk lingering by
the threshold.

"Farouk!" Massoud cried.

The helper vanished.

"Erim, close the door," Massoud said. "Farouk is an excellent assistant, but such an eavesdropper . . ."

Samadhi smiled once more. "Haven't quite learned your
lesson yet, eh?" he asked.

Massoud shot him a peevish glance, saying nothing more
until Erim returned.

"Now then," the Numalian began. "To business. A new
Expected One has arisen."

Erim groaned.

"Does your stomach hurt, Erim?" Samadhi asked.

Erim shook his head.

"Perhaps you fear that we'll dispatch you and your companions to take a look at him."

"Perhaps, *Sibi,*" Erim replied.

"Your prescience is astounding," Samadhi said. "Con-
gratulations."

"Please, Masters," Erim begged. "Can't you get anyone
else?"

"You've done such a fine job so far," Massoud answered.

"Then why not reward us, *Sibi?*" Erim implored. "Don't
send us. It was terrible the last time. People lose their minds
when their Messiahs are subjected to such skepticism. The
crowd simply went mad. The stones flew like hail—I was sure

I was finished. We had to leave Razzaq bleeding in the dirt. When I looked back, I saw them smashing his skull . . .''

"Enough," Massoud broke in. "Razzaq was one of my favorite pupils. I needn't be reminded of what happened."

"We're sending the three of you, and that's all there is to it," Samadhi said. "You might as well accustom yourselves to the idea."

"Of facing such danger just to please the Khan, *Sibi*?" Erim said. "We're Batu's catspaws. He uses us to discredit these men so can he destroy them without provoking an uproar."

"Do you think we're unaware of that?" Massoud asked.

"No, Master," Erim replied. "But has it occurred to you that the Order should side with the Kadjafi people, not the Mirkuts?"

Massoud's eyes widened, their white rage startling against the blackness of his skin. "Should the Order side with a blasphemer simply because he preaches liberation? Would such an evildoer necessarily be better than the Mirkuts? Indeed, would God smile on a revolt led by such a man?"

"I have heard, *Sibi*," Erim said, "that neither you nor Master Samadhi are happy with these investigations."

Massoud snapped: "You did not hear it from me!"

"Nor me," Samadhi added. "The Council has spoken. We have our orders. And our private opinions are none of your business."

"Please, Masters," Sharif said. "Erim misspoke."

"Oh?" Massoud asked.

"He hasn't been himself lately," Sharif went on. "He had a bit of underdone beef yesterday. I knocked him about rather badly sparring—"

"Make up your mind," Massoud said testily.

"It was the beef," Sharif decided.

"Do you share his lack of enthusiasm?"

"Not at all, *Sibi*," Sharif replied. "The Order is my life. And if the Order wishes to concern itself with heretics, that's good enough for me."

Massoud and Samadhi displayed a certain disquiet upon hearing this response, although they said nothing.

"Masters?" Sharif asked, puzzled. What answer had they been looking for?

"What about you, Nawhar?" Samadhi asked.

Nawhar replied: "The Order's actions regarding these maniacs have always seemed perfectly legitimate to me."

"Good," said Samadhi. "You and Sharif should exercise a steadying influence on Erim, then. Keep him out of trouble."

"Why not simply let me stay here, Master?" Erim asked.

"Because, whether you like it or not, you are a born inquisitor," Samadhi replied. "You hate error, and are fearfully good at recognizing it. Just as Nawhar is fearfully good at sniffing out fraudulent miracles. You two are a potent combination—especially with Sharif along to protect you."

"We're flattered, surely," Erim said. "Still—"

"For the last time, Erim," Massoud said menacingly. "Enough."

"As you wish, *Sibi*," Erim said.

"This new imposter," Nawhar said. "What does he call himself?"

"Essaj Ben Yussef," Samadhi answered. "He's a woodcarver's son from Amran. The latest reports have him preaching in the vicinity of Bishah, up in the mountains."

"Bishah?" Erim asked.

"Yes, your old haunt. In any case, this fellow's been making quite a name for himself, primarily as a miracle worker."

"And he claims to be the Expected One?" Nawhar asked.

"Not explicitly," Samadhi continued. "He refers to himself as the Son of Man, whatever that means. He's apparently a master of ambiguity, full of parables that can be interpreted any number of ways. But the Mirkuts are convinced he's a troublemaker. And certainly, the pattern of his so-called 'miracles' suggests an attempt to fit the prophecies."

"But has he actually preached rebellion?" Erim asked.

"That's not our concern," Massoud said. "We're interested in the nature of his claims, and whether those claims are true. Nothing else."

"And if someday we discover the genuine article," Erim said, smiling grimly, "what will we tell the Khan then?"

"We'll advise him to gallop home to the steppes and never

look back," Massoud answered. "God willing, on your return, you'll be entertaining yourself considering the choicest way to word the message."

"God willing," Samadhi added. "But I would not count on it."

Two days later, shortly before their departure, Sharif, Erim, and Nawhar went to see the Grand Master. A bodyguard admitted them—in response to the killing of Iyad, men had been assigned to each of the Masters.

Ahwaz's quarters were on the third floor, and the windows looked out over the ocean. Since his stroke, his bed had been moved next to one of the casements, so that he could admire the view and feel the breeze. When the visitors entered his bedchamber, the old man's face was turned away from them, and he appeared to be gazing out the window; but as they came closer, he did not stir.

"Must be asleep," said the bodyguard.

"Perhaps we should leave," Nawhar said, scratching at the back of his neck.

"No," Ahwaz said faintly, slowly looking towards them.

"*Sibi*?" Sharif asked. "Are you sure it's all right?"

"Of course," Ahwaz said, very thickly. He was evidently having one of his bad days. "Anything for my three favorites. But to what do I owe this honor?"

"We haven't been to see you in a bit, and we're leaving tomorrow."

"Leaving?" Ahwaz looked puzzled for a few moments. "Oh. Of course. Well, I'm certainly glad you've stopped by. As a matter of fact, I was just dreaming about you. One of you, at any rate."

"Who?" Sharif asked.

"Erim was having a conversation with the Grand Master Ghaznavi."

"Really, *Sibi*?" Erim asked. "How delightful. What did Ghaznavi look like?"

"Just like his statue, down in the crypt."

"Was he grateful that I restored his reputation? On the matter of his reptiles, that is?" Ghaznavi had stirred up a considerable controversy with the thesis that the world had once been dominated by huge reptiles, whose likenesses he had divined by the study of petrified bones and skulls; at the time, his theory had been laughed out of court. But Erim, following excavations in the area of Bishah, had shown that Ghaznavi had been right all along.

"As a matter of fact, he *was* grateful," Ahwaz replied. "And he was demonstrating his gratitude by reminding you that his three-horned lizard was *not* found near Bishah."

Erim laughed. "An odd way to do it."

"Precisely what I thought," Ahwaz said. "You seemed very puzzled yourself. But he seemed to think he was doing you a great kindness. And he was very emphatic about it."

"Did he have any other wisdom to impart?"

"Yes. He took your hand and said, 'He cannot die.' "

At the words, Erim felt a strange thrill down his spine. "*He*?"

"That's just how you answered in the dream," Ahwaz said.

"And what did Ghaznavi say then?"

"Nothing. He disappeared. You woke me soon after." Ahwaz shook his head. "I've had such strange dreams since the stroke."

"Did Nawhar and I figure in any of them?" Sharif asked.

"Yes," Ahwaz answered. "Last night I dreamed you two were knee-deep in the Gura River."

"Doing what, *Sibi*?" Nawhar asked, plainly disgusted by the thought.

"Catching turtles for Massoud."

"What did Massoud want them for?" Sharif asked.

"He said,'Wouldn't you like to know,' and refused to tell me."

"Such insubordination," Erim laughed. "Did you remind him that you were the Grand Master?"

"He was unimpressed. 'Well then,' he answered, 'You should certainly be able to figure it out for yourself, shouldn't you?' Then he pointed out a turtle on a nearby log, and instructed me to fetch it. But it slid into the water before I could lay my hands on it."

"What were your dreams about before the stroke?" Erim asked.

"Digging for treasure, mostly," Ahwaz said, with a trace of embarrassment. "And never finding any."

"I dream about flying," said Nawhar, distantly.

Sharif laughed. "You know what that means." He nudged Nawhar with his elbow. Nawhar gave a sharp hiss at this indignity.

"No, I don't," he said.

"Your mother was scared by a bird," Sharif replied.

"What nonsense," said Erim. "What do you think, *Sibi*—?"

They looked back at Ahwaz. The Grand Master was asleep once more. They slipped noiselessly from the room.

✛

# Chapter 5

In the morning, under a gray sky, the three rode north on the New Bishah Road. Flanked by farmland, it ran along a low gravel causeway; every hundred yards or so, there was a culvert to allow the passage of irrigation. Dull red among the green, the canals were filled with muddy water now, but it was all rainfall; the system was closed during the rainy season, superfluous for the time being.

Off to the east, the Gura had overflowed its banks as it always did this time of year; it looked like a vast brick-colored lake. The original Bishah Road had run much closer to the river, and had usually been flooded out every spring; the new route had been built by the Sharajnaghim, and the tolls had once fattened the Order's treasury. But, as with the irrigation system, the road now belonged to the Khan.

*And the profits,* Erim thought as he and his companions approached the first toll-barrier. *How he squeezes them out.*

Yet Erim knew that Batu was not primarily interested in revenue. Control and maintenance of the roads was a military matter. So it was with the irrigation. During the invasion, the

Sharajnaghim had flooded the fields, starving the Mirkuts and obstructing attacks on Qanar-Sharaj from the north and east.

Up ahead, Erim saw a guard emerge from a tent beside the barrier. Several shaggy ponies were tied to date-palms nearby. Casually adjusting the strap on his spired helmet, the Mirkut watched the Sharajnaghim draw near.

"No trouble, please," Sharif told Erim.

"Trouble?" Erim asked.

Two more Mirkuts appeared. All three were armored in laced leather scales. After a brief discussion with the others, the first rounded the barrier and came forward, raising his hand.

Sharif produced a silver piece and gave it to the Mirkut. Small, swart-faced, the barbarian regarded it carefully with his slanted eyes before signalling his comrades. They raised the barrier. One pointed to Erim and chattered something to the man next to him. They began to laugh wildly.

Erim knew some Mirkut, though not enough to tell what they had found so amusing. The remaining Mirkut added an observation of his own, the funniest yet, if his comrades' re- action was any indication; he and Erim locked eyes for a mo- ment. Evidently the easterner was profoundly affronted by what he saw there, and his brown hand flew to the hilt of his curved sword.

Erim wondered if the man had any idea of how easily he could be snuffed out. The Sharajnaghi had a throwing-knife up either sleeve, and could have put them both in the Mirkut's eyesockets before the fool's blade was halfway from its scab- bard. . . .

Erim thrust the idea away. Killing the barbarian would have provided him with considerable satisfaction, it was true. But he could not allow himself to give in to his hate. Forcing a smile to his lips, he said, in Mirkut:

"No offense."

The guard grunted with contempt, kicked gravel at Erim's horse, and stepped aside. The Sharajnaghim rode through. When they had gone some distance, Sharif leaned towards Erim.

"Thank you," he said.

"It was nothing," Erim replied.

The sky grew steadily darker. A downpour soaked the trio to the skin, but along towards noon, the overcast cracked open. A glimpse of blue was to be expected now and then, even in the short grey Kadjafi spring; but the clouds burned off completely. By midafternoon, the heavens were a pale, hot azure from horizon to horizon, and the Sharajnaghim raised their hoods against the sun. Such a break in the weather was quite unusual. It could only mean one thing.

"The rainy season's over," Sharif said.

"And the Khan's going to raise the irrigation fee—" Catching a dim rumble from behind, Erim twisted in his saddle, squinting southward. Helmets gleaming, a large company of Mirkuts was galloping in their direction. "I think we'd best move aside."

The three rode down off the causeway, into a fallow field.

"That *was* real silver you gave the guard, wasn't it?" Nawhar asked Sharif, apparently in dead earnest.

"I think I'll just leave you in suspense," Sharif answered.

As if to heighten Nawhar's fear, several of the foremost Mirkuts veered to take a closer look at them, although the rest paid the Sharajnaghim no attention whatsoever. Small as the riders were, they nonetheless look disproportionately large atop their little steppe ponies. The sight was almost laughable—and thus horribly deceptive.

"Where do you think they're bound?" Sharif asked Erim once the easterners went by. They were clearly intent on slaughter, their quivers stuffed with red-feathered arrows; it was Mirkut custom that such shafts, once drawn, had to taste blood.

"Who knows?" Erim replied apprehensively.

As the afternoon wore on, they passed through several hamlets; there was no sign that the Mirkuts had wreaked the slightest harm in any of them. But a cloud of dark smoke appeared to the north, and shortly before sundown, the Sharajnaghim encountered the barbarians returning southward at a leisurely pace, jesting and singing. They grinned at the wizards; some waved.

Their quivers were nearly empty.

The sky purpled and the light grew ruddy. Ahead, Al-Asriyeh lay astride the road, a small village surrounded like the others by a ring of date-palms. The straw roofs of the houses had collapsed, the brick shells that remained smoking like squat chimneys. Apart from the smoke, nothing moved.

Eyeing the palms, Erim discerned what appeared to be tufted shoots extending from the bases of the trunks. But he knew from experience that they were arrows, buried in men who had been used as targets by the Mirkuts. With all the shafts, and the ruddy light washing everything a dull red, the bloodsoaked victims were hard to make out; but as the distance closed it grew easier to distinguish them. Some seemed to have been shot thirty, forty times. Erim swore.

Suddenly he was eight years old again, returning through the fields to the wreckage of *his* village, finding his father tied to the family's date-palm. There were many arrows, but two fixed his gaze—

Just as they had transfixed his father's eyes.

Sharif's voice wrenched him back to the present. ''Come, Erim. We'll go round.''

*Yes,* Erim thought. There was nothing to be done. He knew that even the livestock were dead. In all likelihood, someone had been harboring rebels. He wondered if any had been caught.

*Their chief should have claimed he was the Expected One. At least he would have gotten a hearing.*

Not for the first time, he half-wished that the Mirkuts would extend their ruthlessness to the false Messiahs.

*Spare us the trouble.*

But the Khan, frightful in crushing mere political opposition, was more circumspect when religion was involved. In his own way, he seemed to be some kind of believer, a monotheist after the fashion of the savage nomads of the east; moreover, he was completely tolerant of all faiths, much more so than the Kadjafim. He preferred to let his subjects settle their own re-

ligious disputes, saying he had no idea which side God was
on, and did not wish to offend Him.

On the other hand, self-styled liberators could not be allowed
to preach insurrection, even if they did claim a divine sanc-
tion. . . .

*Enter the Sharajnaghim,* Erim thought.

They made camp well after dark, several miles north of the
devastated village. Erim ate little. Sharif and Nawhar made no
attempt to draw him out, knowing his mood would pass. Erim
was by nature a cheerful soul; even the slaughter of his family
had not altered that.

But tonight he brooded, on the oppression of his people, and
the Deliverer who had been promised. His thoughts returned
again and again to Essaj Ben Yussef, the man he was almost
certainly going to help destroy. Strangely, or perhaps not so
strangely, Erim could only picture him as his father—riddled
with arrows, head to foot.

The image remained even after Erim sank into uneasy sleep;
but in his dreams, the riddled man was neither his father, nor
Essaj. And he was not bound to a ruddy tree, but raging in the
midst of a huge dark chamber, strewing the floor with corpses,
a mighty sorcerer at the heart of a storm of blood.

*He cannot die,* a voice kept saying.

It remained clear and hot for the next several days. The rainy
season was over, beyond a doubt.

There was some traffic on the road, mostly caravans heading
south from the mountains; a merchant named Mashallid invited
the Sharajnaghim to sample his hospitality one night.

"So, you stopped at Bishah on the way here?" Sharif asked,
over a joint of lamb. "Did you hear anything of a fellow called
Essaj?"

"Essaj Ben Yussef?" Mashallid replied. "Of course. He's
the sole topic of conversation up that way."

"Did you actually see him?" Nawhar asked.

"No. But I certainly got an earful. Miracles, miracles, miracles."

"What kind?"

"Exorcisms, healings."

"The easiest sort to fabricate," Nawhar said. "All you need is an accomplice."

"One who can foam at the mouth on cue," Mashallid said.

"It's a simple trick," Nawhar said. "There's a powder that lathers on contact with saliva. One bite on a pellet, and a man becomes a mad dog."

Erim studied his friend. Nawhar had certainly prejudged this one; perhaps he was justified. But Nawhar's God was too distant for Erim's tastes.

"These Messengers of God never hold up to scrutiny," Marshallid said. He looked slyly at his guests. "You're going to question him, aren't you?"

"Yes," Nawhar said.

"You should be less obvious about it."

"Why?" Nawhar asked.

"Have you no fear of his followers?"

"We're required to inform him that he's under investigation. Give him every chance to change his tune."

"And save his life," Erim added.

"Well, good luck then," Marshallid said. "Reveal him for what he is. Last thing we need is a rebellion. Bad for business." He thrust a wine-skin Nawhar's way.

Nawhar declined.


They pushed on at dawn. To the north, the Andohar range looked within an easy day's ride. But Erim was not deceived, having come this way before. The mountains were still a good fifty miles away—only the clarity of the arid air made them appear closer.

Even so, the land was changing. The Gura swung away to the east. Cultivated plain yielded to shepherds' country, rolling hills studded with occasional outcroppings of orange sandstone.

The slopes rose steadily. Crests grew jagged, the swales deeper. Stands of cedar appeared.

Late one afternoon, the Sharajnaghim came to the place where the Bishah Road met another highway at the bottom of a valley.

"Winds its way northeast from here," Erim said. "It leads to Khaur-Al-Jaffar."

"I don't see any Anarites," Sharif said, almost disappointedly.

"Still, they *do* use this road on their way down to Thangura." Erim indicated a walled, whitewashed compound occupying a level stretch partway up the northern slope. "If it'll make you any happier, I suppose there might be some at the inn."

"Then I say we shouldn't stop," Nawhar answered.

"The food's good," Erim replied. "I know the landlord."

"We'd better water the horses, at least," Sharif said. "Who knows? We might have the place entirely to ourselves."

Small and overweight, a young man met them at the gate. Even though he was plainly a Kadjafi, his eyes were slanted like an easterner's. By his expression and shuffling gait, Erim guessed at once he was feebleminded. The Sharajnaghim dismounted.

"Water?" Sharif asked.

The simpleton pointed to the left. The trough lay in front of a large stable. On the right, up against the western wall, stood the landlord's dwelling, a house with a sloping tiled roof; across from the Sharajnaghim, a two-story building formed the north side of the courtyard. Boisterous shouts and laughter pealed through latticed windows.

"Noisy crowd," Sharif said.

The three led their beasts to drink. Nearby, the manger's double doors stood open; Erim entered.

There were at least two dozen stalls. Twenty held huge black horses. Erim eyed a magnificent stallion in the first stall on the right. Hung over the divider was a black leather saddle, beautifully crafted, but completely devoid of ornament, looking almost as though it was made of lacquered metal. He had seen such saddles before.

*Anarites,* he thought.

The stallion snorted and nickered, stamping. Farther down, an elderly fellow came out of a stall. Seeing Erim, he dropped his hay-fork.

"Good God," he said, voice falling to a whisper: "You're a Sharajnaghi, aren't you?"

Erim had to laugh. "Yes."

"That fool Ashag let you in, didn't he?"

"The boy at the gate?"

The old man nodded. "How many of you are there?"

"Just three."

"You can't stay here. Black Anarites."

"I know."

"Please," the old man said, "go before they realize you're here."

Returning to the threshold, Erim motioned his companions into the shadows.

"Twenty," Sharif said, once he learned what they had blundered into. "Hmmm."

"Why didn't they see us come in?" Nawhar asked.

"The common-room has a sunken floor," Erim replied. "The windows are too high."

The stable attendant came up. "What are you waiting for?" he demanded.

Before they could answer, a series of shrieks, heartrending in their agony and need, rang out of the common-room. A red bottle crashed through a lattice in a shower of wooden fragments.

"What's happening in there?" Sharif asked the attendant.

"They're bullying a merchant," the old fellow said. "They want him to sell his daughters."

"Why not just take them?" Sharif wondered.

"What would be crueler?" Erim put in. "Watching helpless as your daughters were raped? Or living with the knowledge that you'd sold them?"

There was a sizzling crack, unmistakably the discharge of a magic bolt. Two more followed in quick succession, and the door of the common-room suddenly flew off its hinges, landing flat on the ground with a puff of dust, a middle-aged man in striped robes lying on top of it.

"I *told* you I could blast him up the stairs, Wazir!" a voice bellowed, to hoots of laughter and applause. A tall man in black swaggered out, his head shaved but for a long blond topknot. He entered a stance. Watery and transparent in the sunlight, a bolt snaked from his fist and struck the middle-aged man in the groin. The victim clutched himself, drawing his knees up towards his chest.

"I offered you a good price!" the Anarite cried. "What more do you want? They're only your daughters. If you must cherish your children, have sons." He laughed. "Of course, we'd take them too."

He struck the man with another bolt, this time in the face. The back of the merchant's skull struck the door with a thud. His legs straightened spasmodically.

"What do you think?" Sharif asked his companions.

"You're *not* planning to go out there," Erim whispered. "Tell me you're not—"

"Bring them out!" the Anarite shouted, moving to one side. Several others came forth, dragging two young women. Bare limbs flashed amid the captives' torn garments. One of the women was black-haired, her skin milk-pale; the other was dusky, with a kinky red mane.

The Anarite chief went to their father, crouched, and seized him by the cheek. "That's it!" he cried. "Wake up! I want you to see this. We're going to do the sows right here in the dirt, and you're not going to profit at all. For a merchant, you have very little business sense."

He cupped his hands. "Come on!" he cried. "Everyone out! We'll take turns."

Fifteen more Anarites scrambled into view.

"What do you think?" Sharif asked again, this time more insistently.

"Too many," Nawhar answered.

"He's right, Sharif," Erim said.

Eager hands ripped at the women. The sisters screamed, rags flying about them.

Howling a curse, their father lunged up at the leader, grabbing at his tormentor's shoulders. The black-robe's own backward leap pulled the merchant to his feet. The merchant pulled a knife from a scabbard on the Anarite's belt; driving a knee into the father's stomach, the black-robe wrenched free. Swords drawn, his followers closed in.

"Hold!" he cried.

But their blades had already found the merchant's flesh. As the Anarites withdrew, he was on his hands and knees, head hanging, a long straight sword still in him, driven through his back as though it had fallen from the sky, the point protruding from his chest. Black in the shadow of his body, a single long stream of blood ran from the tip to the ground.

Half-naked now, the daughters scrabbled towards him, wailing. He looked at them like a weary animal, barely able to hold his head up. His arms gave, bowing outward, the point through his chest sinking into the ground. Slowly his body slipped down along the blade.

"What do you think?" Sharif asked a third time.

"Are there still twenty of them?" Nawhar asked.

"If we can keep them from flanking us—"

The women tried to pull the sword out. The Anarites hurled them to the ground and ripped their garments away, leaving them naked but for their sandals. Others began to strip off their own robes.

Sharif looked at Erim and Nawhar, shrugging. "I'm sorry," he said, and strode from the manger.

"*You're* sorry!" Erim demanded. He stamped, slapped a palm to the back of his neck—

And followed.

Nawhar rushed up at Erim's side. "Madness," he said.

As he passed his horse, Sharif pulled the halves of his quarterstaff from his saddle. Sliding the pieces together, he twisted them till they locked, all the while continuing towards the Anarites.

Their chief noticed the Sharajnaghim at last.

"And what's this?" he cried.

The Anarites who had stripped began frenziedly to struggle back into their clothes, the rest spreading out behind their captain. The women got to their feet, grabbing up fragments of cloth, trying to cover their nudity.

The leader signalled. Two of his men seized the sisters, holding blades to their throats.

"Are you going to hide behind those women?" Sharif asked, halting at last.

"Just a precaution," the Anarite chief replied. "But considering that you are three, and we are a score, I doubt they're in danger. Just as well. They're better company when they're alive. Somewhat."

"I thought you Anarites prided yourselves on your hatred of flesh," Nawhar called.

"We do," the Anarite answered. "And we were about to express it."

"Let them go," Sharif said. Erim came up on his right, Nawhar on his left.

"We're dead men, I hope you know that," Erim whispered.

"Pretend they're Mirkuts," Sharif whispered back. "And take the ones holding the women."

Hearing a popping sound, Erim looked at Nawhar, who was clenching and unclenching his fingers, working their arthritic joints.

"Do you really mean to do this?" the Anarite leader cried. Sharif nodded.

"Who then shall we say we've killed?"

Sharif spat. "My name, dog, is Sharif Ben Shaqar."

The Anarite smiled. "Did you hear that, men? We have a famous one here—"

Sharif let go of his quarterstaff. Standing on end for a moment, it toppled lazily. The Anarite's gaze left Sharif, following it groundward.

Sharif entered a Dragon Stance and flattened the man's nose with two cataract-bolts.

Hands over his face, the Anarite dropped to his knees. Sharif drilled four more strikes into the overlapping fingers. Hammered backwards at the knuckles, digits snapped, blood exploding between them. The Anarite went over with his legs folded under him.

It all happened so quickly that Erim was taken quite by surprise. Luckily the men holding the sisters were startled as well.

Erim's hands darted for his hidden knives. His targets were still gawking at their fallen captain when the blades took them in the temples, driving through bone in scarlet spurts. The sisters fell backwards onto the collapsing bodies, the dead hands gripping them yet.

A black-robe on the left started to enter a stance, but Nawhar was well ahead of him. A barrage of green strikes pummelled the Anarite's mouth. All but detached, the man's upper lip flapped sideways across his cheek. Glued together with blood, a clot of broken teeth dropped onto his chest. He took two clumsy backward steps and struck the ground like an empty sack.

"How did that happen?" Sharif asked the remaining Anarites. "It seems *you* are now but—" He paused.

"Sixteen," Erim hissed.

"Sixteen," Sharif continued. "Who's next?"

The Anarites looked round at each other, plainly at a loss.

Sharif whooped, making a sudden wild gesture. Most of them flinched, but four raised shields and went over to the attack.

Instantly resuming his stance, Sharif absorbed their strikes, doubled them and hurled them back, visiting the full force of eight combined bolts on the foremost black-robe. The man's shield might as well have been cobwebs; his ribcage gave with a sound like branches cracking beneath a boot. Blood spraying from his mouth in a vast scarlet cough, he catapulted back, arms trailing, hands clapping together.

The others seemed to have no idea of what Sharif had done to him. Topknot whipping forward over his face, a second man died, forehead staved in; a third fell stunned before the fourth broke off his attack, raising an additional shield.

"Thirteen," Sharif said, without any help from Erim this time.

The remaining Anarites stood motionless, watching him. The women wrestled free of their dead captors.

"Knives," Erim told them.

The sisters struggled with the hilts, set their sandalled feet on the dead men's necks. An Anarite started towards them.

Two intense white beams jabbed from Sharif's palms. Kneecaps shattered, the black-robe's legs wobbled out from under him, and he took the ground on his face.

"Twelve," Sharif told the man's comrades.

The women jerked the knives free and ran to Erim. Pressing them into his hands, they vanished behind him.

"The one in the middle!" an Anarite cried. "We have to flank him! Don't worry about the ones on the sides! They're not as—"

Erim put a knife in the man's throat. "Dangerous?" the Sharajnaghi asked.

The Anarite pulled the blade out, examining it with a curiously neutral expression as blood jetted from his wound. His face whitened, and his eyes wandered from the blade. The knife dropped, and he seemed to wilt, falling.

"Eleven," cried Sharif.

On the right, several Anarites whispered to each other. They edged towards Nawhar, suddenly breaking into a run. Nawhar blew the foremost off his feet before it became obvious that they were simply making a dash for the gate.

"Now you are but seven," Sharif told those remaining in the courtyard.

"Let us go," one implored.

"What about the rest of you?" Sharif asked.

"Spare us," they cried.

"Take your wounded," Sharif commanded.

As fast as they were able, they hauled them across the packed earth. Erim and Sharif followed the fallen chieftain as he was pulled along, heels dragging. The man looked dazedly at them out of a mask of blood.

"That's Sharif Ben Shaqar," his conqueror reminded him.

With the help of Ashag and the stable attendant, the Sharajnaghim shut the gate behind the black-robes. Ashag began capering.

"Very good, Masters," he said. "Bad, bad men. Bang! Crunch!"

"Think they'll come back?" Erim asked Sharif.

"Would *you*?"

"I might be tempted," Erim answered. "There is such a thing as revenge. A subject to which I have devoted a great deal of thought."

"They'll be licking their wounds for weeks—" Sharif paused. Ashag was in front of him, grinning.

"Bang!" the simpleton said, smacking fist against palm. "Crunch!"

"I can't believe you did it," the stable attendant told Erim.

"I never had the slightest doubt," Erim said.

Sharif shot him a look.

"Larger doubts, perhaps," Erim admitted.

Sharif cracked a grin. Laughing, they turned—

Only to catch sight of the women crouching by their father's corpse. Instantly their mirth vanished.

✝

# Chapter 6

Nawhar took the cloaks from two dead Anarites and gave them
to the sisters; noting how carefully he averted his eyes, Sharif
could not help wondering if he was acting out of decency, or
because he was offended by the mere sight of naked female
flesh. Some combination of both, Sharif decided. Nawhar was
frightfully intelligent; Sharif would have been the first to admit
it.

But Nawhar was also confused. And a prig.

Sharif, on the other hand, had already decided which of the
two women was more attractive. Given the situation, he felt
mildly ashamed, although he was willing to forgive himself.

The darker sister, the one with the curly red hair, was far
and away the better-looking of the two—that was all there was
to it. The closer he and Erim came, the prettier she seemed,
even with all the tears. She did not look like a pure-blooded
Kadjafi; he guessed she was part Numalian. Some people
looked down on Numalians, but he admired their women, at
least. Exotic faces appealed to him.

The other sister was handsome enough, but much more stan-
dard fare. Pale skin was a trait much prized by his countrymen,

if not by him; her hair was long and straight and jet black. She was definitely Erim's sort.

The two seemed to be about the same age, twenty or so. Given the difference in their looks, Sharif assumed their father had two wives.

A sweaty rotund man came out of the common-room, followed by several younger fellows in aprons.

"Hafez Shammar," Erim told Sharif. "The owner of this establishment."

"Anyone else in there?" Sharif asked Hafez.

"No," the innkeeper replied. "The other guests fled when the Anarites came." He indicated the black-robed bodies. "Will you help us bury these swine?"

Erim went to the one with his knife in its neck. He pulled the blade out, wiped it on the man's garment, and sheathed it.

"Let their friends do it," he said. "Your stable's full of their horses. We could tie the bodies on, drive the whole lot out."

"The bastards did a lot of damage inside," Hafez said. "Their animals would cover my losses."

"Do as you please," Erim answered. "But think—the three of us are leaving tomorrow. And the survivors just might want their mounts."

"An excellent point," Hafez answered.

The Anarites had halted several hundred yards down the road, by a large outcropping. Once the corpses were roped to the saddles, Ashag and the stableman started the horses down towards them.

The Sharajnaghim went over to the women.

"What was your father's name?" Sharif asked.

"Khaldun," the pale sister said. "Khaldun Al-Maari."

"Would you like us to bring him inside?" Sharif continued. "We could . . . ah . . . bury him for you tomorrow."

"He must be washed," the pale sister said numbly.

"Not for a while," Erim said. "I don't wish to be indelicate, but—it would be better if we waited till his blood thickened. Otherwise—"

Nodding, the sisters rose, wiping their eyes. Hafez sent one of his helpers for a blanket. While they were waiting for him to return, Sharif eyed the corpse. The skin had already turned yellow. The dark girl was fanning her hand back and forth, keeping flies away from the wounds.

Hafez's man reappeared. Sharif helped the sisters roll their father onto the blanket. The merchant stared blankly upwards, his eyes slightly crossed. Unlike the rest of his skin, his face had gone very dark, and had been deeply imprinted by the gravel it had lain upon. The women each kissed him, then folded the blanket up over him. Sharif took him by the shoulders, Erim by the feet, and they went down into the common-room.

"Come," Hafez said. "We'll put him in the cellar for the time being." Getting a lamp, he led the way. Depositing the corpse and going back up, the Sharajnaghim surveyed the wreckage the Anarites had left.

The floor was littered with broken clay bowls and bottles; wine was splattered everywhere. Only a few of the tables remained upright.

Sharif dispatched Nawhar to keep an eye on the Anarites. Then he and Erim helped Hafez and his men clean up.

Darkness gathered outside. After several hours, the room was restored to a semblance of order—just as a dozen travellers appeared out of the night.

Hafez served the calf he had been preparing for the Anarites. Sharif and Erim turned their thoughts to the women. The sisters had retired to their room. One of Hafez's helpers started upstairs with a platter and wine for them; the Sharajnaghim intercepted him. Sharif knocked on the door.

The dark woman appeared. Behind her, Sharif could see her sister sitting on the bed. They were fully dressed now. The Anarites' cloaks lay on the floor.

"You should eat something," Sharif said.

She took the platter from him. "Thank you," she said.

"What's your name?" he asked.

"Zehowah," she answered.

*Zehowah*, he thought. *Wonderful*.

"And your sister's?"

"Khalima."

"My name's Sharif, as you might have heard. My friend here is called Erim. We're very sorry about what happened to your father."

For the first time Zehowah looked him in the face. Her eyes were large and light brown, breathtakingly lovely and sad. "Couldn't you have saved him?"

"We were trying to decide what to do," Sharif said. "There were so many of them."

"I understand," Zehowah replied. Sincerely, Sharif guessed; it was a great relief. He could not bear to have this beauty thinking ill of him.

Khalima came up behind her sister. "In any case," she said, "we owe you our deepest gratitude."

"We'll bury your father tomorrow," Erim said.

They shook their heads.

"We can't leave him here," Khalima said. "We must bring him home to Thangura."

"Do you have horses?" Sharif asked.

"In the stable," Zehowah said.

"It's going to be very hot," Erim said. "Are you sure you want to bring him all that way? You might get sick. . . ."

"We can't leave him in this strange place," Khalima said.

"You have enough to worry about," Erim answered. "Two women alone on the road—"

"Which way are you going?" Zehowah asked.

"North," Sharif replied. "Up towards Bishah."

"Bishah," Zehowah said. Her expression grew distant; something had apparently occurred to her. Absently she handed the platter back to Sharif. "Perhaps . . ." A smile passed over her lips.

"What?" Sharif prodded.

She turned to Khalima. "If we could just speak to Lord Essaj . . ."

"Essaj?" Khalima asked uncomprehendingly. Then her eyes widened, and she clapped. "Of course! Why didn't we think of it before? Do you think he'd come back with us?"

"We could bring the body," Zehowah suggested. "Bishah's much nearer than Thangura."

"Hold on a moment," Sharif said. "What are you talking about?"

"Would you let us come with you?" Zehowah asked.

"With your father's body?" Erim demanded. "Why?"

"Have you heard of Essaj Ben Yussef?" Khalima asked.

"Yes," answered Erim and Sharif.

"He has powers," Khalima went on. "Father went to him to be healed. . . ."

"Of what?" Erim asked.

"Consumption," Zehowah answered. "He was dying. Coughing up blood."

"But Essaj cured him," Khalima added.

"So?" Erim demanded. "What has this to do with your father? Even if we assume you're telling the truth, can Essaj raise the dead?"

Zehowah nodded, her face the perfect picture of certainty.

"Oh, please . . ."

"We saw him," Khalima said stoutly. "He raised a little girl."

Erim and Sharif could barely restrain their laughter. In all of their investigations, they had never encountered such an outrageous claim.

"It's true," Khalima insisted.

"You're sure she was dead?" Erim asked.

"We're not doctors," Zehowah said. "But her *parents* were sure. She'd been bitten by a cobra."

"Did you see the snake bite her?" Erim pressed.

"No, but . . ."

"Then how do you know she was bitten?"

Zehowah looked puzzled. "What difference does it make?"

"If you're going to believe someone was raised from the dead," Erim said, "don't you think you should have some evidence? Especially when you're planning to bring your father's body all the way to Bishah in the hot sun?"

"Are you going to help us or not?" Khalima demanded.

"We'll escort you, certainly," Sharif said. "As for the rest . . ."

"You think we're crazy, don't you?"

"Not at all," Erim said. "I'm sure you witnessed something

startling. But whether it was a real miracle—that's a different question.''

''Are you saying Lord Essaj is a charlatan?'' Zehowah asked, as though she could not quite believe her ears.

''That's precisely what we've been sent to find out,'' Erim answered.

''You're going to investigate him?''

''Yes,'' Sharif said. He expected them to explode at that; instead, they seemed delighted.

''God has sent you to glorify him, then,'' Zehowah said, raising her pale palms and her magnificent chin. ''You will prove to all the world that Essaj is the Expected One. Splendid.'' She smiled.

''You'll see,'' said Khalima. ''You'll like him.'' She looked at Erim, dark eyes shining with enthusiasm. Sharif noticed Erim returning her stare with some interest. ''He does the most amazing things.''

''Father really *was* sick, you know,'' Zehowah said. ''We weren't wrong about that.''

''Perhaps not,'' Sharif allowed. ''And perhaps the little girl really was raised. But we're *not* going to bring your father. You have no idea what an ordeal that would be.''

''Then Essaj will come here,'' Zehowah said adamantly. ''He loved father.'' Taking the platter back from Sharif, she told Khalima, ''We really *should* eat something.''

''And we should leave you to it,'' Sharif said. ''Come, Erim.''

''We'll knock in the morning,'' Erim added.

Once the Sharajnaghim were back down in the common-room, Sharif chuckled. ''The things people believe.''

''Amazing, isn't it?'' Erim asked.

''Handsome women, though,'' Sharif continued. ''Especially Zehowah.'' He sighed. ''*Ze-how-ah.*''

''I prefer her sister, to be honest,'' Erim said.

''Too bad their brains are cooked,'' Sharif replied. ''Still, I suppose one must make allowances.''

''Allowances?'' Erim asked. ''If one's taken a vow of celibacy, how many *must* one make?''

''I'm Sixth Level now,'' Sharif answered. ''I can take a

concubine if I want. Half the Masters have them. The vows
are outmoded. That's why no one pays attention to them anymore.''

"Then why do we still take them?''

"You're the theologian. You'll have to answer that for yourself. Besides. *You've* strayed.''

A pained look crossed Erim's face. "Poor Rusaifa,'' he said.
"I should've married her. They'd have let me keep her. They'd
have had to.''

"What God has joined together,'' Sharif said. "Myself, I'd
rather have a concubine. That way *I* don't have to keep her.''

"That's beneath you. You're better than that.''

"Maybe,'' Sharif answered, almost ruefully. Indeed, unlike
Erim, he had been true to his vows. So far.

*But now I've met Zehowah*, he thought. And if she was not
an excuse for oathbreaking, he could not begin to imagine what
an excuse would be like.

He went to relieve Nawhar at the gate. The moon had risen;
standing just outside the arch, Nawhar was a shadow against
the road. Seated on a stool, Ashag was helping him keep watch.
There was an unlit torch in a bracket on the side of the gate;
Sharif asked why they had left it dark.

"So I can see the Anarites more clearly,'' Nawhar answered.

The hillside was sandstone, orange in daylight but yellow-
green beneath the faint blue moonglow; the fire the Anarites
had built stood out garishly, silhouetted figures moving back
and forth in front of it.

"What have they been up to?'' Sharif asked.

"Gravedigging, I think,'' Nawhar replied. "What about
you?''

Sharif told him of the conversation with the women. Nawhar
was badly piqued to learn that they would be along for the
journey.

"Resurrection,'' he said. "The very idea that the Almighty
would intervene in such a matter—''

"I quite agree,'' Sharif said.

"Then why should we humor them?'' Nawhar asked. "Female company is the last thing we need.''

"Speak for yourself,'' Sharif answered.

"I can see you're being tempted already."

"What of it?" Sharif said good-naturedly. "There's no use arguing with me. I'm not equipped for it. Go find Erim—although I suppose I should warn you that he's already up-braided me too."

"He's no one to talk. That Rusaifa woman—what a vulgar story."

"There, you see? You two have something to argue about after all."

"I notice you didn't bother to consult me," Nawhar said. "Do you care that this arrangement is going to distress me profoundly? I joined the Order *precisely* to avoid such entice-ments."

"Enticements?" Sharif said. "You mean you actually—"

"I hate going abroad in the world," Nawhar broke in. "Even on such a worthy mission. I'm happy at Qanar-Sharaj."

"Happy?" Sharif asked. "You know, I don't think I've ever heard that word on your lips before. First I learn that you can actually be tempted by women, then I discover that you're capable of happiness—what will it be next?"

"I enjoy my studies," Nawhar said. "And the disputations. Isn't it obvious?"

"Not exactly," Sharif said. "I mean, you always seem ab-sorbed in them, but in a rather grim way."

Nawhar scratched his shoulders. It made Sharif squirm just watching him. "I'm in my element dealing with abstractions. Sometimes I can ignore this infernal itching, the pain in my joints. Forget that I'm trapped in this horrible flesh."

"Come on," Sharif said. "Being an animal isn't so bad."

"For you, perhaps. You're handsome and strong. Maybe I might see things differently. But I've been given *this* body."

"So it's God's fault, eh?"

"No. My parents', for bringing me into existence. And mine most of all. I ensnare myself with distractions. Prevent myself from seeing beyond this veil of illusion. But I will never blame God. How many times must I say it? God is spirit." Nawhar pinched his hand, mouth twisting with disgust. "Not *this*." He looked at Ashag. "And not *that*."

Completely uncomprehending, Ashag smiled at him, goblin-ugly.

At first light Erim and Sharif woke the sisters. Securing fresh garments for the corpse, they went down to the cellar, bringing water and washcloths, a lamp, and a blanket. They had decided it would be better to clean the body before eating; that proved a wise choice.

During the night, vastly more blood had leaked from the body; the bottom of the blanket it was wrapped in had been completely soaked, and still a dark pool had spread. Puddle and stains had mostly dried, but patches remained damp; unravelling the corpse from the blanket and peeling off its clothes were loathsome tasks, filthy and difficult, as the dried blood had glued the fabric solidly to the body in places. Then came the sickening drudgery of scrubbing away the clotted masses clinging to the cold skin.

*If Essaj can raise this, he is truly a miracle worker*, Sharif thought, puffing at the stench.

The dead man's eyes had begun to sink; the imprint of the gravel was still in his face. His skin had gone from yellow to grey, with huge dark-purple blotches all along his back where his blood had settled. The wounds on the upper surface of his body had long since dried, but the ones on the bottom still oozed a thin red fluid, which stopped after a few dabs with a cloth.

The smell grew steadily worse. Khaldun's bowels had clearly been pierced. The man's stomach was already swollen, and each time they shifted the body, gases hissed from between the lips and out of the wounds. They had to stop several times and go upstairs, shutting the door behind them and gulping air for several minutes before returning to their work.

Yet at last the corpse was clean. They dressed it, wrapped it in the fresh blanket, and brought it upstairs. Hafez sent a man down to wash the floor.

Laying the body down in the courtyard, the Sharajnaghim went back inside to clean themselves, change, and eat. When they returned, Khalima and Zehowah were kneeling beside their father, showing no sign of the hope and assurance they had demonstrated the night before.

Some of the other guests were already about, expressing condolences. The stableman brought tools from the manger, and Hafez and his other menials came out. Taking up the body once more, the Sharajnaghim followed the innkeeper from the compound, Nawhar joining the procession as it passed through the gate; he had been on watch again, even though the Anarites had left during the night.

Hafez brought them to a spot where there was enough soil for the burial, surrounded by a ring of tall cedars; Erim and Sharif dug the grave.

"Not too deep," Zehowah cautioned.

When they were done, Sharif recited the Prayer for the Dead; then Khalima uncovered her father's face, and she and her sister kissed him one last time. After gently tucking the fold back into place, they stepped back, and Sharif and Erim lowered Khaldun Al-Maari into the grave.

"You'll see," Khalima told them as they picked up their shovels once more.

# Chapter 7

The evening after the three inquisitors departed Qanar-Sharaj, Master Khaddam went, as usual, to the Women's Quarters to dine with his concubine, Sigrun. She was a Kragehul from the far north, taller than most Kadjafi women, taller indeed than most of the men; she could almost look Khaddam himself in the eye. Her hair was red-gold, and her round cheekbones were set off by a firm chin. Light freckles ran across the bridge of her snub nose. Her body was muscular and firm, though she had convinced herself that she was getting fat; she was much put out by the fact that she had gained an inch or so across the hips since turning thirty, even though Khaddam had told her repeatedly that he did not mind at all.

"If I wanted a thin little slip of a girl, I would have found myself one," he said, settling himself on the cushions beside the low table in the center of the room. She harrumphed, bringing him his veal and rice, and gave her stock answer:

"I don't care what you think," she said. "*I* don't like how I look. I'm turning into a cow."

"Cows don't worry about their weight," he answered. "What can I say? If I compliment you on your appearance, you tell me my opinion's worthless. If I inform you that I'm the envy of the whole Order, you dismiss all my colleagues as mere men."

"Well, what *do* men know? Show them a big bosom, and they lose their minds. If it wiggles, men will watch it. What kind of an attitude is that?"

"One that is divinely ordained," Khaddam replied. "Men were created to be enthralled by things that wiggle. Besides, what would you prefer I appreciate you for? Your brain? I do. As far as I can make out, it works just fine."

"A thinner figure," she shot back. "If I had one. How is the veal?"

He pulled off a piece, holding it with his thumb and two fingers. Taking a bite, he nodded in satisfaction. "Excellent. Won't you be joining me?"

"I shouldn't."

"Yes, you should. Then you wouldn't be nibbling all day long. And putting on the weight. And lamenting to me about how you're getting fat."

She considered this argument, ultimately deciding to compromise. She had no intention of eating, but at least she could stop complaining.

"Will you be staying?" she asked, sitting across from him. She lived for their nights together. Twenty years her senior he might have been, but he was an excellent lover. And better still, his conversation was fascinating. He was always bringing her books; she read them in the afternoons while he was away. She much preferred that to gossiping with the other women. They were such a lot of, well—cows.

"No," Khaddam said, "but I'll be back later."

"Where are you going?"

"I have some unfinished business. I was overseeing a practice session—Fifth-Levellers pretending they're magicians. Samadhi thought everything was going along quite nicely, but I decided they needed some extra work."

"You don't like Samadhi much, do you?" Sigrun asked.

"He's all right," Khaddam answered. "If anything, he reminds me of myself—when I was his age. Ambitious and insufferable. I suppose some might say I'm *still* insufferable.

. . . As for him, it's simply unfortunate that Ahwaz made him my aide."

"Surely you could persuade Ahwaz to . . ."

"I would prefer not to. Not unless Samadhi gives me genuine cause. For the most part, he's executed his duties quite well."

"You've never told me," Sigrun said. "Why is his post connected with yours at all? What does spying have to with sorcery?"

Khaddam had some more veal, washed it down with wine, then answered: "The first Master to take a serious interest in intelligence was named Ghaznavi . . ."

"The one with the ancient reptiles—who sent Zorachus to Khymir."

"Very good," Khaddam said. "Before him, the Order was very haphazard about the whole business of gathering information. And in spite of the fact that the affair in Khymir was very nearly a disaster, his organization of the Order's various intelligence efforts proved invaluable in other ways."

"And he was Master of Sorcery as well as Grand Master," Sigrun said, working it through.

"So that Intelligence became identified with the Wizard's Chair," Khaddam continued. "Of course, this simplifies matters a bit. Technically, Ghaznavi ceased to be Master of Sorcery upon his elevation. But he remained the real chief of Intelligence, even though his successor as Sorcery Master, Khuroum, was the nominal head. Ultimately a separate Chair was created for Intelligence, but it remained subordinate to Sorcery nonetheless." He wrenched off another piece of veal. "So. You've been reading about Zorachus."

She shivered. "A terrible story."

"Indeed. He remains to this day the only real traitor the Order has ever produced. A Seventh-Level Sharajnaghi—and High Priest of Tchernobog."

"But that was the least of it," Sigrun said. "All that slaughter. And what he intended for the human race . . ."

"Total extermination," Khaddam said. "But he was only being logical, after a fashion. It actually followed quite naturally from what the Priests of Tchernobog had been preaching all along. Of course, some say he received the idea directly from Tchernobog. But he embraced it wholeheartedly.''

"Are the Anarites like the Khymirians?'' Sigrun asked. "As bad as the Cult of Tchernobog?''

"No. The Black Priesthood was far more sinister—and powerful. Particularly under Zorachus's regime. Some have described his reign as the most perfect approximation of Hell that this world has ever seen. And as far as I can tell, it's no exaggeration.

"The Anarites, on the other hand, have fallen from the True Faith, to the extent that they ever had it. In some respects they're more like bandits now than priests. Mere criminals or secular rulers, far more concerned with their slave-trading than worshipping the Black God. But their evil—and their power— still stems from him. He tolerates their deviations so long as they fulfill his larger ends. They'll be our mortal enemies so long as their order exists.''

"What has Samadhi learned?'' Sigrun asked.

"Very little. General Khassar—the Khan's spymaster—told him he knew nothing about Iyad's death.''

"Might he be lying?''

"Probably not. Indeed, Khassar hinted broadly that he'd be delighted if we discovered some real evidence. The Anarites have become far too unruly. And we're better suited to destroying them than the Mirkuts. The Khan remembers how his horsemen fared in the mountains. What he gained was hardly worth the bother.'' He looked down at his plate. "I've hardly eaten at all.''

"Are you in a hurry?''

"Yes.''

"I'll keep quiet.''

He smiled and finished as quickly as he was able. They rose and embraced.

"I'll be waiting for you,'' she said.

He kissed her on the lips, giving her behind a squeeze. "Splendid,'' he said. "If you're a cow, then I say more cows.''

"Moo,'' she replied sourly. "Now leave me with my sorrow.''

* * *

Some time later, as she was struggling through Ibn Mazruli's turgid *History of the Sharajnaghim*, she dozed off on her bed. It only seemed a moment before the first thunderclap woke her.

At least she thought it was a thunderclap. But looking out the window, she saw a clear night sky, dotted with stars. The air hung dry and motionless.

Someone was shouting. Getting up, she put on her robe and went to the door. Several of the other women were looking out; Zubeydah, Samadhi's concubine, was holding her baby in her arms. The child was squirming and whining, working itself up into a good crying fit.

Sigrun sneered slightly. If ever Khaddam allowed her a child, she would surely have a better one than little Hosni there. She liked babies, indeed lusted for one of her own, but Hosni was ugly and very temperamental. Hers would all be handsome and sweet.

"What's all that shouting?" cried Massoud's wife, jet-black Chabela.

There came another detonation, much louder than the first. Hosni jumped in his mother's arms, shocked silent. More doors opened. Children were crying all up and down the hall. Hosni joined in.

Sigrun and Chabela set off in the direction of the blasts, making for the intersection at the north end of the corridor. Hardly had they reached the juncture when a third explosion echoed through the passageways, followed quickly by a fourth; this time Sigrun felt the blasts in the soles of her bare feet. Dust sifted from the ceiling.

She looked to the left. Smoke poured through the archway at the far end, rolling along the ceiling.

Suddenly the grey flashed red. There was yet another roar, and a visible throb passed through the smoke. It seemed to Sigrun as if she had been slapped across the ears. Thrusting her hands over them, she dropped to one knee, nostrils filling with a sweetish, hot smell. Ears aching, she worked her jaw slowly back and forth.

The miasma thickened beyond the arch. A man staggered

out of it. The smoke appeared to cling to him—or was his body itself smoking? His robes were in rags, scorched, stained with red. There was no way to tell if they had originally been grey or white. The man was too far away for her to recognize his face, but he was much the same size as . . . She gasped, racing towards him.

His injuries were hideous, his blood-shiny features furrowed with gashes. A huge wing of scalp trailed over his forehead, and one eye was gone. His tattered garments seemed to have been driven into him in several places. Ribbons of skin dangled from his fingers.

"Sigrun," he croaked, and dropped to the floor.

It was Khaddam.


Word raced through Qanar-Sharaj. Doctor Shoua rounded up his available assistants and rushed to the Women's Quarters, thrusting aside the many Adepts and acolytes crowding the halls. Along the way, they found several corpses; badly mutilated, two of the dead seemed to be Mashad Akif and Jamal Bustani, the youngest members of Khaddam's "Knot of Serpents." Lying in Sigrun's arms, Khaddam himself was still alive when Shoua arrived, but just barely.

"Is there anything you can do?" Sigrun asked Shoua desperately.

The doctor was a tall, lanky individual, hawk-nosed, nearly bald. He swore when he saw how deeply Khaddam's garments had been thrust into him.

"Lay him down flat," he said. "Gently, gently."

Sigrun eased Khaddam to the floor. Khaddam groaned, a foam of blood pulsing on his lips. His remaining eye wandered crazily, finally settling on Shoua.

"Healing-trance," he said feebly, then apparently lost consciousness.

Shoua signalled for his bag. "Always telling me how to do my job," he said, laying two long fingers atop one of the great veins in Khaddam's throat.

"What are you going to do?" Sigrun asked.

"Rouse him sufficiently to enter the trance," Shoua replied. "I have a drug. . . ."

He unwrapped a knife with a channel along the blade, and shook a bit of white powder into the groove. Sigrun gasped as he plunged it into Khaddam's arm.

"It's all right," Shoua answered. "He'll wake any moment now. . . ."

Khaddam's eye opened. He coughed blood, tried to sit up. Shoua clapped a hand to his shoulder, pressing him back down.

"Save your strength," Shoua said. "Your·mind won't be clear long. The drug is making you bleed much faster. You must enter the trance, quickly."

Khaddam nodded, sliding his hand into Sigrun's. He closed his eye once more and began the spell.

"He's going to bleed to death," Sigrun whispered to Shoua.

Shoua put his fingers to his lips. Sigrun and the onlookers fell silent.

Khaddam's voice grew fainter and fainter. Sigrun prayed silently, tears rivering down her face. Khaddam's lips stopped moving. Sigrun's breath caught in her throat.

Shoua put his fingers to Khaddam's neck once more. "It's all right," he said. "He completed the spell."

"But will he live?"

"He's lived this long," Shoua answered, rising. He turned to his assistants. "Put him on the bed in her room."

# ✤

# Chapter 8

Shoua remained with Khaddam through the night, administering drugs to help him fight off infection, and supervising two massive infusions of blood utilizing the recently rediscovered techniques of Takfir Aliphar. Keeping out of his way, Sigrun stationed herself in a corner, praying silently to the Kadjafi God and certain Kragehul deities as well. When at last the sun rose, Shoua sent his assistants from the room and went over to her, weary but smiling.

"The crisis is past," he said, wiping his hands with a damp rag.

Sigrun wept for joy; they hugged each other. Then she bustled out and promptly set out making a splendid breakfast for him and his men.

"It's been too long since I've had food like this," Shoua said, after finishing one of her justly famous pastries. "Khaddam is a lucky man. He should marry you."

"You know it, and I know it," Sigrun replied. "But he can be rather thick."

Shoua laughed. "That's a word I've never heard applied to him."

"Well, let's just say I see a different side of him," Sigrun answered. "What about you? Have *you* ever considered marrying again?"

Shoua shook his head. "I couldn't bear losing another wife. Besides, even if I did find someone, she probably wouldn't be able to cook like you."

"There would be advantages to that," she said. "She wouldn't always be *eating* her own cooking." Suddenly she thrust a finger at Shoua. "And don't you tell me I'm not fat!"

"Heaven forbid," he answered. "You're fat, most assuredly."

"You don't mean it."

"No, I don't."

"You're all alike."

"Yes," he agreed.

Even though Khaddam was out of danger, he remained in the trance; Shoua took his leave, but returned regularly, changing bandages, removing fragments of metal that had been partially disgorged from Khaddam's flesh by the healing process.

Finally Khaddam regained consciousness. Lifting a protective pad, Shoua examined the eye that had grown in the emptied socket. It was still smaller than the other, with a milky cast across the iris.

"Can you see out of it?" he asked.

"Just light and shadow," Khaddam replied, blinking. "It's very painful."

"That's normal," Shoua answered. "It should be fully functional by tomorrow. Here, I'll put the pad back on." It was attached to the dressing that covered the top of Khaddam's head; Shoua lowered it back into place.

"How long was I in the trance?"

"Three days."

"I *thought* I was in a bad way," Khaddam replied. He looked at Sigrun. "And I'd wager you haven't had a wink of sleep."

She shook her head. "For three days? Are you joking? I collapsed like a dead woman the morning after. No one could wake me."

"Ah," Khaddam said, clearly having hoped for a different

response. He turned back to Shoua. "Were there any more attacks?"

"No," Shoua answered. "Shall I send for Samadhi?"

Khaddam nodded. "Akram and Massoud too, I think."

Shoua dispatched an assistant; the three arrived presently. Samadhi had already questioned every available eyewitness; only Khaddam's testimony remained. Sigrun kissed him on the forehead, and departed.

"So," Khaddam said to Samadhi, "another sending."

"The witnesses said a figure in armor . . ." Samadhi began.

"Four of them, to be exact," Khaddam said.

"Four?"

"A series of them, one within the other."

"Perhaps you should start at the beginning," said Akram.

"Very well," Khaddam answered. "As you know, I was with Jamal and Mashad. They'd agreed to guard Sigrun's door during the night. We were on our way here after the practice session.

"As we walked along, I noticed a discoloration on the wall. . . ."

"Discoloration?" Samadhi asked.

"In the whitewash. It was yellow at first, but it quickly turned brown . . . Another appeared beside it, then another."

"Someone was conjuring," Samadhi said.

Khaddam nodded. "I heard a clanking sound from the hall we'd just come out of. When I looked back, I saw a tall figure moving towards us. It looked like a man, cased in steel, head to foot. But the armor was unlike anything I'd ever seen. It appeared to be made of short blades. . . ."

Massoud looked puzzled. "Blades?" he asked. "How were they arranged?"

"Side by side, with the edges pointing outward."

"Are you *sure*?" Massoud asked.

"Yes. Does that mean something to you?"

"Perhaps. Please continue."

Khaddam resumed: "The thing's arms were very long, and it had shoulders like an ape. 'Khaddam Al-Ramnal,' said, even though I couldn't see a mouth. Its voice sounded like struck metal.

"Mashad and Jamal were begging for orders. I ignored them, watching the sending. It moved very slowly. For a moment I told myself that something so sluggish could hardly be much of a threat.

"Then I heard the rumbling. The figure began to swell, and red light showed between the blades. I had no idea of what was about to happen, but it was clearly time to flee.

"We dashed up the corridor, and had just rounded a bend when there was a tremendous blast behind us. Looking over my shoulder, I saw powdered mortar flying from the wall, hundreds of white puffs.

"Thinking the danger must be over, we went back to take a look.

"Beyond the corner, the hall was full of smoke. From what I could see of the walls on either side, they were badly pitted, floor to ceiling. Blades stuck out here and there. The explosion had blown the figure apart.

"I heard doors banging open in the distance, men shouting questions. We continued forward.

"Wind ripped along the corridor. The smoke parted, and there stood another of those things.

"'Khaddam Al-Ramnal,' it said, and started towards us, smaller than the first figure, but much quicker.

"Greyclads rushed up in back of it. I ordered them to stop, but they were all shouting, and I don't think they heard me. I decided to conjure.

"Forceletting was unnecessary—I'd given a demonstration during the practice. A Shroud-That-Crawls appeared between the sending and the greyclads. It completely covered the demon, pulling tight.

"The sending went motionless. It looked like a squat white column. Even if it exploded, I was sure the shroud would contain the force. After all, what could possibly rend a Shroud-That-Crawls?

"The greyclads went very near the sending. I ordered them to halt again—this time they obeyed.

"The figure began to expand. The shroud lit with that red

glow. But the warning-signs passed in an instant. There wasn't time to drop—even to blink—before the sending exploded. I saw it all.

"The shroud absorbed much of the force. Some fragments ripped through, and came whistling our way, but most of the blast vented in the opposite direction. The greyclads vanished in the flames. The shroud whirled toward us, disappearing in midair.

"Hot wind struck my face. I felt fragments pluck at my clothes, but no pain. Somehow they'd missed me—it hardly seemed possible. I squinted through the smoke.

"Yet another figure stood facing us, even smaller than the last.

" 'Khaddam Al-Ramnal,' it said. Like a runner at the start of a race, it bent forward, then came pounding towards us at a full sprint.

"I raised a force-screen across the corridor—I didn't hope to hold the sending, only slow it down. The demon swept into it and jerked to a halt.

"Mashad and I turned to flee. It was then that I saw what had happened to Jamal.

"He was lying on his back, still breathing, even though his head was open. His brains were *steaming*.

"A warm stream crawled down my brow. Had I been hit after all? My leg began to ache, and I looked down. My thigh was completely red.

"Akif was tugging at me. The clanging started again. The sending was through the barrier.

"Akif and I rushed back around the corner. We saw some acolytes, ordered them to get back in their rooms. After we passed, we heard shouts, then screams. The brown-robes had waited too long.

"But they'd simply gotten in the way. *I* was the target.

"We came to a stairway. Reaching a landing halfway down, I looked back.

"Something round was bouncing towards us. Farther up the stairs, the sending was hammering down behind it—without its head.

"I raised another barrier, but the head bounced through before it solidified, spinning by me. I started down the steps once more.

"Mashad was ahead of me now. The head passed between his legs, tripping him, beginning to glow. He fell directly on top of it, rolling into a ball about it. Just as he reached the bottom of the steps, it blew him apart.

"Bits of him came flying up the steps. Metal screeched off the walls—I think I even saw the piece that put my eye out. I coughed, tasted blood. Strangely, the fact that I'd been hit in the lungs didn't disturb me near so much as knowing I'd been blinded in one eye.

"Suddenly the whole stairway lit up. The sending behind had burst, destroying the barrier. I felt a terrible blow across the back. Blood leaped from holes in my chest—fragments had gone clear through me. It was a moment before I realized I was flying. I struck the stairs, the walls . . . everything blurred. One last jolt, and I found myself flat on my back at the bottom of the steps.

"My skull *rang*. I heard footsteps clattering, but they sounded very distant. Shaking my head, I looked up into the stairwell.

"A fourth figure was racing downwards, hardly more than three feet tall. Knowing I couldn't hope to outdistance it, I glanced about wildly.

"I was surrounded by dead greyclads—the blast that killed Akif had felled them as well. I grabbed the nearest as the sending launched itself from the steps, red seams opening all over it. The instant I pulled the body over me, the demon exploded.

"The corpse slammed against me. The back of the poor fellow's head cracked into my nose. I felt jabs in my fingers, my arms and legs—they were all partly exposed. But as far as I could tell, nothing tore through the greyclad's body. Obviously, the demons' explosive power decreased in proportion to their size.

"I tried to push the corpse aside, but my strength was almost gone. I became desperate: was another sending about to crawl underneath with me? Screaming, heaving, I managed to tip the corpse upward, and it slid off.

"I sat up, pawing blood from my face. There was no sign of a fifth demon. But even though I'd been so frightened, I felt no relief at all—I was in too much pain. Getting to my feet, I limped off. Somehow I stumbled into Sigrun's arms. You know the rest."

The others were silent for a time.

"I've never heard of such a demon," Akram said at last. "Samadhi?"

The spymaster shook his head.

"I have," Massoud said. "That is, I've heard of things such as Khaddam described. Automatons, not demons, animated and transported by magic. I once devoted a great deal of thought to creating such devices. Indeed, I would even go so far as to say that these metal figures sound for all the world like the product of my own research. Perfected, of course—" He paused, noticing that Samadhi was studying him very closely.

"Go on," Samadhi said.

"Why are you staring at me that way?" Massoud asked.

"It's nothing," Samadhi said, looking away.

"If it's nothing, you can tell me," Massoud answered.

"Don't trouble yourself about it."

Massoud's face tightened. "I was in my laboratory when Khaddam was attacked. I have at least three witnesses."

Samadhi laughed. "Did I accuse you?"

"I just *admitted* I was working on such a project," Massoud said. "If I was the murderer, why would I draw attention to that fact?"

"Massoud, please," Samadhi answered. "I don't suspect you. What possible motive could you have for attacking Khaddam and Iyad?"

"Iyad?" Massoud demanded. "So you think I killed Iyad too?"

"Now stop this," Samadhi replied.

"Perhaps *you* should stop it," Massoud answered, seething.

"This is getting out of hand," Khaddam said. "Samadhi was only pointing out that Iyad's killer probably attacked me too."

"Khaddam's right, Massoud," Akram said. "Samadhi

meant nothing by it. You only increase suspicion by such out-bursts.''

"*Increase* suspicion?" Massoud cried. "Samadhi, am I un-der investigation?"

"Of course not," Samadhi told him. "But if you persist in acting this way . . .''

Whereupon the Numalian exploded: "Perhaps if I were a Kadjafi I'd be less suspect, eh?"

The charge was so unexpected, so illogical, that after the initial shock they simply had to laugh. Numalians *were* often abused by Kadjafim, in spite—or perhaps because—of their reputation as intellectuals; but the *Comahi Irakhoum,* with its emphasis on merit, was one of the few Kadjafi institutions that had eradicated such prejudice. There had been several Nu-malian Grand Masters.

"We *know* you, Massoud," Khaddam said. "You're not capable of murder. . . .''

"I loved Iyad," Massoud said, practically on the verge of tears. "Everything I have I owed to him."

"We know that too," said Akram.

Massoud swabbed at his brow with his hand. He was sweat-ing profusely. "Please excuse me," he said. "I fear I've made a fool of myself. . . .''

"Apology accepted," Khaddam said. "You're among friends.''

"Between Iyad's death and this new attack, my mind's been in a turmoil. Perhaps I should go back to my chambers and try to regain my composure."

"As you wish," Khaddam said.

Once Massoud was gone, Samadhi said: "Quite a perfor-mance.''

"To put it mildly," Akram answered.

"What are you going to do?" Shoua asked Samadhi.

"Given such behavior, I'd be remiss to rule him out."

"As a *suspect*?" Akram demanded.

Before Samadhi could answer, Khaddam said: "He had noth-ing to do with the attacks."

"How do you know?" Samadhi asked.

"First, as you yourself indicated, there's the matter of motive."

"But we may have seen a motive just now," Samadhi countered. "Consider what he said about his race. He's never shown the slightest hint of insecurity. But if he secretly resents us all . . ."

"Then as you said," Khaddam objected, "he's done an excellent job of hiding it. Rather too excellent for your theory, I think."

"But what about that outburst?"

"Shock at Iyad's death, just as he said."

"I don't know," Akram said uneasily. "He's seemed very much himself these last few days. Frankly, I expected him to show more grief."

"He's embarrassed himself in the past," Khaddam said. "Do you remember how he wept when Hammad died? Afterwards he *swore* he'd exercise more self-restraint. He simply lost control when he was accused."

"I *didn't* accuse him," Samadhi protested.

"You didn't see that look on your face," Khaddam said. "Admit it. You were wondering about him."

"True," Samadhi answered.

"But can you actually imagine Massoud committing such crimes?" Khaddam asked.

"Only with some difficulty," Samadhi conceded.

"And furthermore," Khaddam said, "would you grant that the attacks are connected?"

"I'm not a great believer in coincidence."

"Neither am I," Khaddam replied. "What then are we left with? We have good reason to believe the Anarites were responsible for the first sending. We have some reason to suspect Massoud in the second—but not much. If indeed the attacks *are* related, the Anarites were responsible for the second as well."

"And how do you explain the similarities between the sending that attacked you and Massoud's automata?"

Khaddam shot back: "How do we know the figures were automata, and not demons? Massoud didn't deal with them. I did."

"I removed fragments from you while you were in the trance," Shoua said. "If the sending *was* a demon, nothing would have remained."

"A valid point," Akram said.

Khaddam shrugged it off. "But if Massoud *is* reponsible, why *would* he mention the similarities himself?"

"Guilty conscience—" Samadhi said.

"You'll have to do better than that," Khaddam snapped.

"Would you prefer I didn't investigate him, then?" Samadhi demanded.

"Do as you think best," said Khaddam. "But once again. The Anarites are behind all this. Mark my words."

# Chapter 9

Nawhar's itching eased as he and his companions pressed farther into the high country. The heat diminished, and he was sweating less. Intermittent breezes brought precious moments of pure relief.

Still, it remained quite warm. They passed a dead sheep by the side of the road; the air was foul with its stench. It was well that they had not brought the corpse of Khaldun Al-Maari.

*Flesh*, Nawhar thought in disgust. For a morbid moment he found himself imagining the horrors that were even now proceeding within Khaldun's body.

*As he is,* Nawhar told himself, *you will be*.

The itching flared across his stomach. It felt as though beetles were crawling on his skin. He rasped at himself with his nails.

*You're rotting even now.*

The doctors at Qanar-Sharaj had never discovered why his skin troubled him so. Master Shoua himself was mystified by Nawhar's symptoms. The disease was not the least susceptible to treatment—no salve or ointment affected it in the slightest. Perhaps a healing-trance might have done some good, but Nawhar had never been able to master the technique.

There was a twinge in his shoulder as he scratched himself—
his other ailment clamoring for attention. He took out a short
length of dried bark and began to chew it. Unlike the itching,
the pain in his joints could be lessened by drugs; but there was
no cure, and Shoua had said the condition would progressively
deteriorate. It was a readily identified ailment, typically an
infirmity of age, though not uncommon among the young. It
was always the worst in the mornings; Nawhar had to do elaborate stretching exercises. Zehowah and Khalima had seen him
at them, and he had heard them laughing.

*Sows,* he thought as he rode along. He had no use for them
whatsoever. Erim and Sharif might allow themselves to be
enchanted. He was made of sterner stuff.

True, he *had* acknowledged to himself that they were beautiful, and aside from those giggles, they had been quite charm-
ing. Khalima in particular he found rather attractive—she
seemed the more intelligent of the two.

But he had taken his vows; and moreover, the women were
followers of Essaj! Even now, they were doing everything they
could to sway Erim's judgement—cunning little beasts, they
had already grasped that Sharif's judgement counted for nothing.

Of course, to his credit, Erim was as yet unmoved by the
sisters' claims.

"Those teachings aren't extraordinary at all," Erim was
saying, as the party passed into the shadows of a thick stand
of cedar. "Nothing to convince me that he's the Expected
One."

"But he says we should love our neighbors as ourselves,"
Khalima protested. "That we should do to others as we would
have them do to us. I never heard anything like that from my
parents. Or our priest in Thangura, for that matter."

"Well," Erim said, "I'm not to blame for the deficiencies
in your upbringing. And just off the top of my head, I could
quote you five philosophers who said exactly the same thing.
Take Al-Muttanabbi. He made such pronouncements seven
hundred years ago. And no one batted an eyelash."

"But Essaj speaks with such authority," Zehowah said.

"I'm sure he does," Erim answered. "He's obviously made

a tremendous impression on you two. Still, the world is full of men who act like authorities."

"Yourself, for one," Khalima said.

"Hah!" laughed Sharif. "Stuck you, Erim."

Nawhar looked at him narrowly. Indeed, the woman had scored a point. Yet what good did it do to encourage her?

"Serves me right," said Erim, smiling at her. "Well, then. Take nothing I say on authority."

"Except that?" Khalima asked.

"Hoo now!" said Sharif. "She's covering you with blood, Erim."

Nawhar swore under his breath. Obviously Erim had been about to add that she should judge his arguments simply on their own merit. Sharif was so thick. The more superficial a point was, the more it impressed him. Coaching him for the Sixth-Level doctrine trial had been a perfect nightmare.

"I was simply going to say that you should judge my arguments on their own merits," Erim said. "I might also mention that I'm not claiming to be the Lord's Anointed. You're aware, of course, that others besides Essaj have made that claim?"

"They were false Messiahs," Zehowah said. "Essaj is the *real* one."

"The Son of Man," Khalima said.

"Son of Man," Erim mused. "An interesting title, but rather enigmatic. What does it mean?"

"Just what it says, I suppose," Khalima replied.

"But we are all sons—or daughters—of man. Why is he *The* Son of Man?"

Neither Khalima or Zehowah had an answer for that.

"Perhaps you should ask him," Zehowah answered.

"We will indeed," said Nawhar.

Shortly after midday, in a clearing on the crest of a thickly wooded slope, they paused beside the road to eat. Bishah was now in sight, a large walled city, standing atop the next ridge, its red towers and domes a vivid contrast against the mighty blue mountain-wall that rose behind. Standing astride the main caravan-route from Tarchan, it was a major trading center, the heart of a thriving commerce in cedarwood. Its people had specialized since time immemorial in selling timber, as well as various forms of woodworking; the inhabitants of the small villages nearby did the actual harvesting. The trees were carefully nurtured, sections of forest replanted as soon as they were cleared.

Erim handed Khalima a piece of flatbread, saying: "I spent a year up here, looking for bones."

"Why?" she asked.

"Let's say for curiosity's sake. We Sharajnaghim like to imagine that we're interested in just about everything."

"What kind of bones?"

"Ones so old they've turned to stone," Erim replied. "Remains of creatures that lived very long ago. These outcroppings hereabouts are a very good place to look. The right *kind* of stone. A little farther to the north, you see, the rock turns to granite, like those mountains over there. You never find anything in granite. But here, in these hills, it's all sandstone. And sometimes, if you're lucky, you can find entire skeletons, just waiting to be pried out. Monsters that lived before there were any human beings at all."

Khalima looked puzzled. "But weren't men the first creatures that God made?"

"So, your father taught you Scripture, eh?"

"I can read," Khalima announced proudly.

"We both can," Zehowah added.

"Remarkable," said Sharif, looking at the dark beauty dreamily.

"But back to these animals of yours," said Khalima, apparently with genuine interest.

"Well," Erim resumed, "Regarding the Scriptures, there are two stories. In one, man is made first. In the other, he's made last."

"But which do you think is true?"

"I try not oppose one text against the other. I'm committed by faith to acknowledge the truth of both. Which does, undeniably, lead to certain confusions. But I, for one, don't think that God cares at all about surface consistency. Not when he speaks to us."

"Consistency?"

"Making everything agree with everything else. You see, I think there's only one thing that makes perfect sense. Only one *perfect* thing at all. And that's God.

"Now somehow He has to tell us about His perfection, so that we'll know that He's God. But we're too small to take it all in, or make sense of it all. We're *im*perfect. And so He doesn't worry about the details, because we wouldn't be able to make sense of them no matter what. Do you follow me?"

"I'm not sure," said Khalima.

"Let me see if I can explain. When the Scriptures were written, a thousand years ago, learned men had a different idea of what the world was like. They knew less than we do now. And when God explained Himself to them, He spoke in terms they'd understand.

"Now some might say that that means the Scriptures are less valuable today, because we know more, and we can see what appear to be mistakes in them. I take a different view. I think we *have* learned more about the world. But the more we've learned, the more we've seen that our view is very limited. And someone in the future might well regard our new 'knowledge' much the same way that we regard the knowledge of the people who wrote the Scriptures.

"Yet from God's point of view, our knowledge of virtually *anything* is next to nothing. So He's hardly doing us a disservice if He explains Himself according to ideas men had a thousand years ago, so long as He gives us the essential truths, such as the fact that He created everything, which of course is literally the case. And literally miraculous. The truth is, it would hardly be a blessing if the Scriptures actually told us *how* God makes things happen. We wouldn't be able to understand the Scriptures then. Any more than we understand the world."

"I still don't think I follow you."

"Very well, then. Perhaps you should think of it this way. Have you ever heard a story that you loved very much, but not all of it fit together? The characters did things no one would do, or things happened that were impossible?"

"Yes," she said.

"But nonetheless, as a *story*, it all made sense? You were

willing to put up with the rest, because the parts that made sense were so good?"

"Yes, I know what you mean."

"But do you think the person who made up the story did all that by accident?"

"I don't know."

"Well, it depends on the storyteller, I suppose. But the really good ones know they can't make everything in their stories make sense, because they've only got a little story to work with, and they can't just sit there endlessly explaining everything. They can only give you the *appearances* of things—just enough to convince. To give you faith, as it were. A storyteller's like the Grand Vizier who put up beautiful villages that were all facades, so that the King might see something other than wasteland as he passed through his realm. The Vizier knew that there was no point in making whole buildings. In the same way, a good storyteller tells you what he thinks you need to know.

"That's what this world is like, at least in my opinion. Compared to its author, it's just a little story. Real, but less real than He is. And even the Scriptures are just a little story within that story. And if you look at any of it too closely, you no longer see the story, but only the words. And when you do that, you lose track of the truth."

Nawhar had been listening intently to all of this. "So," he said, "the world we live in is like the Grand Vizier's facades?"

"To an extent," Erim replied.

"How then is that different from thinking it's all an illusion?"

"Because I think the facades are really there," Erim said. "They're not *illusory* at all. We might be interpreting them incorrectly. But the very fact that we interpret them in a particular fashion—the very fashion that renders us susceptible to the Grand Vizier's artifice—implies that there is a large element of truth in our perceptions."

"You've lost me again," Khalima said.

"He isn't talking to you," Nawhar snapped.

* * *

After finishing their meal, they proceeded into the valley. It was miles across, and there were several villages, where the Sharajnaghim inquired about Essaj. Word had it that he was preaching north of Bishah. As the afternoon drew on, and shadows lengthened among the cedars, they decided to spend the night in the city.

They were partway up the northern slope when faint shouts reached them on the wind, interspersed with howls and roars. The farther the Sharajnaghim ascended, the louder the cries grew, ringing through the woods.

"What language is that?" Sharif asked.

"I don't know," Erim said.

"Black Malgronese?" Nawhar ventured.

Presently they came to an expanse filled with vaults and mausoleums, Bishah's necropolis. A high cliff bordered it on the north, dozens of ornate tomb-facades chiselled into the stone along its foot. The city's red walls rose flush from the cliff-top, the road winding up to the gate along a great carven ramp.

The cries seemed to be coming from one of the cliff-tombs. Many people had been drawn by the din, Kadjafi and Mirkut soldiers among them. The road was completely blocked.

"What's happening?" Nawhar asked a tall Numalian on the fringe of the throng.

"A demoniac," came the answer. "Can't you hear him? He's been breaking open the vaults, ripping bodies to pieces."

For the first time, Nawhar noticed black shapes moving between the whitewashed walls—vultures.

Other voices suddenly echoed from the tomb. There was a series of shouts, all in Mirkut, then cries of pain.

The Numalian added: "Four men from the garrison went in to try and restrain him—"

The first voice rose to drown the Mirkuts out. Its words were still unintelligible, but presently Nawhar began to recognize some of them, growing aware of numerous strands, an intertwined babble of sentences spoken simultaneously in several different languages, interspersed with roars and barks.

A Mirkut staggered out of the tomb-mouth. A second appeared, dragging a third. There was no sign of the fourth. Their comrades in the crowd rushed over and helped them to the road. Vultures croaked and bounded skyward, then settled once more.

Nawhar and the others rode forward, the throng parting to let them pass. Reaching the Mirkuts, they dismounted.

"What did you see?" Sharif asked one of the stricken men.

"He has powers," the fellow replied in thickly accented Kadjafi, fingers pressed against the side of his head. Blood streamed down his neck. A companion came near with a linen cloth. The wounded one lowered his hand, revealing a ragged hole where his ear had been ripped from his head. "His face— terrible. It hurts to see him. Terrible, terrible." He began to weep like a child. "Shagdai's still in there. All his fingers— bitten off."

Erim told Nawhar: "I don't think that's one of your pellet-chewers in there."

Nawhar nodded. Even though he had never encountered a genuine case of possession, he had no doubt that the phenomenon existed. Why a spirit would sully itself by invading a physical host, he had no idea; it seemed almost the ultimate perversion to him. But if one could imagine angels in rebellion against God Himself, one could imagine more.

A middle-aged man thrust his way past the Mirkuts, a woman with grey hair running along behind him, pulling at his wrist.

"I've sent for Essaj, Akhtal," she cried. "These men can do nothing."

"They're Sharajnaghim," the man replied. "They can exorcise demons. And Essaj isn't here."

"But, Nihat—"

"Silence, woman!" he shouted. He eyed the wizards. "That's my son in that tomb. Possessed by a devil. It'll kill him before it's through, and God knows how many others. Can you help us?"

"You're followers of Essaj Ben Yussef?" Nawhar asked.

"*She* is. I'm not. Will you help?"

"I've never performed an exorcism," Erim said.

"Neither have I," Sharif said. "But we know the ritual. How much can there be to it?"

"That depends on the demon," Nawhar said. He addressed the Mirkut Sharif had spoken to: "What did it call itself?"

" '*Horde*,' " the easterner answered, wincing as his comrade dabbed at the side of his head with the linen. "It said, 'My name is Horde.' "

"Never heard of him," Sharif said. "Hedge-demon."

"Not necessarily," Erim answered.

"So? What difference does it make?"

"What if it's something completely beyond our experience?" Erim asked. "There are demons we couldn't possibly cope with."

To which Sharif replied: "The sort that possess people aren't very powerful. Generally."

"Generally," Nawhar emphasized. "Then there are the others. Fallen angels. Grand Master Ahwaz tried to exorcise one. It killed its host and every member of the household, and very nearly killed Ahwaz—"

"But will you help us?" the father pleaded.

"Yes," answered the Sharajnaghim, all at once.

The demoniac had fallen silent; but as the three stepped over the low wall bordering the necropolis, a torrent of laughter, seemingly many voices at once, poured from the tomb.

"Come back!" cried Khalima. "Wait for Essaj!"

They ignored her, threading their way among the sepulchres. Most were simple stone receptacles with thick slab lids, roughly four feet high. Others were imposing structures, some the size of houses, with domes and carved archways, and elaborate locks upon their gates.

But such safeguards had not defeated the demoniac. Several mausoleums stood open, their shadowy interiors strewn with splintered coffins and ragged sprawling shapes.

Neither had the vaults of the lowly been spared; a dozen lids at least had been smashed, the caskets beneath broached. Bodies had been wrenched up into sitting positions, their heads torn off and switched; here a child's lay upon the shoulders of a large warrior in chain mail, there a helmeted skull rested atop a nude female mummy.

Yet most of the cadavers, or pieces of them, had simply been strewn upon the ground. The vultures ripped and slashed at the freshest. The smell was all but unbearable, the air thick with flies.

Nawhar clapped a hand over his nose, stomach roiling. Flies lighted on his skin; beneath his robes, far beyond their reach, his diseased flesh reproduced their crawling. He was surrounded on all sides by decay, by the physical universe at its most revolting; insects drawn by a banquet of corruption had turned their attention—naturally—to his own rank carcass.

The crawling beneath his robes intensified. He could feel his skin rising, visualize the red rash spreading like blood in milk; the crawling became an itch that verged on pain, moving across his shoulders, under his armpits. . . .

*Ignore it,* he thought. *Just an illusion. Concentrate on the task at hand.*

Calling on deep reserves of contempt, he forced a temporary wedge between himself and the carnal muck encasing him. Soon he could barely feel the flies lighting on him; the stench lost its fetid power. The nettles in his flesh grew duller.

"Deny the body," he whispered. "Deny the filth. . . ."

Erim looked back at him. He had caught Nawhar at this ritual before. Shaking his head with what might have been disapproval or pity (or easily some combination of both), Erim turned once more.

"Deny the flesh," Nawhar continued. "Deny the rot. . . ."

Presently the Sharajnaghim reached the steps of the cliff-tomb. The demoniac's laughter had faded; the looming archway stood mute. Much taller than Nawhar had thought from a distance, it seemed to lean ominously over them.

They proceeded up the stairs. At the top they prayed, drained off a measure of repellent force, and uttered a spell. Filtered pink through blood and flesh, light throbbed from their left palms, dim under the late afternoon sun. The pulse steadied to a constant glow.

"Now," Sharif said. "Slowly."

They passed under the arch, into a wide corridor lined with squat pillars. The colonnade receded into thick blackness; the air was hot and parchingly dry.

"I don't see any coffins," Sharif whispered as they walked along.

"They'll be up ahead, in the main chamber," Erim replied, fanning flies away from his mouth. A rectangle of deeper gloom grew visible in the darkness ahead. "Through that doorway, I suppose."

"Stench isn't so bad," Sharif said.

"I expect no one's been buried in here for a while."

"Then what's drawing these—"

There came a fierce, powerful buzzing, as though some huge hive had opened before them. A black cloud billowed out of the door. Flecks of light glittered on thousands of tiny wings and chitinous bodies; so dense was the teeming mass that it looked almost like a solid sludge of flies, a tarry wall rolling along the passage.

Some distance from the Sharajnaghim, it halted, a circular opening appearing in the middle. The aperture widened steadily, the rim surrounding it beginning to rotate. Black spurs crept inward and outward, like points on a circlet of thorns. The flies had assumed the shape of a gigantic spiked wheel. The wizards stood silently, pondering this prodigy.

At last Sharif laughed and walked boldly towards it.

"What are you doing?" Nawhar demanded.

"It's an invitation," Sharif replied. "He wants to us to go through."

"And that's a reason to oblige him?" Nawhar demanded.

As if in answer, Sharif broke into a sprint and hurled himself headlong towards the opening in the wheel.

The aperture contracted spasmodically. Nawhar gasped to see the spikes licking inward at Sharif.

But the opening instantly widened once more, allowing Sharif to pass. He dropped from sight on the far side. A moment went by before he reappeared, beckoning.

"Come on," he said impatiently.

Erim muttered something and followed. The opening contracted once more. Nawhar thought the spikes drove closer before retreating this time.

Sharif hauled Erim up on the far side. "What are you waiting for?" he asked Nawhar.

Nawhar sucked in several deep breaths, eyeing his companions. Erim waving him on, he started forward, but paused at the last moment before the wheel of flies.

"Nawhar," Sharif said, exasperated.

Nawhar retreated, raced forward again. He bounded airborne, soaring towards the center of the wheel. As he neared the opening, he saw it tightening yet again.

Time seemed to slow. He was floating through the tunnel, the pillars passing lazily on either side. The sensation was pleasant; also terrifying. He suspected after all that speed was of the essence, and here he was, drifting along. . . .

*The others made it,* he told himself. But the wheel was not merely contracting this time. The spikes seemed to be *lengthening*, reaching for him like tentacles.

He entered the hole, the flies brushing his body. Then everything went dark, and his hurtling form sank under a great weight. Tiny legs plucked at his face. Wings beat at his skin. The wheel had collapsed upon him. As he struck the floor, he realized he was completely smothered in flies.

Not daring to open his mouth, he stood up, staggering under the heavy blanket, ripping at himself, fingers digging inches deep before they touched flesh. He crushed the handfuls he held, began to swat himself, smashing, beating, the flies bursting and liquefying under his blows.

He felt other hands slapping at him. He reached up and tore the mask of flies from his face, gulped air, felt another mask settle over his features. He began to grow dizzy, sinking to his knees.

Erim and Sharif kept slapping him; through the hideous buzzing in his ears, he heard their distant shouts.

"I'm going to use bolts," Sharif cried. "I'll blast them off you. Hold on!"

Nawhar felt a muffled impact against his chest. His clothes were suddenly wet.

A second impact struck his left arm. Pulped flies sloughed away like a rain of mud. Nawhar swiped the insects from his face, opened his eyes for an instant just in time to see a third blast blazing towards him. Slime burst from his right arm and shoulder, splattering his cheek.

"Lie on your belly!" Sharif cried.

Nawhar put his hands over his face, hurling himself onto his stomach, crushing thousands of insects beneath his weight. He tried to distance himself from the horror, but it was useless; his senses assaulted him. The ooze seemed to be merging with his flesh. The buzzing grew so intense that he was sure his very skull had been invaded. . . .

Sharif's bolts raced up and down his back. Nawhar grew dimly aware that the tide had turned. The insects were crawling from his ears. Moment by moment, the buzzing grew fainter.

At last it faded altogether. He could no longer feel any flies on his skin. He rose, gasping, beslimed from head to foot, standing in a sump of wet smashed chitin.

"The rest went back through the arch," Sharif said. "Are you hurt? I tried my best to control the bolts, but—"

Nawhar just stared at him spitting, shivering. The ooze had gone very cold.

"Are you hurt?" Erim asked.

Nawhar shook his head slowly. Numbly he wiped slime from his face.

"He singled me out," he said. "It was a trap—for me."

Sharif began: "Well, if that's the worst he can do—"

"Worst?" Nawhar cried, unable to endure the rest of Sharif's shallow exhortation. He felt as though he had been violated; completely unable to communicate the horror of it, he screamed and swept his arm at Sharif, splattering him with fluid. Sharif blinked.

Erim stepped between them. "Do you want to go back?" he asked Nawhar.

"Back?" Nawhar said. Shaken as he was, the thought had not occurred to him. Was Erim suggesting he had lost his nerve?

"Admit that he defeated you?" Erim prodded.

Nawhar shook his head vehemently, realizing that he was no longer trembling with cold, but rage—whether at Erim or the demon, he was not sure. "How could you ask me that? After what he did to me . . ."

Erim read his face. "That's better."

"Yes," Nawhar answered, seeing his friend's intention now,

struggling to restrain his anger and disgust. "Give me a few moments."

He discovered that the ooze covering him was drying swiftly. More accurately, it seemed to be evaporating from his body. The thought that the filth would soon be gone calmed him considerably.

He looked at the crushed flies on the floor. The sump was shrinking steadily, simply disappearing.

"I'm all right," he announced.

"Good man," Sharif said. Nawhar saw what seemed to be genuine respect in Sharif's eyes; perhaps Sharif had some appreciation of what he had gone through after all. Authentically touched, Nawhar almost smiled, feeling a warmth towards Sharif that he had never known before.

"Now," Sharif continued, "let's show that hedge-demon the error of his ways."

Nawhar nodded, raising a silent prayer that Sharif's estimation of the threat should prove correct.

They started forward once more. As they approached the threshold of the burial-chamber, dark red smears could be seen on the walls of the corridor.

"What do you make of those?" Erim asked.

"Looks like blood," Sharif said, and touched one of the marks. "Still wet."

The smudges seemed to have been made with some kind of broad brush. In places they formed crude letters.

"Can't read it," Erim said.

Nawhar and Sharif studied them. Both were experts in deciphering old manuscripts and difficult script.

"*Horde*," Sharif read.

"Anything more?" Erim asked.

"*Lord of the Flies*," Nawhar answered. The title meant nothing to him, beyond the obvious; but as he spoke it aloud, a dreadful intuition shook him. "He's one of the Great Demons."

"How can you tell?" Erim asked.

"I can feel it."

"Maybe we should go back after all," Erim said.

"No," Nawhar said. "Who else is there?" ——

Sharif's eyes shone. "That's good enough for me."

They went to the doorway.

Ahead lay a large circular chamber under a domed ceiling. The curving wall was lined with niches, but these had been emptied, the coffins spilled out onto the floor, smashed into fragments or overturned. Bones were scattered everywhere, many still sheathed in rags and parchment skin.

Directly across from the entrance, caskets and parts of caskets had been lashed together to form a great jagged chair. Enthroned upon it was a huge man in a tattered knee-length tunic, head on his chest. A mere child in comparison, a Mirkut sat on his massive knee, drenched in blood, his head also hanging, one of his hands buried to the knuckles in the other's mouth. The giant seemed to be chewing on it.

Behind the throne, a black spiked wheel was emblazoned on the wall. It shimmered slightly, and Nawhar realized it was made up of flies. The bloody brush had been applied on either side—*Hail Traitors,* the message read.

The giant spat the Mirkut's hand out. All the fingers were gone. The Mirkut groaned, stirring fitfully atop the giant's knee. The demoniac looked up slowly at the Sharajnaghim, grinning literally ear to ear.

*It hurts to see him,* the other Mirkut had said. Now Nawhar knew what he meant. The Sharajnaghi felt an actual scorching sensation; it was like standing too near a fire. Nawhar had never dreamed that such malevolence could be expressed on a human face. It seemed far too perfect for flesh.

"Ah," said the giant. "It's you."

Taking the Mirkut by the hair, he lifted the man's head, revealing the abraded red meat that had once been a face, scraped featureless but for the gaping hole of the mouth.

"What do you think of my brush?" asked the Lord of the Flies.

## Chapter 10

Erim had never known such fear.

*I told them,* he thought, heart pounding against his ribs. *We should have gone back.*

But if Sharif was frightened, he gave no sign of it. "In the name of God the Almighty," Sharif said, "Maker of heaven and earth, I command you to put him down."

Still holding the Mirkut by the hair, the demoniac extended him at arm's length, shook him so that his legs swung violently to and fro—and dropped him to the floor. The Mirkut crumpled in a wheezing heap.

"There," said Horde. "Satisfied, traitors?"

"Why do you call us that?" Sharif demanded.

"Don't speak with him!" Erim cried. "Command!"

But Sharif had already risen to the bait; and Horde was not about to let him escape.

"I call you traitors because that is what you are," he went on. "You don't know it yet. But the seeds are there. You will betray everything you love. Your friends, your Order—"

"Never," Sharif answered.

"Never?" Horde asked. "How do you justify such confidence? Can you see the future, little one? I can. And your sins will be scarlet, I promise. One of you will stand back as his love is slaughtered. Two will deliver the third up to be slain. One will kill another. And one will fight on *my* side when the final battle is joined . . ."

"He's trying to confuse us," Nawhar said.

"I don't have to confuse you," Horde replied. "Your little minds are quite murky enough."

"Silence!" Sharif cried. "In the Name of God, I—"

The demoniac laughed. "I've heard that Name before, maggot. I'm quite familiar with all the Names, as a matter of fact. We were very close once, He and I. I still remember His warmth, His light. You would have to invoke Him many times before I felt the slightest pang. I am great and mighty, traitors. I am no hedge-demon."

"Silence!" Sharif cried. "It is God Himself who commands you—"

Horde laughed again. "It is *you* who command me. You, my rightful prey. You have no authority. And you have nowhere near enough time."

He stood, colossal in the shadows. A stamp of his foot, and two mummies rose from the floor. He lifted his arms; their skeletal hands reached out.

"Bring me their tongues," he said.

Joints creaking, the mummies started forward, cerements trailing, hissing over the stone.

Erim and Nawhar were still assuming stances when Sharif launched two cataract-strikes. Brittle and ancient, the mummies came apart like paper and twigs, torsos blasted from under their heads. The skulls struck the floor like dried gourds, flattening in puffs of dust.

Horde sighed. "The flesh is weak, as Nawhar might say. It seems I'll have to do this myself."

He stepped down from the throne.

"I'll bind him!" Sharif cried. Entering a Griffin Stance, he uttered a spell.

Halfway across the floor, Horde began to struggle, caught in unseen fetters.

"Force him to his knees!" Erim shouted.

Sharif nodded. Horde bent forward as though there were a loop about his neck; his arms snapped straight down. Gradually one of his legs buckled. Grinding his teeth, great tendons standing out on his throat, he sank to one knee.

"With the power of God, I adjure you," Sharif roared. "*Come out of that man!*"

"Come out?" the demoniac gritted, craning his neck from side to side. "Shall I come out?"

"Obey the Servant of the Lord!" Sharif cried.

The giant nodded. "Shall I come out—*THROUGH HIS EYES*?"

His head jerked up. The organs bulged, whites fading as they stretched; then the orbs burst. The Sharajnaghim flinched as droplets struck them. Clear fluid crawled down the giant's cheeks.

"Better," said Horde, and brushed his massive hands along his arms, as if to sweep away the invisible strands restraining him. Effortlessly he rose to his feet. "Eyes are such a nuisance. They come between you and the truth. Worse still"—he wrenched a scrap of tissue out of one eyesocket and flicked it to the floor—"they go blind."

Once again, he started forward.

"Stun-bolts," said Sharif.

The Sharajnaghim switched stance and released a storm of blue crescents. The whole chamber lit up, carved pink sandstone tinged purple by the glare of the strikes. Pummelled steadily backwards, the giant pitched at last into his makeshift throne, smashing the coffins, half-disappearing beneath the wreckage. His legs jerked once, and went motionless.

Maintaining their stances, the Sharajnaghim eyed him cautiously.

*It can't be this easy*, Erim thought.

But the giant remained still. Slowly they crossed the floor, going very close.

Off to the side, the Mirkut groaned. The little easterner raised himself on one elbow and flopped onto his stomach, fishing about blindly with his good hand.

"See to him," Sharif told Erim.

Erim swore, hesitating.

"If we can help him—" Sharif began.

"I know," Erim answered. Crouching, he turned the Mirkut over. One glance, and he averted his eyes instantly, gasping.

The man bubbled a few unintelligible words. Erim forced himself to look again. As much as he hated the easterners, he could not help but be moved by the man's plight. He doubted the Mirkut could possibly survive; even if he did, to go through life without a face—

"Worse than death," a voice agreed jovially from beneath the coffins.

The wreckage shifted. Erim jumped to his feet just as it exploded in all directions, the demoniac rearing up out of the flying wood. Fending off spinning fragments, the wizards retreated frenziedly.

"Did you actually think you stunned me?" Horde asked. "What lofty opinions you have of yourselves!"

"What now?" Nawhar panted to Sharif.

"Indeed," said Horde. "What now, Sharif?" And with that, he bounded directly towards him.

Entering a Dragon Stance, Sharif answered with two cataract-strikes. For all the effect they had against the onrushing shape, they might as well have been directed at a hurtling boulder. Lighting in front of him, Horde swept Sharif's hands aside—the motion seemed astoundingly casual to Erim—grinned full into his face, and butted him in the forehead. There was a loud crack. Brow split open, Sharif stumbled backwards, toppling.

Horde turned towards Erim. "Now *that*," he said, "is stunned."

Erim blinked, suddenly aware of an awful pressure on his forearm; when had the demoniac grabbed him? It was as if the intervening instant had simply been removed.

"You should listen to Nawhar," the giant said, taking the limb in both hands. "Bodies truly are a bad idea; which is why I enjoy mocking them so much. Think: if you weren't just a little puppet made of bones and meat, I wouldn't be able to do *this*—"

With a sharp motion, he snapped the forearm in the middle.

Broken bones lifted a little tent in Erim's sleeve, two tiny pale points protruding through the cloth; the glow in his palm went out. He gaped in horror, watching his sleeve go black with blood, waiting for the agony.

"Or *this*—"

Horde wrung Erim's forearm as though he were twisting a rag. The pain struck the Sharajnaghi at last, a hammerblow that sent water spurting from his eyes.

"Or *this*—"

Horde lifted him high up by the wrist. His whole arm one long shriek of torment, Erim twisted in midair. Wincing the tears away, he looked around wildly for Nawhar.

Nawhar stood nearby, in a Griffin Stance. He seemed to be whispering to himself, halting every few words, starting again.

"Conjuring, are you?" Horde asked him. "Having trouble, worm-feast? Did you enjoy the flies?"

Swinging Erim by the arm, he let go of his wrist, flinging him feet first towards Nawhar.

Nawhar dodged. Sailing past, Erim landed heavily on his side, arm slapping against the stone. There was a horrendous jolt of fresh pain, then numbness. Nawhar helped him to his feet.

"Finished the spell," Nawhar said.

Wiping his eyes, Erim looked round at Horde.

Above the giant, a shape like an inverted tree hung from the ceiling, branches snaking. The limbs ended in human hands, dozens of which had locked onto the demoniac's body.

Horde seemed unconcerned. Completely motionless despite the tugging hands, he might have been a statue bolted to the floor.

"A poor choice, Nawhar," the giant said. "This creature *will* answer to the name you called. But only because it's forgotten its true name. The one *I* gave it—a million years ago."

He pronounced a single harsh syllable. The hands recoiled from his body. Pressing his own together, he raised them high above his head and swept them apart violently.

The tree split as though it had been riven by a huge axe, the halves banging upwards against the ceiling before they vanished.

"Now," Horde said. "About those nasty squirming tongues of yours. No more exorcisms for you."

Nawhar and Erim fell back before him, praying.

Sharif rose to his feet, blinking, one hand to his wounded forehead. Insanely, he decided to hold his ground, summoning a demon of his own.

Squatting on its haunches, a dark bulk like a great bear or ape materialized in front of Horde. Rearing up, it unfolded a brace of long heavy arms, six at least.

Horde snorted with contempt and, even as the arms enfolded him, brought a malletlike fist down between two short horns on the creature's skull. The head was driven instantly from sight below the curve of the beast's shoulders; it happened with such speed that Erim thought the creature had been decapitated. But Horde seized the head and lifted it back into view, twisting it savagely so that its ursine face peered back at the Sharajnaghim.

"Look what you forced me to do, Sharif," Horde said, the head dematerializing between his palms.

Erim tugged at Sharif. "It's no use!"

Sharif swore, shaking his head.

"He'll kill us all!" Erim cried.

"And that's not the half of it," Horde said.

"I'll hold him," Sharif said, slinging blood from his eyes.

"I don't think so," the demoniac replied.

"Run!" Sharif cried.

Erim pulled loose from Nawhar, and they staggered from the chamber. The archway at the far end appeared impossibly tiny and distant, the setting sun just descending beneath the lintel. Light flooded into the corridor. Squinting, Erim raised his good arm before his eyes, the other brushing warm blood onto his leg as he ran.

He heard Sharif summoning another demon, then pounding footbeats.

"Keep going!" came Sharif's voice.

"Is he coming?" Erim asked over his shoulder, the footbeats rolling up hard and close.

"Yes!" Sharif answered frantically.

Erim tried to force more speed into his strides. Increasingly lightheaded, he wondered if he would faint before reaching the arch.

"Can't you run any faster?" Sharif cried.

Maddeningly resistant to Erim's efforts, the exit never seemed to come any nearer. Weeping in frustration and terror, he was about to sink to the floor when he and Nawhar crossed the threshold. Erim had no idea of how it had happened.

But there he was jolted by the realization that he had heard only one set of footsteps behind him. He turned drunkenly, and—

There stood Horde.

The demoniac was cradling Sharif in the crook of one mighty arm as though he were a baby, his other hand working in Sharif's mouth. It had been the demoniac's voice all along.

Erim reached for the throwing-knife inside his bloodsoaked sleeve. The arm was still wrenched out of shape; the knife was not where he expected. Grinning at him, Horde pulled Sharif's tongue into view.

Erim's fingers fumbled onto the handle. He hurled the blade.

Loosing Sharif's tongue, Horde caught the knife by the tip as though plucking a mosquito from midair.

Erim and Nawhar backed down the stairs, the demoniac following, tossing the blade aside.

"Where are you going?" he laughed, thrusting his hand back into Sharif's mouth. "I'll have this out in a moment—"

He paused, empty eyesockets staring past them. A hollow silence descended. Startled to see him halt, Erim and Nawhar stopped as well, staring breathlessly.

The giant emitted a low growl, upper lip curling. Wagging his head, he paced this way and that like a frustrated beast.

"What do you want with me?" he bellowed at last, foam bursting from his lips.

Erim was astounded. Had he detected a note of fear?

"Put him down," a calm voice answered, so soft Erim barely heard it.

Horde snarled and lowered Sharif to the steps.

*You can't have seen that*, Erim thought, mystified by the demon's compliance. He and Nawhar looked round.

A man was coming up the steps, holding a half-eaten apple. He was solidly built, with broad shoulders and a powerful chest, his hands rough-looking and very big. He had the appearance of someone who had spent a life at hard physical labor, though there was also a strange youthful quality about his face. His hair was tied behind his head, and he had a dark moustache but no beard.

Stopping at last, he smiled at Erim and Nawhar. His teeth were almost comically perfect; yet somehow, on him, the effect was not foolish at all.

"It's going to be all right," he said, handed Nawhar the apple, and looked up towards the demoniac. Leaning forward, one hand on his hip, the other on his knee, he addressed the giant as though talking to a disobedient dog:

"Come out of that man."

There was a sound like a titanic whipcrack; Erim jumped as a fog of dust rose from the steps and the cliff-face, as if there had been some tremendous detonation beneath the earth. His robes thrashed violently; his ears popped.

Fists clenched like hammers at his sides, the demoniac arched backwards, a mighty tumult of voices pouring from his throat. He seemed to shrink radically; something huge and terrible was departing his distended flesh, a fallen angel, Erim had no doubt of it, in all likelihood a close lieutenant of Tchernobog himself.

*But why?* Erim thought, drunk with awe and bloodloss. *Why is he fleeing?* The question was like a whirlwind in his skull. How had a simple command, unaccompanied by ritual, without even an invocation of God, wrenched such a spirit from his prey?

The voices faded. The demoniac's hands unclenched, shaking and twitching. He swayed upright for a few more seconds, then dropped beside Sharif.

Erim heard the beating of many wings, and turned to see the vultures rising from the ground. Squawking hideously, they circled for a moment high in the air, a black wheel against the darkening sky, before flying directly into the side of the cliff.

Trailing dark feathers, bodies rebounded from the stone face, plummeting to the ground.

The stranger took his apple back from Nawhar.

Nawhar and Erim stared at him mutely. The man took another bite, raised his eyebrows and smiled slightly, as if to say: *What did you think of that?* Then he pointed a thumb at Erim's broken arm.

"Would you like me to fix it for you?" he asked, his mouth full of apple.

Consciousness teetering, Erim nodded. He saw the man touch the bloodied limb, but felt nothing through the numbed flesh.

"Why don't you take the weight off your feet?" the stranger suggested.

It made eminently good sense. Erim sat down, sagging back against the steps.

"Who are you?" he asked.

"My name is Essaj," the man said, an instant before Erim surrendered to oblivion.

✠

# Chapter 11

Khaddam leaned back from his desk, shaking his head. "You can't be serious," he told Samadhi.

"If you wish, I could repeat the tests," Samadhi replied. "But I don't believe it would serve any purpose. The fact is that the sending that attacked you was dispatched *inside* Qanar-Sharaj. The spell clearly induced reactions in various substances, particularly the whitewash on our walls."

"The discolorations I noticed," Khaddam said.

"Yes."

"They couldn't have been caused by routine conjurings? Spells from a practice-session?"

"No," Samadhi answered. "The evidence was quite distinctive."

Khaddam considered this. "What about the demon that killed Iyad?"

"I haven't been able to improve on my original results. The demon—demons—were conjured within a radius of seven miles."

"Which includes Qanar-Sharaj, of course," Khaddam said.

Samadhi went on: "And I have still more disturbing news."

107

"Well?"

It was a few moments before Samadhi answered. "My findings indicate that the second sending was dispatched in the immediate vicinity of Massoud's laboratory."

Khaddam's face pinched in disbelief. "What?"

"It might even have been sent from the laboratory itself."

"Can you find out for certain?"

"Possibly. But Massoud won't allow me to perform the requisite tests."

Khaddam went over to his window. "He claimed that several witnesses were with him at the time of the attack."

"Yes."

"Did you question them?"

"They support his story," Samadhi replied. "But—"

"But what?"

"That doesn't necessarily exonerate him."

"Go on."

"The automaton might have been hidden in another location. If he worked the spell before they arrived, leaving out the final few words, he could have triggered it in their presence without much difficulty—"

"Completed it in a whisper," Khaddam said.

"He wouldn't even have had to enter a stance."

Khaddam turned. "The Influences would have to have been remarkably favorable."

"They were," Samadhi answered. "I examined the entries in the Book of Masters. He was at the height of his cycle."

"But it simply doesn't make any sense," Khaddam insisted. "He has no motive."

"None that we'd consider sufficient, perhaps. But we're not murderers, are we?"

"Neither is Massoud," Khaddam snapped.

"Is that simply your intuition, or do you know something that truly excludes him?"

Khaddam conceded: "My intuition."

Samadhi's infuriating smile passed fleetingly over his lips. "Believe me, I *would* rather it wasn't Massoud . . ."

Khaddam's eyes flashed. "Are you saying that I can't accept your theory because of mere personal vanity?"

Samadhi laughed. "Well, you have gone a considerable distance to blame it all on the Anarites."

"And how do you know they're *not* involved? At the very least, the killer patterned his first attack on their methods."

"To draw attention from himself," Samadhi countered.

"Perhaps. But there's also the other explanation. That we have an Anarite in our midst, who's trying to lay it all at Massoud's door." Khaddam paused. "And if indeed Massoud is involved—that is, if *he's* their man—that would give us *his* motive."

"A possible motive," Samadhi said. "Frankly, though, I can't believe that we've been penetrated. He could easily be acting on his own, launching the attacks for reasons we can't guess."

"I suppose he might simply be out of his mind," Khaddam allowed. "Certainly, if he is the killer, he's not covering his tracks too well."

"Perhaps we should have Shoua examine him," Samadhi suggested.

"I think that might be in order," Khaddam said.

Taking the place of his assistant Ezzedin Moukarbal, who had fallen ill, Massoud was just ending a lecture on cosmology when Master Shoua entered the hall. The doctor and his bodyguard took a seat in the rear as Massoud began to entertain questions from the students.

"*Sibi*," one said, "you mentioned in passing that travel to— and *from*—another universe had been accomplished—"

"Four hundred years ago," Massoud said. "By the Grand Master Shafiq Al-Wazzam. Whose techniques have since been lost, I might add."

"And he actually returned, *Sibi*?"

"Yes—that's the amazing part."

"But why should such a feat be so difficult to duplicate, Master?"

"We don't know, obviously," Massoud answered, fetching a laugh.

"Might he have been summoned home?" the student asked.

By someone on this side? We routinely conjure beings from other universes."

"No," Massoud said vehemently. "No, no, no. Beings that exist throughout *all* the known universes, but in modes we can't perceive. Always present, but on another plane. There's no *travel* involved, even though that language is commonly employed, even by Masters. The actual process involves the rearrangement of material on our plane into an eidolon, a self-approximation or abstraction of the being that has been conjured. This is why, for example, entities in alliance with Tchernobog manifest themselves in such hideous forms—their abstraction of themselves as physical entities is wholly conditioned by their intense distaste for God's physical creation."

"But how do conjured beings acquire matter, *Sibi*?" another student asked. "Out of the air?"

"Some do," Massoud said. "Which can be deadly in an enclosed space, resulting in the suffocation of anyone present. More typically, structures have been known to collapse, crushed apparently by the sheer pressure of the surrounding atmosphere.

"There are also demons who kill simply by manifesting themselves near a living being—bodies within a certain distance are denuded of flesh to form their eidolons.

"But for the most part, conjured beings draw only tiny amounts of matter from any particular physical locality. Given their mode of existence, all space is present to them. And when they withdraw from their eidolons, the matter they have purloined returns to its original location."

A third student rose. "Might I return to Master Shafiq for a moment, *Sibi*?"

"Certainly," said Massoud.

"This other universe that he visited—what was it like?"

"Very similar to ours," the Numalian answered. "In fact, he found himself on a world inhabited by human beings. But he discovered, rather to his surprise, that they were incapable, for the most part, of performing magic. Ultimately he discovered that their Fall had occurred in the first human generation."

The student worked through the implications of this. "So

that the Darkening of the Will and Intellect was *universally* transmitted to subsequent generations?''

"Yes. This had an an entire range of consequences. Besides their inability to perform magic, the people in that world were physically far less capable than us, as well as less intelligent. They were also more susceptible to disease and pain. The process of slow degeneration which we are even now experiencing was vastly accelerated."

"Not to change the subject, *Sibi,*" the first student said, "but given our *own* degeneration, why is it that the first wizards in our world were not as powerful as subsequent mages, such as Moujiz or Zorachus?''

"Or Sharif?" Massoud asked, eliciting more laughter. "The answer lies in the fact that innate power can't substitute for knowledge. True, those early wizards were closer to the unfallen generations, and therefore possessed far more native strength than we do. But *expressing* it was quite another matter. Zorachus, on the other hand, could draw on two thousand years of experience and invention. Furthermore, if we found him among us today, I strongly suspect we could teach him some very unpleasant lessons." He paused. "Any more questions?''

There were none.

"Very good," he said. "Dismissed."

As the hall cleared, Shoua came down the steps. Massoud's bodyguard joined Shoua's at the rear of the chamber.

"So, Shoua," Massoud said. "What are *you* doing here?''

"I just examined Ezzedin," Shoua said. "I thought I'd see what sort of replacement you made."

"Well?"

"You seemed to be doing all right."

Massoud laughed. "Thank you."

"I noticed, however, that you presented some of your opinions as established fact."

"The chief advantage in being Master of Doctrine," Massoud answered. "I take it you were referring to my theories on demonic eidolons."

"Yes," Shoua said.

"Well, as far as *I'm* concerned, they *are* proven. But if

you'll recall, I mentioned that most Masters employ other language.''

"I believe you did at that."

"Does that raise your estimation of me as a replacement?"

"Indeed," Shoua replied. "So. How have *you* been feeling?"

Massoud looked at him warily. "Why do you ask?"

"Ezzedin's fever might be contagious. Have you had a sore throat? Headache?"

"No," Massoud replied. "I've felt just fine."

"Excellent."

Massoud's eyes slitted. The look made Shoua quite uncomfortable.

"Tell me," the Numalian said, "what did you and Samadhi discuss this morning?"

"What do you mean?"

"I heard that he paid you a call."

Shoua scrambled for a story. "He seemed to think he was coming down with something."

"*I* didn't come up in the conversation, did I?" Massoud asked.

"Not that I recall."

Massoud was some time replying. "I hate to have to say this, Shoua. But I think you're lying."

Shoua tried to force a note of genuine outrage into his tone: "Lying?"

"Samadhi sent you here."

"I assure you, Massoud—"

"He asked you to observe me, didn't he?"

"Why would he do that?"

"Why don't you tell me?"

"Really, I don't have the slightest idea of what you're talking about."

"You're not cut out for this kind of thing, Shoua," Massoud said. "Spying doesn't become you."

"I *told* you why I came—"

Massoud cut him short: "You came to look for signs of insanity."

"Nonsense."

"I have no *motive* for killing anyone, so I *must* be mad, isn't that it?"

Shoua laughed, pretending astonishment. "You've jumped to all these conclusions simply because I visited Samadhi?"

" 'Jumped to all these conclusions,' " Massoud sneered. "First Samadhi accuses me of murder. Then he demands to run tests in my laboratory. Then he summons you to his quarters, and you turn up here, asking about my health. . . ."

"I am, after all, a doctor," Shoua protested.

"Precisely why he'd send you. Stop insulting my intelligence. I'm under investigation, and you're helping him."

Shoua's gaze fell.

"Admit it."

Shoua nodded.

"Get out," Massoud said freezingly, eyes shining.

"Massoud," Shoua answered, "hasn't it occurred to you that you're doing everything in your power to place yourself under suspicion?"

"What do you mean by that?" Massoud demanded. "That I'm acting like an innocent man, unjustly accused? Slandered by those he thought were his friends?"

"I *am* your friend," Shoua said. "And I thought I could dispel Samadhi's suspicions by examining you."

"A likely story," Massoud snapped.

"Please, Massoud . . ."

"Get *out!*" the Numalian shrieked. At the back of the room, both bodyguards whirled.

Shoua turned and mounted the steps. Leaving the hall with his guard, he went directly to Samadhi.

"How did you ever get so good at this, old man?" Sigrun gasped, as Khaddam settled beside her.

"Hundreds of years of practice," Khaddam replied. "*Old man.*" He snorted. "I'm only fifty-two."

"And a very *spry* fifty-two, at that," she said, stretching luxuriously.

"You say that word very well."

"Which one?"

"*Spry*. Say it again."

She turned over onto her stomach, whispered it into his ear with all the lasciviousness at her command, and licked him. Taking her by the hair, he kissed her mouth, powerfully and deeply.

"I love the way you taste," he said, as she laid her head on his chest.

She giggled. "I've noticed."

He cupped one of her buttocks. "What do you think? Another session, after you've caught your breath?"

"No," she said firmly. "You do your work too well. I'll be all tickly, I just know it."

"You always say that."

"And it's usually true."

"Then there are those other times," he reminded her. "Please. I'll sleep better. It would take my mind off things."

She rubbed against him tentatively. "Ask me again in a bit," she said, drawing a knee up across his leg.

"All right," he said. There was a thin breeze from the casement, chill upon their sweaty flesh. With a deft movement, Khaddam swept a blanket over them both. Sigrun wriggled a bit, trying to get her feet underneath.

"So," she said after a time. "How did it go between Massoud and Shoua?"

"Didn't you speak to Chabela this afternoon?" Khaddam asked.

"She hasn't been very talkative lately," Sigrun replied.

"Understandable."

"But what happened?" Sigrun pressed.

Khaddam answered: "Massoud heard that Shoua had been to see Samadhi. He guessed why Shoua had come."

"And?"

"They quarrelled. Massoud shouted at him, demanded Shoua leave the lecture-hall."

"Whereupon Shoua reported to Samadhi that Massoud was behaving very strangely indeed," Sigrun guessed.

"Correct," Khaddam replied. "He went so far as to say that Massoud had exhibited signs of a madness known as Martyr's Disease. Those afflicted believe they're being hounded for no reason. They see persecutors everywhere."

"But if Massoud's innocent," Sigrun said, "then he *is* being persecuted."

"That's not quite right," Khaddam said. "So far he's been his own worst enemy. I still believe he can't possibly be guilty. But if he continues in this fashion . . ."

"What will you do?"

"Samadhi feels we should watch Massoud very closely, recruit one of his assistants, perhaps. Given the situation, I could hardly refuse. Of course, we'd need the Grand Master's permission . . ."

"But what if Massoud found out?" Sigrun asked. "Wouldn't that infuriate him even more?"

"Certainly," Khaddam said. "Which, I fear, would only drive him to act in an even more suspect manner. If he *is* the killer, that would simplify our task. But if he isn't—"

"Isn't there any way Samadhi can perform his tests?" Sigrun asked. "That would settle the question once and for all, wouldn't it? Couldn't he simply break into the laboratory when Massoud isn't there?"

"Once again, we'd require permission, and I expect that Ahwaz would insist we inform Massoud beforehand. Which is only fair, I suppose."

"What will happen if Samadhi discovers that the sending *was* dispatched from the laboratory?"

"It still wouldn't prove that Massoud's guilty. Even so, it would narrow it down—to him and those with him."

"But what if you find that he *was* responsible?"

"We'd try him," Khaddam said, "and turn him over to the authorities for execution."

Sigrun shivered.

"Don't worry," Khaddam said. "It's not going to come to that."

"Yet if it *isn't* him," Sigrun wondered, "who could it possibly be?"

"I don't know," Khaddam answered. "But whoever the killer is, he's doing a splendid job of incriminating Massoud. He has intimate knowledge of Massoud's research, and he's *improved* upon it. He's also very good at anticipating Massoud's reactions, and exploiting them. I always knew Massoud had an irascible streak, but I would *never* have guessed he'd behave so foolishly. We're up against a very formidable opponent.''

"A member of the Council?"

"Not necessarily. A Fifth- or Sixth-Level Adept, perhaps, someone whose true talents have been—how shall I put it—underestimated?"

"A Black Anarite?"

"That's still my best guess. But I must admit, I'm none too confident of it."

"None too confident?" she asked. "That's not *my* Khaddam Al-Ramnal."

"If a man can't speak his mind to his mistress, what's the point of having a mistress at all?"

She began to rub herself against him once more. "You can't think of any others?" she said. "It's been a bit, you *spry* old man."

"Am I going to get a good night's sleep after all?"

"Anything to keep your strength up," she replied, her hand wandering down his stomach.

✛

# Chapter 12

In the refectory the following evening, Kourah Kislali, one of Samadhi's assistants, was quietly pondering certain aspects of the investigation when Nabil Aref, a Sixth-Level follower of Massoud, deposited himself on a cushion across from him.

"So, Kourah," Nabil said, running his finger over the varnished surface of the low table which separated them, "What exactly does your Master have against *Sibi* Massoud, anyway?"

At that, a hush fell over those nearby.

But Kourah thought their apprehension completely misplaced. There would be no trouble. He fully intended to remain calm.

"Nothing that I know of," he replied, carefully avoiding Nabil's gaze. He looked hungrily at the plate of meat and bread that a brown-robe had placed in front of him just moments before. "Lamb. My favorite."

Nabil's finger squealed on the wood. "Trying to change the subject?"

"And what *is* the subject?" Kourah answered, scratching his forehead.

"Your precious *Sibi* Samadhi," Nabil said. "And why he's decided to torment My Lord."

"Please. I'm famished. I had a very difficult day—"

"Preparing false evidence against *Sibi* Massoud, no doubt," said Nabil's friend Yasir Merghani, settling on the cushion to Nabil's left.

Kourah lifted his face at last, staring wearily at them. "*Sibi* Samadhi and I are simply doing our duty. Perhaps if your Master would be a bit more co-operative—"

"You'd have an easier time blackening his reputation?" Nabil asked.

Kourah almost answered, thought the better of it; to his relief, *Sibi* Ghazal rose at the head table to recite the mealtime prayer. Adepts and acolytes got to their feet. But all the while Ghazal spoke, Nabil glared across at Kourah.

"Bless these Thy gifts, O Lord," Ghazal said. "Let us be truly grateful for Thy bounty, and deliver us and all the people from famine."

"Hear us, O Lord," answered the rest.

Ghazal motioned them to sit.

"And deliver us from all traitors as well," muttered Akbar Meheishi, another of Samadhi's assistants, who sat at Kourah's right.

"What was that?" Nabil asked.

"Nothing," Akbar said.

A brown-robe poured wine into Nabil's goblet.

"Who are you calling a traitor, Akbar?" Nabil asked.

"Well," said Akbar, "since I said nothing, I couldn't have called anyone a traitor. But since you're convinced you heard something, why don't *you* tell us who I was referring to?"

"My Master," Nabil answered.

"Massoud?" Akbar asked. "Good Lord! I was referring to men like Zorachus, of course. Can it be you know something that I don't?"

"Be quiet, Akbar," Kourah said, and looked imploringly at Nabil. "Please, brother. We don't want to argue with you. We bear your *Sibi* Massoud no malice, I assure you. . . ."

"Liar," Nabil said, and hurled his wine at him.

Kourah's mouth flew wide, the vintage sour on his tongue. Eyes stinging, he reached up, wiping his face.

Akbar tensed himself for a lunge across the table. Opening his eyes, Kourah took his arm. "No," he said. "This is child-ish."

"But—" Akbar said.

"No," Kourah said firmly. "We should go."

Akbar leaned back, grunting assent a moment later. They started to rise.

Jeering, Yasir hurled his wine at Akbar.

Akbar ducked and flung his heavy clay plate edge-first into Yasir's forehead. To Kourah's horror, it left a deep red gash. Slumping, Yasir appeared already unconscious when Akbar sprang across the table, jolting into him, knocking him back-wards.

Nabil scrambled up. Akbar slid off Yasir, narrowly avoiding a kick from Yasir's friend. All along the tables nearby, brown-robes and greyclads leaped to their feet, shouting.

"Stop it!" Kourah shrieked. "In the name of God, stop!"

No one listened. A cohort of Nabil's seized Akbar from behind. Nabil snapped his foot into Akbar's stomach. Akbar doubled forward, but Nabil straightened him with a kick to the face.

Kourah ached to leap to Akbar's aid; but his first duty was to the Order, not his friend. Akbar had been the first to resort to violence. Intervening on his side would only heighten an already senseless situation.

The man holding Akbar let him go. Akbar fell to his knees. Loosing a vicious laugh that cut through the surrounding din, Nabil brought his knee up into Akbar's eye. Akbar's head recoiled, the struck eye still wide open. In that instant, Kourah knew that Akbar was dead, and was just about to hurl himself at Nabil when someone struck him crushingly in the kidney, and he sank down paralyzed with pain.

The melee spread rapidly. Ghazal and Akram rushed down from the head table, shouting. By the time they managed to restore order, a dozen men lay bleeding on the floor. Akbar and Yasir were dead.

The Masters sent for Shoua, Samadhi and Massoud. While the Numalian and the Spymaster tried to calm their followers, Shoua and his men examined the injured. Those that could had already entered healing-trances.

Felled by a blow in the side of the head, Nabil lay quivering, unable to rise; Shoua crouched next to him, taking his hand.

"Can you hear me?" the doctor asked.

"*Sibi*?" Nabil asked dazedly. "*Sibi* Shoua?"

Shoua bent closer, trying to peer into his pupils.

"I'll be all right," Nabil said, pulling his hand away from him, turning his face.

"I'll be the judge of that," Shoua said. "Let me look at your eyes."

"I don't need your help, My Lord," Nabil said, feebly trying to fend him away.

"Why are you doing this?" Shoua demanded.

"Why are you helping Samadhi, *Sibi*—?" Nabil's breath hitched, then released in a rattle; an unmistakable vacuousness transformed his eyes. Shoua wondered how many times he had witnessed that hateful change.

Someone was standing next to him; turning, he saw it was Massoud.

"He's dead, isn't he?" Massoud asked.

Shoua nodded.

"Satisfied?" Massoud demanded.

Samadhi came near with Ghazal and Akram. "If you must blame someone, blame me," he told Massoud.

"If you must feel guilty," the Numalian answered, "rest assured that I do."

"Brothers," Akram said under his breath, "take this quarrel elsewhere. Half the Order is listening."

"I have nothing more to say," Massoud answered.

Signalling his faction to follow, he strode from the hall.

"I cannot believe this is happening," Shoua said.

"Master!" cried one of his assistants, beckoning desperately beside a fallen greyclad.

Shoua hurried off.

* * *

Later that evening, Samadhi and Khaddam went to the Grand
Master's quarters. Ahwaz had already been informed of the
fight.

"Terrible, terrible," he said, the words coming thick and
slow from his lips despite his obvious agitation. "Are we all
going mad?"

"Not all, perhaps," Samadhi said. "But I fear for Massoud's
sanity, at the very least."

"I will have a talk with him," Ahwaz said, forcing his reply
out. "I don't know if it will do any good. . . . But he must be
more firm with his men. And you, Samadhi—you must keep
a tighter rein on yours."

"Massoud's provoked this," Samadhi protested.

"What does it matter?" Ahwaz asked.

Samadhi subsided.

"The situation could become quite grave," Khaddam said.
"We've come for permission to take certain steps. In our opin-
ion, we should make every effort to indict—or exonerate—
Massoud as soon as possible."

"You want authority to conduct tests in his laboratory?"
Ahwaz asked.

"Yes, *Sibi*," Khaddam asked. "How—"

"I may have had a stroke," Ahwaz said, "but I can still
think. And I have my sources of information."

Khaddam smiled. "As well you should, Grand Master."

"Do we have your permission?" Samadhi asked.

"Yes," Ahwaz said. "I'll have my secretary draw up the
warrant in the morning. But I think you should wait a day or
two. Allow all that hot blood to cool."

"I don't know if that's wise, *Sibi*," Khaddam objected. "As
I said . . ."

"Trust my judgement," Ahwaz said.

Khaddam bowed.

"Are there any other measures you wish to take?" Ahwaz
continued.

"We wish to approach one of Massoud's followers," Samadhi said.

"Recruit a spy, in other words?"

"Yes. I have a man in mind."

Ahwaz considered this. "I take it you intend to keep watching Massoud even if your tests prove . . . inconclusive?"

"It would be prudent," Samadhi said.

"I agree," Ahwaz answered. "But this whole business turns my stomach."

"Understandable, *Sibi,*" Khaddam said.

Ahwaz studied Samadhi. "Does it turn your stomach, spymaster?"

"Of course, My Lord," Samadhi said, showing a puzzled expression.

"I'm pleased to hear that," Ahwaz said.

Shoua and his assistants transferred the injured to the infirmary. Setting broken bones, performing surgery, they worked until well after sunrise. Retiring at last, Shoua dropped instantly into richly deserved sleep.

Moustapha his bodyguard woke him far into the afternoon; together they proceeded to the refectory, where Shoua led the prayers, adding pleas for the souls of the dead and the swift healing of wounds, both physical and spiritual.

Dinner was tense and somber. Massoud and Samadhi were in attendance, watching their followers, who were kept well apart. Armed with quarterstaffs, a company of Akram's finest fighters stood guard along the walls, watching for the first signs of trouble.

Afterwards, Shoua returned to the infirmary, where Massoud's followers and Samadhi's had been installed in separate wards. Several of last night's victims—all having been able to enter trances—had been discharged. As for those who had required surgery, they seemed to be recovering, much to Shoua's gratification.

Presently he went back to his quarters. A note had been slipped under the door:

*I deeply regret my behavior towards you these past few days. I realize now you were only responding to a legitimate request from Samadhi, and I am horrified by what happened in the refectory, for which I bear no little responsibility. Would you*

*please come to see me? I will be in my laboratory, ready to*
*co-operate in any examination.*

*Your friend, Massoud.*

"What does it say, *Sibi*?" Moustapha asked.

"Massoud wants to speak to me," Shoua said.

"Will you go?"

"There's nothing to fear," Shoua answered. "Even if he *is*
the murderer—which I very much doubt—I can't imagine he'd
be so foolish as to attack me in his own laboratory. Still, I
suppose I should notify Samadhi."

Collaring a passing brown-robe, Shoua sent him off with the
message, then went to the laboratory.

Moustapha knocked on the door. It promptly swung wide.
Shoua could not see who had opened it, but assumed that one
of Massoud's men, Farouk perhaps, must be standing behind
it.

Massoud was over on the far side of the chamber, sprinkling
food into one of his furnace-ant colonies. He had one hand
over his nose; Shoua knew from experience that the insects
generated a powerful, acrid smell. Noticing the doctor, Massoud lowered the lid and latched it, waving him in.

Shoua stepped over the threshold.

As the door opened, Moustapha also guessed that someone was
behind it; but he could see no shadow beneath. Puzzlement
became alarm.

"Master!" he cried.

Shoua appeared not to hear him. Moustapha began to follow,
but found his progress blocked by an unseen, slippery mass.
Its surface was raspy beneath the slime, and yielded to the
touch; he stepped back, gasping in surprise and disgust. Try
as he might, he could see nothing of the barrier. Shoua and
Massoud were clearly visible on the other side.

He shouted again, without success. Drawing his sword, he
slashed at the obstruction. As his sword connected, the invisible
mass lashed back instantly, throwing him against the far wall
of the corridor.

Wind knocked out, he slid to the floor. Breathing was impossible. A tremendous hand seemed to have locked about his chest.

Shoua was very close to Massoud now. The Numalian madman was about to strike again, and Moustapha could do nothing but watch. Raging at his own powerlessness, he managed somehow to force air into his lungs. It was like inhaling fire. He got to his knees, then his feet. Puffing, every breath sheer agony, he staggered back to the barrier and slashed at it again. This time there was a clang; a vicious impact quivered up through the blade.

On the other side, Massoud turned away from Shoua, standing with his arms down at his sides. Shoua laid his hand on the Numalian's shoulder.

Moustapha reached out. The pliable mass was gone, replaced by a hard, smooth, undulant surface—or perhaps a series of objects, laid side by side. Somehow, they were horribly suggestive of—

Beyond the barrier, Massoud turned at last.

Only it was not Massoud.

*No,* Moustapha thought, panic overwhelming him. *It can't be.*

"I was very pleased to receive your note," Shoua said, as he advanced from the doorway.

Massoud merely stared at him.

"It's my fondest wish that we'll be able to put all this ugliness behind us," Shoua continued.

At that, Massoud's mouth moved, but no sound came forth. Shoua was close enough now to lip-read:

*Mine also.*

"Is there something wrong with your throat?" Shoua asked.

Massoud nodded, pointing to it.

"Ezzedin lost his voice too—"

With a motion oddly reminiscent of something rotating on a potter's wheel, the Numalian turned.

"Massoud?" Shoua asked.

He heard a gurgling noise. His first thought was that Massoud was under attack.

*It wasn't him,* Shoua thought, touching him on the shoulder.

*God forgive us, we goaded him so badly, and it wasn't him . . . .*

Massoud did not respond.

"Brother?" Shoua asked. "Are you all right?"

Massoud remained motionless, completely quiet now. Shoua started to go round.

Form blurring as he spun, Massoud wheeled once more. Shoua's face pinched in disbelief.

Iyad stood before him now. His throat swelled and pulsed as though some large living thing were rising from his gorge.

Shoua looked back at the door. Moustapha was pounding on something the doctor could not see.

Shoua raced over to the threshold. Even as he approached, the doorway began to darken. The last he saw of his bodyguard was Moustapha gesturing wildly, apparently trying to warn him of something coming up from behind.

Shoua pivoted, sword flying from its scabbard. Iyad was a scant three yards away. Both arms were extended, one ending in a scarlet-dribbling stump.

Shoua slashed off the remaining hand. Iyad paused as though he had never considered such a possibility, lowering his arms. The bulge was gone from his throat now; his mouth began to open, an oval shape protruding between his lips.

Shoua swore. It was an image of his own face; and it too began to open its mouth.

Barely an inch from brow to chin, a third face emerged. Two tongues lolled from its mouth, like tiny red earthworms.

Shoua screamed and struck at Iyad's neck. The head up-ended, hanging from the shoulders by a thread.

But the body continued upright. And out of the stump of the neck a tiny hand appeared, covered with blood, gripping the rim of flesh.

Shoua stepped forward, bringing a powerful diagonal slash down Iyad's chest and belly. The little hand vanishing inside its neck, the body staggered back and dropped to one knee.

At the jolt, its abdomen opened in a flood of viscera. As the offal struck the floor, a small figure leaped up out of it, barely the size of a newborn baby, monstrously thin, its torso hardly thicker than its emaciated legs. Its head was huge atop the shrivelled body, with a spike-nosed goblin face, bitter and vindictive, the teeth like needles. Its diminutive hands gripped a great cleaver.

"*Chop!*" it cried in a shrill voice, brandishing the weapon. "*Chop! Chop!*"

Assuming a stance, Shoua blasted it back against the still-kneeling corpse. When it tried to return to its feet, he struck it four more times. The cleaver flew from its hands. The huge head split, and the little body curled up like a dead wasp's, Iyad's corpse folding over it.

Shoua looked about wildly. For the first time he noticed how the room had changed. Where walls met floor and ceiling, angles were softening, becoming curves. Whitewash had gone pink, and was steadily reddening. Branching, veinlike structures appeared, pulsating. The floor softened under his feet, the surface growing slick.

The door was gone. Where it had stood, an unbroken wall of glistening flesh met his gaze. He became aware of a distant thumping, pounding in time to the pulsation of the veins.

He spun. The entrances to the rear chambers still remained; as he recalled, there was an exit that opened on a courtyard. Dashing around the beheaded corpse, he raced towards one of the arches. Narrowing, transforming even as he approached, it began to open and shut, thick glutinous strings hanging across the aperture.

His feet skidded in the fluid coating the floor. Falling, he landed directly athwart the valve. The sides closed upon him, squeezing so powerfully that he thought his ribs must crack; howling, he reversed his grip on the sword, driving it backwards, into the muscle on the left. Immediately the valve opened. He scrambled through, heard it sigh shut behind him, wind gusting onto the back of his head.

Ahead lay a narrow, ribbed corridor; red light sputtered in the veins, shining off the curving sides of the passage. He went some distance before he saw a figure coming towards him around a bend. In the flashing bloody glow, he saw that it was another replica of Iyad.

He assumed a Griffin Stance, loosing strike after strike. Blood vomited from the replica's mouth, a new freshet painting

its chin after each blast. Its shoulders hunched forward as its
chest collapsed; slowly it slumped onto all fours.

"Watch now, watch!" a high fleshless voice giggled behind
the doctor. "Watch how he died!"

Shoua started to turn, but was arrested by the spectacle of
a black forest sprouting from the flesh beneath the replica; a
dozen jointed legs arched over the double's back, digging long
spurs into it. Serrate mandibles thrust into view; the legs forced
the replica downwards, and the jaws threshed into its face in
a fury of blood.

"See how it happened!" the tiny voice giggled. "See! See!"

Shoua looked down.

Apparently little the worse for its split skull, the Chopper
stood at his side, cleaver flashing towards Shoua's ankle.

The Doctor leaped over the blow, smashing his foot down
on the demon, crushing it into the floor, stamping until the
Chopper was indistinguishable from the flesh surrounding it.

Ahead, the replica had been reduced to bleeding rags by the
spiny legs; the head was a glistening pash between the scis-
soring jaws.

Shoua backed slowly away. The jaws went motionless; the
replica began to rise. With a hollow sucking noise, like something being wrenched out of thick mud, a great dark shape
lifted from the floor.

Shoua struggled to make sense of what he was seeing. The
thing was spiderlike, but upside down; another rose beneath
it, the first resting on its back. It was only after they started
towards him, clawed feet thudding simultaneously on the floor
and ceiling, that he realized they were one creature, Iyad's
replica bouncing bonelessly atop the upper half.

Shoua resumed his stance, shouting a spell. The double spider shuttled nearer, venom drooling from the points of its mandibles. A musky, sour smell washed over him. Black legs
reached out for him like pincers, gathered him towards the
waiting jaws. Shoua wondered if he had conjured in vain: where
was his defender?

Suddenly it appeared, a shrew the size of a man; in an
astounding display of ferocity, the creature launched itself at

the spider's heads, teeth snapping everywhere at once, biting off the mandible-points, then the jaws themselves.

The spider tried to retreat. The shrew pursued eagerly, dark blood spraying over its back. Jointed legs began to fold. The spider collapsed, both heads already gnawed away.

Shoua issued a mental command. The shrew wriggled backwards from the hole it had made, spun round, and got up on its haunches, foreclaws folded on its breast. The doctor could not be sure, but it appeared to have a peevish expression on its face—was it annoyed that he had interrupted its meal?

The shrew's body was steaming, the ichor on its fur evaporating; its body seemed not to have swelled an inch. Given its incredible energy, Shoua could easily believe that it had already burned up the food it had devoured.

He caught a distant drumming—another spider was approaching. He eyed the shrew. He had no doubt it would be equal to the challenge, but a better tactic occurred to him. Perhaps escape was possible after all.

Another command, and the creature bounded past him, making for the valve. The entrance was closed now, but as the shrew tore into it, the sides sprang open. The shrew recoiled, sniffing; Shoua ordered it to go through.

Just as the creature entered the quivering aperture, something struck Shoua just above the left heel. He twisted round to see the Chopper, fully intact once more, sweeping its cleaver back for another blow.

Dropping to a crouch, Shoua drove his sword into the demon's face. Shrieking with laughter, the Chopper hurled itself off the point, regained its balance, and leaped onto the sword, racing along the flat with the cleaver raised on high. With a flick of his wrist, Shoua tried to shake the demon off.

Laughter screeching to a deranged peak, it continued along the edge.

And sliced off his hand.

Shoua stared in shock as the Chopper leaped from the falling sword. Dropping its cleaver, it pried the hand from the sword hilt and ran off down the tunnel with the severed member under one spindly arm, Shoua's ring glinting faintly on one of the still-twitching fingers.

The doctor felt no pain from his wrist, but there was a strange nauseous sensation that spread from his stomach to his whole body. He nodded, one part of him objective and curious even now; he had heard of amputation inducing such symptoms.

He was dimly aware of the approaching spider's footbeats; a monstrous shadow sped along the wall behind the first arachnid. Fumbling the sword into his remaining hand, he got to his feet. As he passed through the valve, he realized that his left foot was flopping, dragging. The Chopper had cut the tendon between calf and heel.

In front of him, no trace of the laboratory remained. Indeed, there was only a steeply descending corridor. The shrew was waiting for him, still at the top. With the spider hard behind, they started down the incline.

Almost immediately, Shoua's feet went out from under him on the slippery surface. He slid down the tube at breakneck speed. His mind seemed to leave his skull, trailing behind him; he had a brief vision of his own hurtling body, from some distance up the passage. Then his consciousness flickered and went out.

How long the darkness lasted, there was no way of knowing. Back in his body once more, he found himself sprawled on a soft, moist surface, the shrew standing beside him, its heat washing over him. The creature was snarling, but he could barely hear it over the thudding tattoo drawing ever nearer.

He lifted himself on one elbow, looking back over his shoulder. The spider crawled into view at the bottom of the incline, its upper legs blossoming as it passed from under the overhang. Instantly the shrew darted to the attack.

Shoua never saw the outcome. Off to the left, a third replica of Iyad shambled from a side passage; to the right, two more emerged.

Shoua tried to get up. Unaccustomed to the loss of his hand, he put his weight on the stump. Now at last he felt the wound— it seemed his hand was still there, but plunged wrist-deep into molten metal.

Screaming, he pushed with his other arm, thrusting himself off the floor. He managed to blast one of the doubles over. Then pain and dizziness dispelled his remaining power.

The replicas still on their feet came closer, mouths yawning, his countenance smiling from each.

"It's no use," said the faces within faces. "You're inside now. With us. With yourself."

He swept the sword at them, crying out hoarsely. They walked directly into the stroke, never pausing, grabbing at him. His point plunged deep into the one on the left; he had no strength to pull it out. They eased him gently to the floor, grinning at him with their faces and his, stroking his hair, holding him down.

He heard a moist pattering. Tiny footsteps raced over his groin and up his stomach. Hoisting its cleaver, the Chopper rushed into view.

"Fear not for your hand," the demon said, black eyes gleaming like balls of pitch. "It's somewhere very safe."

The cleaver hissed downward, splitting Shoua's nose from brow to tip. Blurry red dots splattered his vision.

"Chop!" screamed the Chopper, raising the blade once more.

Outside, Moustapha had seen the barrier darken, Shoua vanishing behind it. Crying for help, the bodyguard swiftly attracted a crowd of Adepts and acolytes. They made furious, futile efforts to blast an opening. They conjured, but the beings they summoned proved ineffectual against the barrier.

Samadhi arrived, followed shortly by Massoud. By then, the blackness in the archway had faded to a filthy yellow-green, divided into irregular segments, bordered at top and bottom by strips of chancred pink. Just as Moustapha had guessed, the barrier was a wall of gigantic fangs. Shoua had vanished inside the maw of some huge demonic entity.

Before Massoud and Samadhi could bring their powers into play, the jaws opened; the crowd drew back. Two enormous tongues thrust a body out onto the floor, right hand gone, head hacked and shattered. Staring into the mouth, the Sharajnaghim could see what appeared to be three men in white robes, standing atop the tongues.

All were identical to Shoua. Like a father holding a newborn baby, the one in the middle cradled a hideous goblin-shape. The imp was licking the blade of a cleaver.

The tongues withdrew. The jaws closed with a clack of teeth against teeth. The mouth seemed to grow smaller; then it became apparent that it was retreating at great speed from the threshold. The full face shrank into view, a lurid orange disk, goggle-eyed, covered with small veins.

"Morkulg," Samadhi breathed. "Morkulg the Mask."

The face hurtled into the distance as though flying backwards down a long dark corridor, disappearing at last in the gloom. Like smoke before a strong wind, the blackness vanished. Massoud's laboratory appeared once more.

The Numalian turned to Samadhi. There was no anger on the black's face now, no defiance, only fear.

"What are you doing here?" Samadhi asked.

"I've an experiment in progress," Massoud answered.

"I see."

"I had nothing to do with this!" Massoud cried. "The killer's trying to put it off on me. Can't you see *that*? Would I be so mad as to murder Shoua in my own laboratory?"

"I don't know," Samadhi replied coldly. "How mad are you?"

# Chapter 13

Erim woke to find the demoniac leaning over him, adjusting his bedcovers.

With a yelp the Sharajnaghi rolled to the floor. Moments later his back was to the nearest wall.

"So," laughed Horde, in a somewhat different voice than he had used in the tomb. "You're awake."

For the first time Erim noticed that the giant's eyes had been restored, through some diabolic miracle, undoubtedly.

"Did you sleep well?" Horde asked.

Erim also remarked that the giant seemed considerably *less* giant, and that his monstrous smile was gone. Indeed, the fellow had a rather pleasant appearance for a demoniac.

*Clever,* Erim thought, eyes darting towards the door.

"It's all right," said the man. "The devil's gone."

With that, it all came back to the Sharajnaghi—the appearance of Essaj, the exorcism, the vultures flying into the cliff, Essaj turning his attention to Erim's broken arm. . . .

*Would you like me to fix it for you?*

Erim raised the limb, working his fingers. He was clad in an unfamiliar striped kaftan; he pulled back the sleeve, blinked in astonishment. He had watched Horde snap his arm as though it had been a rotten branch, seen the broken bones jutting from the cloth—

But there were no wounds now.

Nor even the faintest hint of scars.

"He healed you," said the other man.

"What?" Erim asked.

"Me too," the fellow replied, pointing to his eyes.

"I'm dreaming," Erim said.

"He cast out the demon," said the man. "Why *couldn't* he heal me?"

Erim had no answer for that. He had seen healers work miracles; he had never heard of one who could restore eyes to emptied sockets, but it was not beyond possibility. And Essaj *had* exorcised the spirit. . . .

*No*, Erim thought. *He didn't merely exorcise it. He pulled it out screaming with five simple words, a King of Hell, and he didn't even raise his voice . . .*

It was all too much. Erim shook his head.

"Where am I?" he asked.

"My house," the man said. "My father's house, that is. We were all very grateful for your efforts on my behalf. . . ."

"My companions?"

"Still talking to my mother, I expect. I was passing the door, and noticed that you'd kicked your covers off the bed. . . ."

"Where are my clothes?"

"Mother washed them, and she was sewing your sleeve just now. She didn't get all the stains out, but blood's hard to remove, you know. Shall I bring them up?"

"No," Erim replied. "If you'll just take me to your mother—"

The man indicated the door. "After you," he said. "My name's Motamid, by the way."

They went downstairs. Sharif, Khalima, and Zehowah were sitting with Motamid's mother in a room with thick wooden beams running along the ceiling; the chamber was fragrant with the odor of cedar. Nawhar stood off to the side, though there were several unoccupied chairs.

Erim saw that there was no bandage—or wound—on Sharif's brow; had he too been healed by Essaj?

Motamid introduced Erim to his mother.

"I've just been telling your friends about Lord Essaj—" She broke off as her husband came in from the street, shutting the door behind him.

"But did you tell them the truth, Fatima?" he asked.

"I tried my best, Nihat," she replied.

"Nothing but his miracles, yes?" Nihat said.

"He healed your own son. . . ." Fatima began.

"For which I shall be eternally grateful—to the Lord God, who uses evildoers to bring about good. But not to Essaj."

"And what crime has Essaj committed," Khalima demanded indignantly, "That you call him an evildoer?"

"Blasphemy," Nihat answered.

"By claiming to be the Expected One?" Erim asked.

"That—and more," Nihat replied. "*Much* more."

"Would you care to explain?" Nawhar inquired.

"Has my wife mentioned the paralytic that Essaj cured?" Nihat asked.

"Which one?" Sharif replied.

"It was a fortnight ago," Nihat answered. "I was still one of Essaj's followers. I suppose I hadn't really listened to what he had been saying all along. But this time I couldn't ignore it.

"He was preaching in a square. The usual sermon, blessed are the poor in spirit, the hungry, the peacemakers. . . . I stood there nodding my head like all the rest, and why wouldn't I? He hadn't said anything that anyone would take exception to.

"But when he finished, it all changed for me. Some men brought a paralytic forward on a litter. He was a horrible sight, skin and bones, his limbs wasted away.

" 'My brothers have carried me all the way from Khazala,' he told Essaj. 'They said you could heal me. I didn't believe at first, but now that I've heard your voice. . . .'

" 'Say no more,' Essaj answered. 'Your sins are forgiven.'

" 'Thank you, My Lord,' said the paralytic. He was silent a few moments. 'But I was hoping . . . I mean, I do not wish to be ungrateful . . . but . . . could you do anything to ease my suffering?'

"Before Essaj could answer, two priests from the local temple came up.

" 'Teacher,' one said, 'Correct me if I'm mistaken, but did you just say this man's sins were forgiven?'

" 'Yes,' said Essaj.

" 'Yes?' they asked, together.

"Essaj nodded.

" 'But who can forgive sins except God?' the first priest asked.

"I was thunderstruck. The question had never occurred to me, even though it was so obvious. I'd heard Essaj tell several other people that they were forgiven, but the full meaning had never quite penetrated this thick skull of mine. I listened closely to Essaj's response, hoping he'd have some explanation. But his answer only made things much worse.

" 'Consider,' " he said. " 'Which is easier? To forgive a man's sins? Or to heal him?' "

At that, Nawhar interjected: "To heal him, obviously."

Erim motioned him to be silent.

Nihat continued: "Then Essaj said, 'I will prove to you, then, that the Son of Man has authority to forgive sins.' And he took the paralytic's hand, saying: 'Get up, pick up your litter, and go home.' Whereupon the paralytic did just that. The flesh on his limbs had returned while we were all listening to Essaj and the priests. I don't think the man himself had even noticed, until Essaj commanded him to rise. . . ."

"But you no longer believed in Essaj?" Erim asked.

"How could I believe in someone who preached such devilish nonsense?"

"How can you say it's nonsense when you've seen his miracles?" Fatima answered.

"A healing's no proof of divinity," Nawhar said. "Even if genuine, it only demonstrates finite—if extraordinary—powers. Besides, it's a known human capability. Absolution, on the other hand . . ."

Erim interrupted: "But don't you believe that our perception of physical reality is wholly conditioned by sinful human nature? That disease, like everything else, is simply a product of our perverted imagination? Surely a man rendered sinless . . ."

"Would no longer perceive the physical world at all," Nawhar answered.

Erim laughed. "What evidence do you have on that score, one way or the other?"

Nawhar glared at him. "Are you saying you accept Essaj's argument?"

"That's quite beside the question, isn't it?" Erim replied. "I was only pointing out that *you* have no business raising such an objection. But if it would make you feel any better, please remember that *I'm* under no such constraints."

"I'm afraid I didn't follow much of that," Nihat said.

"Consider yourself fortunate," Erim answered.

"When are you going to start your investigation?" Nihat asked.

"As soon as possible," Nawhar replied.

"In a sense, it's already begun," Erim said. "We've seen Essaj in action. For that matter, I for one"—he raised his arm, flexing his hand—"have direct experience of his powers."

"He put my forehead back together, too," Sharif said. "Let's not forget that. And then there was that poor Mirkut . . ."

"The one on the road, as well," Khalima added.

"It's a wonder he didn't raise every corpse in the cemetery," Nawhar said sarcastically.

"I asked him about that," said Zehowah, very seriously. "He said the day was coming. Not soon, but coming."

Nawhar rubbed his temple as though he had developed a splitting headache. "I'm going outside," he announced, and made for the door.

"I'll join you," said Nihat.

Once they were gone, Fatima addressed Erim and Sharif: "I think your friend has already made up his mind."

"Perhaps," Erim said.

"Will you be more fair?" Fatima asked.

"I'll certainly try," Erim answered. "But I must tell you

now—if indeed Essaj claims to be God Himself, things will go ill for him. In this life *and* the next."

Zehowah looked slightly perplexed. "He doesn't make such a claim."

"Ah," said Khalima. "But he does."

"Your husband reported his words faithfully?" Erim asked Fatima.

"I think so," she acknowledged.

"Whatever," Erim said heavily. "We'll ask Essaj ourselves, just to make sure."

"And his miracles count for nothing?"

"If he wasn't a heretic, they'd count for a great deal. But if he is—a man claiming to be the Almighty, for example— then they could only be used as proof that he's a sham. Depending on whether we could discover how he performs them. If we determine that he's using sorcery, or mere tricks . . ."

"But what about your arm?" Fatima asked. "And my son's eyes?"

"*Mere* trickery would be excluded, it seems," Erim acknowledged.

"Yes," Khalima said. "That's because he isn't a fraud."

"For his sake, I hope you're right," Erim replied. "Now, then. Where can we find him?"

"Why should we tell you?" Motamid asked.

"If *you* won't," Erim answered, "I suspect your father will."

Fatima considered the situation for a few moments. "Don't worry, Motamid," she said. "Our Lord cast out the demon within you. These men had no power over it whatsoever. How could they have power over Essaj?"

"So," Sharif said, "you think he'd resist arrest?"

Erim could not help joking: "If I were God, I would."

"You're not God," Khalima said mirthlessly.

"She's scored again, Erim," Sharif said, then returned his attention to Fatima: "Well, then, what about it? *Would* he resist?"

"He would do what serves his purpose," Fatima said.

"Don't we all?" Sharif laughed.

"He would *succeed*," said Khalima, with a certainty that

drove the smile from Sharif's face. Slowly he ran two fingers
up and down his brow. Erim noticed that their path seemed to
describe the wound that was no longer there.

"Where are our horses?" Erim asked.

"Outside," said Fatima. She had been working intermit-
tently on his tunic; now it was done, and she handed it to him
coolly. He went to change.

Upon his return, Fatima told how Essaj was staying with his
uncle Terzif, a wealthy merchant; Essaj's mother Yasmin was
also there, having gone to live with her brother after she was
widowed. Zehowah and Khalima knew the house, but not how
to find it from Nihat's dwelling; Fatima sent Motamid to lead
the way.

"I didn't believe in him either," Motamid told the Sharajnaghim. "I made such fun of my parents. They'd seen him
perform an exorcism; that's why they started listening to him.
I didn't think it was much of a reason. A few days ago I joked
that he'd have to exorcise *me* before I'd put my faith in him."

"And someone was listening," Zehowah replied, riding
alongside him.

"God or Tchernobog?" Nawhar asked from behind. Like
Erim and Sharif, he was walking his mount. "Has it never
occurred to you that Essaj commands demons because he's in
league with them?"

"That's just not true," Motamid said. "I was awake, all
the while Horde was in me. I knew—I could hear—his
thoughts. Horde hates Lord Essaj."

"And why," Nawhar sneered, "wouldn't devils hate their
allies? They hate everything."

"But he *fears* him as well. He was terrified. *And he didn't
know Essaj was coming.* He knew *you* were on your way, but
not him. He didn't think Essaj would bestir himself for an
unbeliever."

"He seemed to be surprised," Erim admitted.

"*Seemed,*" Nawhar replied, raking his nails over his chest.
"Do we know what was actually going through his mind?"

"I told you," Motamid answered. "I heard—"

"What Horde wanted you to hear," Nawhar snapped. "Devils *lie*. If Horde *is* in league with Essaj, he'd try to conceal it.''

"But . . ." Motamid protested, "it didn't happen to you. It happened to me."

"And what kind of witness are you?" Nawhar asked. "One who all but calls a demon into his body? Who believes whatever was put into his head?"

Erim took Nawhar by the elbow, the others going on ahead.

"There's no need to be so harsh on him," Erim said. "He's just an ordinary fellow, understandably confused. He's no theologian."

"A fact some theologians would do well to remember," Nawhar replied.

"Meaning me?"

"Come on," Nawhar said, shaking free.

They worked their way steadily westward, into the area where Bishah's wealthier families lived. Terzif's house was a large wooden structure surrounded by a whitewashed stone wall. Someone was playing a flute; Erim recognized the tune, which he had always associated with scantily clad dancers in taverns.

A palanquin passed by. Inside a corpulent man was talking agitatedly to his wife.

"Prostitutes, tax collectors," Erim heard him say. "I tell you, Terzif's gone quite out of his head."

Two large fellows stood guard at Terzif's gate, thick-set and bull-necked. Erim guessed they were brothers. Both had short-swords thrust into their belts, and he had the distinct impression they knew how to use them.

*So Essaj needs men like this*, he thought, smiling to himself. *Oh, well. The Lord helps those* . . .

"Zehowah!" one cried suddenly, in a startlingly high-pitched voice. "Khalima!"

"The Master will be so pleased to see you!" said the other guard.

The sisters dismounted, and the men took turns giving them what appeared to be all-but-bonecrushing hugs. Zehowah and Khalima staggered back, gasping.

"Where's your father?" the first man asked.

"It's a long story," Khalima said.

"So," said the second man. "Motamid we know. But who are these others?"

"Sharajnaghim, I think they're called," his companion laughed.

"The ones that tried to help Motamid, I expect. But what are their names, Khalima?"

She pointed to Erim. Her eyes met the Sharajnaghi's; it had happened more and more of late. He returned her stare. She seemed to forget the question she had been asked.

"It's Erim, remember?" he whispered.

A pink flush rose to her cheeks. "Erim," she announced. Still looking at him, she waved her hand vaguely in the direction of his companions, mumbling their names.

"What was that?" the first guard said.

She repeated herself, tearing her gaze from Erim at last.

"But who's who?"

"That's Sharif, that's Nawhar," Zehowah answered.

"My name's Mahir," the first guard told the Sharajnaghim. "And that's my brother Moussa. We call him Moussa the Mouse, because he squeaks."

"We both squeak," Moussa said.

"And just as well," said Khalima. "You'd be too frightening if you didn't."

"You mean you're *not* frightened?" Mahir asked.

"We've come to see Lord Essaj," Zehowah said.

"Just in time," answered Mahir. "We're nearly off to the wedding."

"Wedding?" Zehowah asked excitedly.

"Aziz and what's-his-name," Mahir said.

Zehowah clapped, the bangles on her bracelet chiming. "Aziz is getting married!"

Khalima wrinkled her nose. "But to what's-his-name . . ."

"Oh, he's not so bad," Zehowah replied.

"Well," Moussa said, "perhaps you'd better go on through."

They entered the courtyard; servants took their horses. Somewhat to Erim's disappointment, there were no scantily clad dancers to be seen; a thin black snake-charmer in a turban was playing the flute, making an utter fool of the largest cobra that Erim had ever seen.

"It's only a trick," Nawhar said disdainfully. "Snakes can't even hear."

Erim knew that already; still, he was impressed. And somewhat surprised that the snake-charmer's performance had no audience whatsoever. A group of young men stood against the front wall of the house, engaged in a ferocious disputation, several of them shouting.

"Who are they?" Erim asked.

"More of the Master's disciples," Khalima said. "No point introducing you now. They're arguing about who's going to be first again."

"First?" Erim asked.

"When Essaj comes into his kingdom," Zehowah explained. "They're deciding who's going to sit at his right hand."

"Wouldn't Essaj be the one who decides that?"

"You'd think. But they don't always listen to him." She sniffed. "Men."

An elderly steward met them at the door, then went to fetch Terzif. Somewhere, children were giggling; a horse neighed repeatedly.

The master of the house appeared shortly, looking rather like a fatter, greyer version of Essaj. Accompanying him was a tall, strikingly beautiful woman with almond-shaped grey eyes; she looked barely out of her teens. Khalima and Zehowah rushed to embrace her.

"This is my sister, Yasmin," Terzif told the Sharajnaghim.

"Essaj's *mother*?" Erim asked, dumbfounded. Her son looked at least ten years her senior.

"I was very young," she answered casually.

"I see," said Erim.

"Essaj is with my son's children," Terzif said. "Come."

Terzif and Yasmin brought them to an inner courtyard, lined with cedar pillars. Lush grass surrounded a circular pool overspread with water-lilies, a small fountain gushing in its midst. Going around and around on all fours, neighing periodically with uncanny realism, Essaj was playing horse with two young boys. A third stood off to the side; apparently awaiting his turn.

"Look out!" one of the riders cried. "Mirkuts!" Putting a hand to his chest as though he had been shot with an arrow, he toppled to the grass.

Immediately the third child tried to scramble into the spot that had been vacated; but he succeeded only in knocking his other brother from his perch.

"That's enough," Essaj said, rising. "You're getting too rough." He brushed grass from his knees.

"*Look* at those stains," Yasmin said. "What am I going to do with you? You can't go to the wedding like that!"

"No one will mind, mother," Essaj replied.

"Please, go upstairs and change," Yasmin answered. "I'd be so embarrassed . . ."

He laughed. "If it will make you feel any better."

The boys running at his heels, he trotted forward. "I'll be back in a moment," he told the newcomers as he passed, disappearing into a doorway. Erim heard one of the children ask: "Do we have to change too?"

"I suppose," Essaj replied.

Almost out of Erim's earshot now, the boys groaned in collective disgust.

Yasmin gave the Sharajnaghim a mildly abashed look. "Really," she said, "he's a good boy."

Presently Essaj returned.

"Now," he said to the sisters, "about your father . . ."

"He's . . . He was . . ." Zehowah's voice faltered. Tears glimmered in her eyes.

"Yes," Essaj said. "I know."

Erim was taken aback, but only for a moment.

*Fatima must have contacted him,* he thought.

"Will you help us, My Lord?" Khalima asked. "It's several days journey, but . . ."

"As it just so happens," Essaj replied, "I intend to preach in Thangura. We'll be leaving the day after tomorrow."

The sisters cried aloud and flung themselves to their knees. Taking his hands, they kissed them passionately.

He smiled and raised them back to their feet. "Enough of that now. You shall have your father back again—for a time."

Nawhar loosed a hissing, derisive laugh. Essaj turned his way, towering over him. That was nothing; most men towered over Nawhar. But Erim found himself unable to overcome the impression that Essaj was much taller than everyone present— even though Terzif and Sharif were of equal stature. Erim had never encountered a man with such sheer physical presence; there was a kind of intense solidity about him. Not in the least otherworldly, he seemed far too much an animal to be a messenger of God.

"So," Essaj said. "You've come to investigate me."

"We have," Nawhar answered, disdain showing plainly on his face.

"It's not a mission that we relish," Erim felt compelled to add.

"No need to apologize," Essaj replied. "You are under authority."

"If you have no objection, we would like to observe you for a time. . . ."

"And if I *do* object?"

"We'll do our best to observe you anyway."

"Well, then," Essaj said, with an expression of good-natured amusement, "I suppose you'll just have to accompany me on my rounds." He looked to Terzif.

"We could put you up here," Terzif told the Sharajnaghim.

Erim bowed. "Your hospitality is overwhelming. I must admit, I would never have expected it."

"I have nothing to hide," Essaj said.

Erim's first impulse was to believe him; his second was to be deeply irritated—with himself, for even an instant of such credulity.

"Please, Essaj," Yasmin said. "We should be off."

Essaj nodded. "Mustn't be late for the wedding."

# Chapter 14

Walking several yards behind Essaj as he led the way from the house, Nawhar looked narrowly at the man's broad back. He could see perspiration shining on Essaj's deeply tanned neck.

*There he is,* Nawhar thought. *God Himself, and he sweats just like a laborer in a ditch....*

The Sharajnaghi shook his head, marvelling at human gullibility—how could anyone look at a human body, a potential corpse, a nest of smells and stench and excrement, and believe that God would condescend to reside in such a disgusting mass? It was devilish nonsense, just as Nihat had said.

Nawhar felt sweat crawling on his own neck, teasing his nerves, raising a rash. He flung his hand back, nails grubbing his angry skin.

"Perhaps you could ask the Master to help you," said Khalima.

"Help me?" Nawhar demanded, not understanding her at first.

"With your itching."

"Do you really believe that everyone can be taken in as easily as you?" Nawhar jeered.

The sow made no reply.

*Women,* Nawhar thought. *How he hated them!* He took a certain amount of malicious pleasure in noting that Essaj's retinue was full of them—the whole attitude of the crowd was so thoroughly carnal and unspiritual. At least half the man's disciples seemed to be married, and there were quite a few brats along for the trip, as well as several pretty women who appeared to be unattached. *Tax collectors and prostitutes,* Nawhar had heard the man in the palanquin say.

*Has God caught any diseases?* he thought, wondering how often Essaj had recourse to his doxies. *Ah well. I suppose he could always cure himself. . . .*

It was going to be so easy to secure an indictment. Nawhar was sure of it. All he needed was to overhear one claim to divinity, implicit or explicit; and apparently Essaj was none too shy about making such pronouncements. It was a wonder he hadn't been stoned already—Nawhar guessed the local priests had simply been cowed by his followers and "miracles."

The latter *were* impressive, Nawhar had to admit to himself. He had seen Essaj heal Erim and Sharif, not to mention the Mirkuts. The re-creation of the one man's face had been truly astounding—there had been no ritual, no wizardry of any recognizable sort.

But that hardly proved that the healings were from God. Indeed, since divine intervention was positively ruled out by Essaj's heresy, the facts pointed strongly in the direction of magic. And even though fraud was as yet undemonstrable, a conviction for heresy would bring Essaj under the executioner's axe all by itself. Proving the falsity of the miracles would merely corroborate the charge.

*God Himself, executed for an offense against His own honor?* Nawhar thought. *That would be an embarrassment.* Nawhar would have laughed—if he had been the type.

The procession wound its way into the center of the city. Some onlookers swore and shook their fists at Essaj as he approached; Nawhar noticed two priests looking on balefully from the doorway of their temple.

But for the most part, people greeted the small parade with

enthusiasm. At one point a woman halted Essaj, asking him to bless her twin daughters; at another, he was prevailed upon by the owner of a sick-looking foal. Nawhar watched in annoyance as the creature started to kick up its heels, although he did feel some satisfaction when it ran off down a side street with its master puffing along behind.

Finally the company reached its destination, a large walled garden beside an inn.

"The landlord's a friend of the bride's family," Khalima told Erim. They were walking very close; Nawhar noted that Erim's hand frequently brushed hers, as though by accident. Clearly they had been influenced by Sharif and Zehowah, who had already perfected the trick.

*It can only lead to one thing,* Nawhar told himself.

For a moment he found himself imagining Khalima and Erim in bed. *How can she prefer him?* he wondered—then immediately shunted the thought aside. What did he care?

Essaj had stopped to talk with a man at the garden gate; the bride's father, Nawhar guessed.

"As you can see, I've brought Khalima and Zehowah," Essaj said.

"Aziz will be delighted," the father answered. "And the Sharajnaghim?"

"They're staying with me," Essaj said.

"Then they're welcome here."

"And how's that rooster I blessed?" Essaj asked.

"Batu Khan? He's performing magnificently."

"What did I tell you?" Essaj said, and went through.

*He blesses roosters?* Nawhar thought. *He helps animals rut?*

Starting with Yasmin and Terzif, the father greeted each member of Essaj's party, betraying a hint of unease as Nawhar and his companions came forward.

"Thank you for having us," Erim said, bowing.

"I am honored by your presence," the man replied, with a smile that seemed less than sincere.

They entered the garden; it was full of guests. Khalima and Zehowah ran off to talk with several other women.

Nawhar scrutinized his surroundings. Six long tables had

been set up to the left, under a white canopy; to the right was a wooden altar. An old greybearded priest doddered around it sprinkling holy water, dipping a cedar branch into a silver vessel. There were olive trees, and cedars, and some other kind that Nawhar was unfamiliar with, their branches bursting with blue flowers; azure petals drifted lazily to the ground, and the air was heavy with a sweet smell. Sickly sweet, Nawhar thought; he disliked flowers, refusing to be taken in by their transitory beauty.

Studiously avoiding the guests, he stationed himself against a wall, watching the bustle from a distance, feeling an immense superiority. All the faces were so common; but then, what could be expected of people who had come to celebrate a joining of the flesh? The *Comahi Irakhoum* held that procreation was licit, though he flatly disbelieved the teaching—where lay the good in adding new sinners to a sin-infested world?

A very short man, almost a dwarf, noticed him and came over. "I don't believe I know you," he said.

"I don't believe you do," Nawhar replied icily.

"This is my garden," the man said. "Did you come with Essaj?"

"Yes," Nawhar answered.

"You should cheer up. God loves weddings. And there's going to be plenty of food and drink."

"I'm not hungry."

The other shrugged. "Pity."

A yellow-skinned fellow with Mirkut eyes came running up, his kaftan spotted with purplish stains. "Master," he said to the short man, "I was just down in the cellar. Ali's drunk, and he accidentally knocked a hole in the great barrel."

"With what?"

"An axe. He was telling your son about his exploits in the wars, and . . ."

"How big a hole?"

"*Big*. Please, Master, you must come."

The two hurried off.

Nawhar smirked, hoping the hole was large indeed. The less drunkenness at this banquet, the better, although the feast was going to be an ordeal no matter what.

Still, his tribulation might not be in vain—perhaps Essaj would let his guard down completely. The man's ruddy complexion was typical of a drunkard.

The afternoon drew on toward the ceremony. The guests gathered before the altar. Musicians began to play; Nawhar saw Essaj's snake-charming disciple among them. The music was very lewd, as wedding music always was, with throbbing insistent drums and rattles and bells, aimed directly at the loins and the blood.

A lane appeared for the bride and her maids. She was weighed down with brazen trash, baubles that would have delighted a jackdaw; her face was a mask of paint, her eyes dark with kohl.

*Pagan priestesses must have looked like that, back in the old days,* Nawhar thought. *Or temple prostitutes.*

The whole crowd was clapping in time to the music. Even Erim and Sharif had joined in. Nawhar grew sick to his stomach, and his head began to ache from the music; he felt almost as though his friends had betrayed him, somehow. Sharif's behavior was no surprise—he was carnal through and through. But Erim had a fine mind. How could he participate in this? Nawhar felt so alone, the one human being, the one *spirit,* surrounded by soulless animals.

He looked at Essaj, his mind turning once more to the man's claim of divinity.

*God at a wedding,* he thought. Horrified to the core by the idea of the Almighty approving such debauchery with His presence, Nawhar was comforted by the fact that *Essaj's* attendance clearly demonstrated the falsity of his claim.

Not that one had to go farther than the claim itself if one was looking for absurdity. True, Nawhar allowed a certain demented consistency between the proposition and Essaj's attendance. A begotten God, a thing that had emerged from between a screaming woman's legs, might well be a God of marriages, of grunts and slime and thrashing limbs. But it was the consistency of dung, of undifferentiated mud.

Of prime matter.

*We will bring you down, Essaj,* Nawhar thought. *We will*

*put you in a hole and cover you with dirt. We will teach you what it means to be a man.*

The groom appeared now, a gawky fellow with an asinine smile, a cheap gilt crown on his head. Nawhar felt his upper lip curling.

*His Majesty, What's-His-Name. King for a day.*

What debased notions these yokels had! Where was the majesty in a man wallowing on some groaning slut? How could anyone see anything noble in physical pleasure?

What's-His-Name took his place beside the bride; the music ceased. The priest splattered the couple with the water, then fumbled his way into the ceremony, mangling passages from the (suspect) scriptures that endorsed marriage, adding a few inane thoughts of his own. His chief insight, which he trotted out twice, was that marriage was "like life." He seemed to find the thought deeply moving.

Nawhar heard weeping; he looked round to see Zehowah and Khalima dabbing at their eyes, then noticed that every female in the crowd seemed to have tears oozing down her face.

Yet suddenly he had the feeling that *he* was being watched; scanning the crowd, he saw Essaj staring directly at him, smiling slightly. Nawhar returned the stare, doing his smug best to communicate the impression that he saw clear through the man.

But the longer he looked, the more an unpleasant certainty grew that he was trying to communicate a lie. Something impenetrable had appeared in Essaj's expression. The look seemed friendly enough, even concerned; but it also suggested unfathomable depths, calculations of such complexity as to render it quite opaque . . . Why *was* the man smiling? What had occurred to him?

Somehow those questions became quite terrifying; with a shock, Nawhar realized that *he* was the one being seen through, the mere object of an intelligence vastly greater than his own. The realization manifested itself with astonishing vividness; he found himself visualizing the inside of his own skull, a transparent shell illuminated by a fierce light.

But most monstrous of all was an intuition that the light had *always* been present, flooding through him, reading him, fitting him into its timeless, infinitely convoluted schemes. . . .

He wrested his eyes from Essaj, trembling. The glare inside his head vanished.

Yet had it indeed gone? Or had he merely ceased to perceive it? There was a fearsome mystery here. Something more than human was clearly at work. It had already occurred to Nawhar that Essaj might be in league with demons; but was Essaj himself possessed? What had been peering out of that peasant face, scouring Nawhar's mind?

He glanced at Essaj once more. Essaj was still looking his way; as though they had just shared a private joke, he raised his eyebrows. There was no hint of that superhuman intelligence now. It was like looking into the eyes of a child. The other spirit was hidden, withdrawn behind the veil of matter.

*Reality cloaked in illusion,* Nawhar thought.

Profoundly disquieted, he tried to return his attention to the ceremony, only to discover that the couple had taken their vows. How much time had passed?

Hand in hand, they turned to face the crowd. The women began to voice a high ululant cry; it was the traditional method of congratulation, but Nawhar thought it sounded like a swarm of locusts.

The couple proceeded up the lane, taking their place at the head table along with their families. Guests entered the inn and returned with gifts, mostly crockery and other sorts of household items. Terzif gave a small bag full of silver; Essaj contributed an elaborate carving of some fabulous dragonlike animal.

"I made it myself," he said.

Nawhar could not help noticing that the workmanship was exquisite; the man's father *had* been a wood carver, the Sharajnaghi recalled.

Erim leaned forward, squinting at the figure.

"Strange," he said. "It bears a certain resemblance to . . ."

"To what?" Nawhar asked.

"A creature Ghaznavi postulated," Erim said. "I've seen his sketch. He only had a few fragments of a jawbone, and a little bit of spine. One of his wilder reconstructions. Even I couldn't go along with it. Too much guesswork."

"And that carving looks like the sketch?"

"Right down to the sail on the back. That was the part I couldn't accept. There were reptiles that had such sails, but they were from a much earlier period. None of the big meat-eaters had structures like that. Except for Ghaznavi's lizard."

"I wouldn't trouble myself about it, if I were you," Nawhar advised. "Essaj probably invented the creature out of whole cloth. Or maybe his devils fetched the idea into his head, just to confound you."

"I think you have far too little warrant to be talking about demons," Erim replied. "At this stage of the inquiry, at any rate. I also think you should watch your tongue. We're surrounded by the man's followers, or haven't you noticed?"

Presently the guests settled at the tables; the innkeeper and his men served up the feast. There was lamb and veal and rice, together with many kinds of cheeses and breads. Nawhar sat with his companions, though he ate little; his stomach was still troubling him, and the clods nearby did not help. He felt like he was watching animals at a trough.

The wine flowed freely for perhaps an hour. The jests flying back and forth grew steadily coarser.

Then the cups began to go unfilled; some guests started to complain. Wiping his forehead with a rag, the innkeeper spoke to the bride's father.

*They've run out,* Nawhar thought. *God be praised.*

Yasmin joined them. They conferred with her for a few moments, then followed as she went purposefully towards her son, who was seated at the table behind Nawhar. Nawhar twisted slightly to catch the conversation.

"There's no more wine," Yasmin told Essaj. "I said you'd help." She spoke in a low voice, apparently believing she would not be overheard; but Nawhar's ears were very sharp.

"You might have asked me first, woman," Essaj laughed. "I prefer to be asked."

"I know you do, son," she replied. Nawhar glanced round

briefly, just in time to see her pat Essaj on the head. Then she said, apparently to the landlord:

"Do whatever he tells you."

"Master?" the landlord asked.

"You have cisterns?" Essaj said, more statement than question.

"Of course, Master."

"Use what you find there."

"Is that all? Don't you have to come with me?"

"Go and look. And don't cause a stir. This day belongs to the bride and groom. I'm just a guest."

*What humility,* Nawhar thought, revolted by such obvious pretense. It *was* possible to see through the man, sometimes at least. . . .

Out of the corner of his eye, he saw the landlord scurry off, gathering up his assistants. Nawhar thought perhaps he should try to accompany them, in order to observe the "miracle," if it occurred. But it was already too late—he had had no chance to examine the cisterns beforehand. And if they proved *not* to be full of wine—well, so much the better.

"Thank you," said Yasmin to her son.

"But once again—" Essaj replied.

"I know. Ask you first."

When the landlord finally reappeared, he looked much less flustered. To Nawhar's infinite disgust, the waiters returned to their rounds, pitchers full.

"So, Tarak," someone called. "You saved the best wine till now, eh?"

"An excellent vintage!" another voice seconded.

Erim and Sharif held their cups up to be refilled. After his first sip, the latter informed Nawhar:

"You really should try some of this."

"Splendid stuff," Erim seconded.

"Never," Nawhar answered, rising. As he strode away in a cold fury, he caught bits of conversation from the tables on either side; word of the "miracle" was spreading, Essaj's injunction to the landlord notwithstanding.

*Just as he knew it would,* the Sharajnaghi thought.

✠

# Chapter 15

"Where does he think he's going?" Sharif asked.

"I'm not sure," Erim replied. "And I don't think I care."

The rumor of the miracle reached them soon after. Sharif looked down into his cup. The drink was already having an effect; not only did it taste much better than the other wine, it seemed stronger as well.

Considerably stronger.

"Think we should be drinking this?" he asked.

Erim took another mouthful, sloshed it around as he considered the question, and swallowed. "Definitely," he decided.

"Right," said Sharif, downing another gulp himself. "But what if Essaj really *did* do something to it?"

"Well," Erim replied, "if it really *was* a miracle, there's nothing to fear."

"But what if he's a heretic?" Sharif asked. "A black magician? Maybe it's drugged, so he can control our minds."

Erim tasted it again. "No," he announced.

"Good," Sharif answered. "Not that I find your arguments convincing. But I'm really not very good at logic, so . . ."

"So what?"

"I think we should toast Essaj, for this excellent wine."

"No," Erim said. "We're here to investigate him. We mustn't succumb to enthusiasm."

"It's just a *tactic*," Sharif said. "He'll think we're becoming converts, and he'll open up to us."

"What if he reads our minds and realizes we're not sincere?" Erim asked.

Sharif pondered this. "And blows up our heads?"

"Yes," Erim said. "I've seen heads explode. It's not a pretty sight."

Sharif waved his hand. "Ah, I'm not afraid of him. I'm the greatest wizard since Zorachus."

"Greatest of all time, perhaps," Erim conceded.

"Yes. I was going to make that precise point."

"But *you* couldn't deal with Horde," Erim went on. "All three of us couldn't."

"The Influences weren't with me. Maybe they were with Essaj."

"But what if he's *not* a wizard?" Erim asked. "What if he's a genuine miracle worker?"

"Lee me see," Sharif replied. "Are you saying that *God* might blow up our heads?"

Erim nodded.

"Let's toast him sincerely then," Sharif said.

But hardly had he spoken when several men lifted their goblets to Essaj. Apparently with some reluctance, Essaj rose to accept the tribute. Erim and Sharif joined in the general applause.

Khalima and Zehowah were off at another table; they came back breathless.

"Isn't it exciting?" Khalima asked, sitting across from Erim.

"What?" Erim replied.

"The miracle, of course," Zehowah said.

"Well," Erim answered, "however the wine was made, I admire the results." He paused, a fond expression on his face. "It's like a girl I knew once. She was wonderful. I almost married her. But I never found out anything about her past. . . ."

"She was probably made in the usual way," Zehowah observed slyly. Then something seemed to occur to her, and she sat down facing Sharif. Brushing her hair away from her forehead with both hands, she fixed him boldly with her marvellous light-brown eyes.

Sharif felt as though his wind had been knocked out. His face went slack; he had no idea of what to say.

"Are you an authority on these matters?" Erim asked Zehowah.

Zehowah nodded slowly, never taking her gaze off Sharif.

"You've been drinking," Sharif managed at last.

She nodded again.

"That's only part of it," Khalima said. "Weddings get her very excited. She takes after her mother."

Sharif felt something beneath the table. It was Zehowah's foot; she had taken off her sandal. She smiled innocently, teasing him with her toes.

"Mother was a dancer," she said.

"I believe it," Sharif replied.

"Don't you just *love* weddings?" she asked.

He slipped his foot out of his sandal. "Yes."

"Mother met Father at a wedding," Zehowah continued.

"He was marrying *my* mother," Khalima said.

"And what did *your* mother think of Zehowah's?" Erim asked.

"They got on well. And she was delighted to get the other dowry. It came in very handy."

"You know," said Sharif, as Zehowah's other foot caressed his, "there are some who say that a man should content himself with one wife."

"Father came to agree wholeheartedly," Zehowah replied, massaging him gently with her soles. "He said our mothers were always in league against him. . . ."

"Is that so?" Sharif asked, his voice all but cracking.

"I don't think I'd want another woman in the house," Khalima said.

"I wouldn't either," Zehowah added. "Then again, I don't think my husband would need another."

Pulse racing, Sharif believed that also, although he forgot to say so.

Zehowah put her elbows on the table, leaning forward, palms against her cheeks, both sets of toes wiggling salaciously.

"You're very handsome, do you know that?" she asked.

Sharif's mouth opened slowly. His tongue seemed to be covered with sand.

"And what does Essaj think about sins of the flesh?" Erim asked suddenly.

Zehowah leaned backwards; her gaze fell, and she sighed. She gave Sharif one last nudge with her feet, then withdrew them.

"He says they are among the least serious," she replied demurely, settling her hands in her lap.

"I've talked to her about this before," said Khalima.

"It didn't work, did it?" Erim answered.

"Obviously not," said Sharif dreamily.

Erim poked him sharply.

"I've been drinking," Sharif protested.

The afternoon waned. Aziz and her husband retired. Most of the feasters went into the common-room, and a group of Khalima and Zehowah's female friends pried them away from the Sharajnaghim, who turned their attention to Essaj's retinue. Rather to Sharif's surprise, the priest was sitting with the would-be Messiah.

"Remember when your parents brought you to my temple?" the old man was saying as the Sharajnaghim drew near. "We were so astounded by the things you had to say! A twelve-year-old, no less."

"And what *did* he tell you?" one of the disciples asked.

"How we should read the Scriptures, particularly the Creation Stories. And what literal—perfectly literal—interpretation really is. It was all about God putting his ideas into the world, and why the seven days described couldn't have been like our days, because there wasn't any sun at first, and a lot of things like that. To be honest, I didn't really follow a lot of it. But it was the sort of confusing that made you realize that something very intelligent was being said. If you see what I mean."

Sharif understood completely; it was an experience he was quite familiar with.

The disciple looked to Essaj. "You've never told *us* how to interpret the Scriptures, Master."

Sharif whispered: "Exactly your sort of meat, Erim—" Catching a hint of motion off to the side, he turned.

Zehowah was walking next to a small pool covered with blue petals. Without a second thought, he started toward her.

"But not yours, I see," Erim whispered after him.

Sharif flashed him a grin over his shoulder. "How crude," he said.

Zehowah was sitting on a large stone now, dipping her feet in the water. Her face was turned to the west, her perfect chin uptilted; the dying light was orange-yellow on her face, and her kinky red hair seemed to glow. She made rather too much a show of not looking at Sharif as he came up; but when she turned at last, her eyes were hungry.

"Oh," she said. "*Sharif.*"

"Yes," he replied, in a flat voice; he thought—was *certain*—that he sounded incredibly stupid. "It's me."

There was an awkward silence.

"Why aren't you with your friend?" she asked. "Investigating Essaj?"

He shrugged. "No point investigating when you're as light-headed as I am."

"I know what you mean," she replied.

"Have you done much—investigating?" he asked.

"No, but I still understand. If you really care about something, you try not to do it when you're drunk. Because you don't do it as well."

"Yes," he said. "That's what I meant, all right."

"Of course," she said, kicking up a little splash, "there *are* desperate situations."

"Such as?"

"If a house was on fire," she answered. "You'd still have to try to rescue people, even if you *were* feeling lightheaded."

"Yes," Sharif said solemnly. "You might not do it as well . . ."

"But you'd still have to do it," Zehowah said. "And try to put out the fire, of course."

"I hate it when things burn," Sharif said.

"I do too," she agreed. "There's something exciting about it, but you really *do* want to quench the flames."

"Whether you're drunk or not," Sharif agreed.

"This is a beautiful garden," Zehowah said, quite beside the point.

"Would you like me to show you around it?" he offered.

"You've never been here before."

"Would *you* like to show *me* around it, then?" he asked.

"The garden?"

"Yes."

She stood. They set off on one of the paths.

"Where are your sandals?" he asked her.

"Back by the tables. Don't worry, I won't forget them. But I just love to go barefoot. I like to *feel* the earth and the grass." She pointed to the right, off the path. "There's a wonderful tree, just over here. . . ."

"Oh," Sharif said. "Good."

It proved to be a massive oak; she led Sharif to the other side of it, then sat down at its base, patting the ground where she wanted him to sit.

"We can watch the sunset," she said. Off to the west there was a gap in the cedars; the clouds were ablaze against a purple sky. Sharif settled beside her.

"This garden's been here a very long time," she said. "I've heard that the city grew up around it—and the inn. People stopped on their way down from Tarchan. Then they started coming for the timber."

"So," said Sharif. "You're an authority on history as well as . . ." He paused.

"Making children?" She smiled at him, her teeth bright against her brown skin. "Mind you, I've never made any. But I've taken a keen interest in the subject. Mother talked to me at some length."

"She sounds like an interesting woman," Sharif said.

"She made Father very happy—when she wasn't conspiring with Khalima's mother. Khalima's was the better cook, and he talked to her more. She was very intelligent. But he spent more nights with my mother, I think. Not that Khalima's minded.''

"What happened to them?" he asked.

"They were killed"—a choke rose in her voice—"in the bazaar at Thangura . . .''

Instinctively, he put his arm around her shoulder; she nestled up against him, warm and soft, smelling faintly of perfume.

*Well,* he thought. *That seems to have been the right thing to do.* He decided to press for more details of the tragedy; the more comfort she needed, the better, apparently . . .

"Was there a riot?" he asked.

"Two years ago," she replied. "Someone insulted a Mirkut captain. The Mirkut killed him, and things got out of control. . . . Our mothers were just there buying melons." She looked up at him, brushing a tear from her eye. "What were your parents like?"

"I never knew them," Sharif answered. "My mother died in childbirth, and my father went off to die in some war. When I was ten, I showed an interest in the Sharajnaghim, so my uncle turned me over to them. He was glad to get rid of me, I think.''

"Why?"

"I scared him. I'd already learned some magic, you see. A hermit taught me—he lived in a cave outside town. As it turned out, he had designs on me, and he didn't realize that I was already capable of slaughtering him and four more like him. I didn't realize it myself, at first. . . .''

"*Did* you kill him?" Zehowah asked.

"He practically insisted. His pride was injured, I suppose. There he was, older than the hills, and I wasn't even nine.''

"Have you killed many men?"

"More than my share. Does that bother you?"

"I don't know.''

"What does Master Essaj say about men like me?"

Zehowah thought for a few moments. "You're really a soldier, aren't you?"

"I suppose," he answered. "What does he think of soldiers?"

"He healed a Mirkut officer's servant," Zehowah said. "He was very impressed with the Mirkut's faith. He said he'd never seen anything like it among us Kadjafim."

"He didn't tell him to stop soldiering?" Sharif asked.

"It didn't even come up."

"But I heard Nihat say something about 'Blessed are the peacemakers.' "

"Oh, Essaj says that too. But he's not silly about it. Didn't you notice Mahir and Moussa?"

"Both carrying swords," Sharif said.

"Not that Essaj needs protection. But it makes *them* feel better."

He squeezed her shoulder. "You love him very much, don't you?"

"Yes."

"And you're still willing to tolerate me? Even though I'm here to investigate him?"

"Erim and Nawhar are the ones doing that. You're just along to protect them, isn't that so? And besides, they're not going to find anything."

"You're so sure of that."

"As I am of anything in this life. And I know you'd never do anything to harm him."

Sharif laughed. "You've been observing me very closely, have you?"

"Yes—and I've noticed that you've been observing me."

He said nothing, wondering what he should do now. Her hand slipped into his.

"So why haven't you tried to kiss me?" she asked.

He hesitated, then drew her onto his chest and kissed her softly, briefly, on the forehead. He licked his lips; they tasted faintly of cinnamon.

"Am I your sister?" she asked.

He looked at her, puzzled.

"On the *mouth*," she said.

He had some difficulty getting into position for this; still, the reward was exquisite. Feeling her lips against his was marvellous enough, but when hers parted, and she began to use her tongue, he felt he was entering a whole new plane of existence. After an intoxicating eternity, they parted with a mutual gasp.

"What about those sins of the flesh?" he asked, gulping.

"I'm weak," she said, rubbing her head against his chest with an insistent feline motion. "What about your vows?"

"I'm uninterested in them."

Their mouths locked once again. This time he was more aggressive; but while he was concentrating on the kiss, her hands roved all over him. He reached tentatively for one of her breasts. Immediately she placed his hand directly on top of it.

"Are you *sure* you haven't done this before?" he asked.

"As I said, my mother . . ." Her voice caught. "Taught me how to proceed . . ." She gave a little squeal of pleasure. "Yes," she breathed. "Yes. *Exactly* like that. Right on the nipple . . ."

"How do I get into this thing?" Sharif asked, looking for a way to slide his hand inside her garment. The neckline was very tight, and there seemed to be some sort of complicated hasps holding the front together. With a deft mysterious motion she dealt with the fasteners, then guided his hand underneath.

"Yes," she said. "Oh, *yes*."


As the twilight deepened, Erim stood listening to Essaj. Astounding was hardly the word to describe what he was hearing. If this man was the son of a common woodcarver from the backward town of Amran, then the world was a very strange place indeed.

His command of the Scriptures was not necessarily surprising. They were often the only literature that country folk had recourse to, and bumpkins frequently knew them chapter and verse. But his intimate knowledge of the Commentaries—that was a different matter. And he gave every sign of having mastered formal theology.

Yet most amazing of all were his original insights—Erim wracked his brain, but for the life of him, he had never encountered them before. Essaj had begun with arguments that had first appeared in Al-Ghuzdinn's *On The Literal Meaning of the Book of Creation*, but had proceeded rapidly along lines of reasoning that appeared nowhere in that text; stunning in their own right, they also buttressed Al-Ghuzdinn quite brilliantly.

The disciples seemed to be having trouble with all this, but from their determined expressions, Erim guessed they were trying to absorb as much as possible. Interest piqued in a way that had nothing whatsoever to do with the investigation, he had almost worked himself up to intruding with a question when he felt a tug on his sleeve.

"Have you seen my sister?" Khalima asked.

Erim pointed absently, barely looking at her. "She went off that way."

"By herself?"

"With Sharif."

"I might have known," she said.

"And what's that supposed to mean?" he asked, irritated now.

"He's going to get her into trouble."

"*He's* going to get *her* in trouble?"

"You'd better come with me. After all, he's *your* friend."

"She's *your* sister."

"But what if he has to be restrained?" Khalima asked.

"Sharif?"

"Zehowah has that effect on some men . . ."

"What if *she* has to be restrained?"

"Then *I'll* deal with her. Please, Erim. Didn't you see the way they were looking at each other?"

He began to resign himself to it; accompanying her seemed to be his fate. "Will you be angry if I don't go?"

Her eyes flashed. "And I have to wrestle with your half-naked friend—?"

She broke off, looking past him. Erim turned back towards Essaj. Essaj, the disciples, and the priest had all fallen silent, and were staring at him and Khalima.

"Excuse me, Master," Khalima said, grabbing Erim's arm and dragging him off some distance.

"Why don't you just pull me into the bushes?" Erim whispered, dreadfully embarrassed.

"Are you joking?" she answered. "Do you know how that would look?"

"How is it going to look when we stroll in there together?" Erim glanced back at Essaj. Essaj had returned to his discourse, his followers attending him raptly. But the priest was still eyeing the Sharajnaghi and Khalima, shaking his old grey head slowly.

"Do they observe the law in this city?" Erim asked, dearly wishing he could be listening to Essaj.

"What do you mean?"

"Do they flog people?"

"Of course they'd be flogged," Khalima answered. "They'd be flogged anywhere."

"*They?* Who are you talking about?"

"Zehowah and Sharif."

"Well, I was talking about *us*. Are the authorities careful about evidence?"

"I've never given it much thought. I don't live here. Come on."

"Ahhh," he growled.

"Which way?"

He led her past the pool and in among the trees. It had grown very dark under the branches.

"Sharif!" Erim whispered.

"Zehowah!" Khalima hissed.

There was no answer. They pressed deeper into the gloom, following the white-gravel path. There were several interwoven trails; Erim and Khalima covered them all twice, fetching no response.

"Either they're not still out here—" he began.

"Or they aren't listening," she said. "He's going to get her pregnant, I just know it."

"She's a wanton one, isn't she?" he asked.

"No, not really," she replied, sitting on a stump beside the path. "She's never known a man before, though she's come close a few times. She loves Sharif, that's all."

"She told you that?"

"Not in so many words. But I can tell." She paused. "Would he marry her?"

"He's been talking about taking a concubine . . ."

"Oh, that's not good enough," she answered stoutly.

"It's not as if the two of you have any means of support," Erim said. "You could stay at Qanar-Sharaj. There are quite a few women living there now. It's not a bad life at all."

"No," said Khalima. "When father comes back . . ."

"*If* your father comes back . . ."

She shook her head at his perceived obstinacy. "After what you've seen, you still doubt Essaj's powers?"

"I've seen him cast out demons, and I know he has the power to heal. But I *haven't* seen him raise the dead."

"I have," Khalima said fiercely.

He sat on the ground beside the stump. "I can't accept that story at face value, and you know why—"

Suddenly she broke in: "The two of you?"

*Where did that come from?* he wondered.

"What?" he asked.

"You said, 'The two of you.' "

"When?"

"You were talking about how *we* didn't have any means of support. Zehowah *and* I."

He scratched his head. "Did I?"

"You said *we* could stay at Qanar-Sharaj," Khalima said. "I heard you."

"I was just talking about Zehowah," he answered. "I always think of you together. . . . You're sisters. I didn't mean anything by it."

"No?" she asked, displaying both surprise and dismay; he could only think of a sail drooping for lack of wind.

"No," he said.

At least, he hadn't thought he'd meant anything. He *was* attracted to her, but taking her as concubine? He had hardly known her long enough.

"You never think of me?" Khalima asked. "*Just* me?"

"I didn't say that," he answered.

"Yes, you did."

Now that he considered it, he had at that.

She drew herself erect on the stump. "I'm much more interesting than Zehowah," she announced.

"A case could be made for that," he said.

"I have a much better brain. Even Zehowah would tell you so. And I'm every bit as beautiful."

"I agree," Erim answered.

Then came the thunderbolt: "So why haven't you tried to kiss me?"

In the morning, Sharif met them at the gate of Terzif's courtyard.

"I'm standing guard," he explained. "I was up all night, so I guessed I might as well take the morning watch. Sent a couple of Essaj's men back in to get some sleep. They looked so tired." He smirked evilly. "And where have the two of you been?"

Erim fumbled: "We were . . . ah . . . well, you see . . ."

Khalima leaped to his rescue: "Where were you and Zehowah, Sharif?"

"We took a room at the inn," Sharif replied.

"You *didn't*," Khalima said, scandalized.

Sharif nodded. "After we were married."

Erim and Khalima were speechless.

"We went out in the garden," Sharif continued. "One thing led to another—but Zehowah stopped me at the last moment. Said we couldn't go any further. 'What would the Master think?' she asked."

Khalima beamed. "Oh," she said. "I'm so proud of her."

"We found that old priest, and he took us to his temple," Sharif continued. "Not much of a ceremony, as you might expect. Still, we're man and wife. Zehowah's inside with Yasmin. I think Essaj is carving her something." His smile returned. "Now then. Where have *you* been? Off contemplating the moon? Discussing theology?"

Erim took Khalima's hand. They eyed each other.

"This, um . . . priest," Erim said presently.

"Yes?" Sharif asked, eyes brimming with amusement.

"Would you take us to his temple and introduce us?"

"As soon as I'm off duty." Sharif gave a ribald laugh. "Don't you just *love* weddings?"

# Chapter 16

Steel rasped from a scabbard.

Khaddam and his bodyguard whirled, facing the greyclad who had just passed them in the hall. It was Farouk, Massoud's assistant.

Drawing his own shortsword, the guard stepped in front of Khaddam. There was a single clang, followed by a moist thump of penetration. Over the guard's shoulder, Khaddam saw a crimson globule burst against Farouk's cheek.

As his man fell, Khaddam entered a stance and toppled Farouk with two bolts. But Farouk had already hurled his blade.

Khaddam dodged. A silver blaze, the weapon whistled by.

With a wild thrashing movement Farouk came up off the floor. "I'll kill you!" he screamed, producing a second shortsword from his robes.

Khaddam was preparing to blast him again when the bodyguard rose between them. Farouk lashed out, and the guard's blade went flying, biting plaster from a wall. Farouk grunted, thrusting. The bodyguard gave a shriek, his feet lifting from the floor. Three inches of steel sprang out from between his shoulders in a red splash. Jerking the blade out, Farouk hurled the corpse aside.

Khaddam stepped forward, reaching for the hilt of his curved Malochian longsword. Farouk tried another lunge, but Khaddam caught him across the forehead with a whistling draw cut.

Farouk straightened like a man who had just been fearfully insulted. As yet, no blood was visible in the slash that bisected his brow.

Then a thin strip of flesh purpled above the wound. Three thin ruby streams crawled from underneath, two more oozing out of his nostrils. He shuddered, shaking his head as though someone had splashed him with cold water, turned, and collapsed, a last breath blubbering from his lips.

Khaddam went to the bodyguard, felt for a pulse. There was none.

A brown-robe came up, gawking at the bodies.

"Get Master Samadhi," Khaddam told him.

An hour later, Khaddam and the intelligence chief were standing beside one of the lesser pools in the baths. Immersed to mid-stomach, Grand Master Ahwaz sat on the steps. On most days, he divided his time between his bed and the soothing waters.

He dismissed the brown-robe who had been scrubbing his back. The rest of the chamber had already been emptied of unnecessary listeners. Reflected off the water, torchlight threw shifting patterns on the many pillars and the honeycomb vaults of the ceiling; constructed in a style far more opulent than the rest of Qanar-Sharaj, the baths had been built during the days of the spendthrift Grand Master Khatib, who had nearly bankrupted the Order.

"I demand Massoud's immediate arrest," Samadhi said, his voice hollow under the echoing vaults.

"Demand?" Awhaz replied, the word coming viscously from his mouth.

"Request," Samadhi answered.

"What do you think, Khaddam?" Awhaz asked.

Khaddam answered wearily: "Massoud is *not* the killer—"

Samadhi exploded in exasperation: "Farouk was Massoud's *personal assistant—*"

"In addition," Khaddam resumed, "this attack has convinced me still more firmly of Massoud's innocence. He's the victim of a campaign to manipulate our suspicions. It is *painfully* obvious. Samadhi has no real evidence against him. As you know, the tests he ran in Massoud's laboratory revealed nothing—"

"I've explained why," Samadhi said. "Morkulg's presence obliterated the patterns, reformed them."

"And you couldn't discover where Morkulg was conjured?" Awhaz asked.

"No," Samadhi admitted disgustedly. "It was the same as in Iyad's death. A seven-mile radius, nothing more definite than that. But since Morkulg probably killed Iyad, Massoud remains implicated."

"But Massoud was nowhere near his laboratory," Awhaz said.

"He didn't have to be."

"But how could he have known that Shoua had entered the trap? A demon such as Morkulg couldn't have been maintained indefinitely."

"We found an anagram of Shoua's name scratched on the threshold," Samadhi answered. "Some sort of trigger. Shoua summoned Morkulg himself, when he stepped over it."

"Which means, of course, that *anyone* could have set the trap," Khaddam pointed out. "So what does that leave Samadhi with, Grand Master? The fact that Massoud's indignant at being falsely accused? A brief evaluation by Shoua, who provoked Massoud into a justified rage?"

Samadhi hurled his hands up. *"What about Farouk?"*

"Farouk was a perpetual eavesdropper," Khaddam answered. "It's my guess that the killer used him to spy on Massoud. To provide him with details on Massoud's automaton, for example."

"Your *guess,*" Samadhi sneered. "Everything points to Massoud, and you know it."

"Indeed," Khaddam replied. "Each one of these crimes virtually has 'Massoud did this' scrawled all over it in blood.

But could he possibly be so disinterested in concealing his guilt?''

"He's insane," Samadhi said.

"Do you think *insane* is a magic word?" Khaddam asked. "That if you merely utter it, your fantasies become more plausible?"

"Nothing we've discovered contradicts my theories," Samadhi answered.

Khaddam barked a laugh. "You're being led around by the nose, because you have a wide streak of sheer perversity.''

"And what's that supposed to mean?" Samadhi demanded.

"That'll you'll disagree with me no matter what," Khaddam answered. "And mark this well—the killer has noticed. He's watched you closely, and he knows how to exploit your weaknesses. Just as he's exploiting Massoud's. The whole Order's, if it comes to that.

"I'm terrified by what I've been seeing. The halls are seething. Fights every day. Suspicion, rumors, fear. And it's not just your followers and Massoud's any more. They have friends among my men, among Ghazal's and Akram's. And those friends are making up their minds, taking sides, looking over their shoulders, thinking of how to settle scores that have nothing to do with this. Arresting Massoud will only increase the tension. We must find the *real* murderer, Samadhi.''

"And what will you say when Massoud strikes again?" Samadhi shot back. "For the love of the Almighty, Khaddam, he's already tried to kill you twice. Who knows who will be next? *Sibi* Ahwaz? Me?

"You speak of terror. What about my terror? I've made him my enemy. My *mortal* enemy, if I'm right. What does he have in store for *me*? You didn't examine Shoua and Iyad. I did. When I looked at Shoua's head, I saw my own, *my* skull shattered, *my* brains leaking out on that slab! We must arrest him, Khaddam. Lock him away and watch him day and night.''

"Isn't he already being watched?" Ahwaz asked. "I gave you permission.''

"Our spy was killed in a brawl, almost as soon as we recruited him," Khaddam said. "One of Samadhi's men was responsible, as a matter of fact.''

"Do you have any other candidates in mind?" Ahwaz asked.

"No," Samadhi said. "Massoud's followers have locked ranks around him. They're very loyal. It's actually rather touching."

Ahwaz laved his neck with his good hand. "Arrest him," he said heavily.

Khaddam swore. "*Sibi*—"

"I have spoken, Khaddam," Ahwaz replied.

Khaddam bowed his head. "Your will be done, My Lord."

"Help me out of here, would you?" Ahwaz asked.

Khaddam selected a new bodyguard and went to Massoud's quarters, carrying the warrant. A gang of Massoud's men stood near the door.

"What is your business here, *Sibi*?" one asked truculently.

"A question I might ask you," Khaddam answered.

"I'm *Sibi* Massoud's bodyguard," the other said.

"And all these others?" Khaddam asked. "Have they no duties to perform?"

"They are helping me, *Sibi*," the man replied. "Masters are being killed, you know. And since ours is not the murderer—"

Khaddam answered in a clenched voice: "You are an insubordinate fool."

Apparently not the least cowed, the other replied: "And *you* are helping *Sibi* Samadhi to destroy My Lord—"

"No," said Massoud, appearing on the threshold.

"This fellow needs discipline, Massoud," Khaddam said.

"Haji?" the Numalian said.

The bodyguard turned.

Massoud slapped him across the face.

Haji pressed the back of his hand against his cheek. "But, *Sibi*—"

"Master Khaddam is your superior," Massoud said. "And mine." He motioned to Khaddam. "Come in."

"What about my man?" Khaddam asked.

"He can stay outside," Massoud said, and looked sharply at Haji. "I guarantee his safety."

Khaddam nodded, striding past Massoud.

The room beyond was full of models; Massoud was always inventing things. There were miniature siege devices, bridges, ships, objects with wings and screws that Khaddam could put no name to. Fearsome-looking assemblies of gears and springs were ranged along the top of one long table, along with a half-dozen prototype animal traps; Massoud came from a family of royal game wardens in Numalia, and his career as an inventor had begun when he improvised a device for immobilizing elephants, now a commonplace tool in the ivory trade—it enabled harvesters to saw off tusks without harming the animals, thus helping them maintain the size of the herds.

Massoud shut the door.

"What happened to Farouk's body?" he asked. His forehead was shiny with sweat; he smelled heavily of wine.

"I managed to keep most of my men away from it," Khaddam said. "He was beyond pain in any case."

"God in Heaven," Massoud breathed.

"I had no choice but to kill him," Khaddam said.

"I'm glad you succeeded," Massoud said.

"Glad?"

"He was a spy, wasn't he? Watching me for the murderer?"

"So I believe."

"You've been defending me all along, haven't you?" Massoud asked.

"Where you've left me an opening," Khaddam replied. "Damn you, Massoud, you've made a horrible mess of this."

Massoud gave him a look that was more than sheepish. He laughed bitterly. "Here I am, Master of Logic and Doctrine, and I can't even control my own temper. I was horrified by what I said to Shoua, you must believe me . . ."

"I do," Khaddam answered.

"That note that I supposedly sent him—did they ever find it? See that the script wasn't mine?"

"The bodyguard said Shoua put it inside his robe. But it wasn't on the corpse. At least not as anything recognizable. There was a charred place on his chest, and some ashes—we suspect the paper was treated to ignite after a certain interval."

"Or in the presence of the demon that killed him?"

"Perhaps."

Massoud picked up a small hammer, rapping it softly against the tabletop. "Shall I tell you what I think?" he asked.

Khaddam shrugged.

"Samadhi's behind all this," Massoud said.

Khaddam looked away from him.

"You know it, don't you?" Massoud pressed.

"The thought's crossed my mind," Khaddam answered. "But I don't think he's guilty."

"Why not, in God's name?"

"For the same reason I can't believe it's you. It's too obvious. He's a pawn. Unwitting—but also very dangerous. I have some bad news for you, old friend."

"I was wondering why you came," Massoud said.

"Perhaps you should sit down."

Massoud answered with a laugh full of false bravado. He thumped his chest as though he were issuing a challenge. "Let's have it."

"Samadhi has demanded your arrest," Khaddam said. "I argued the case for you as forcefully as I could, but . . ."

Massoud's face wrinkled with disbelief. "Ahwaz *agreed*?"

"Yes," Khaddam answered.

Disbelief became white-eyed rage. "The filthy old cripple!" Massoud shrieked, hurling the hammer at a large model galley, smashing the aft castle.

"Get a grip on yourself," Khaddam said quietly.

"That's easy for you to say!"

"I'm not in the process of digging my own grave," Khaddam replied.

Massoud brought his fist up to his mouth, biting his knuckle. He nodded.

"Ahwaz has elected to err on the side of caution," Khaddam said. "And with some reason, as I think even you would admit. The evidence being trumped up against you might be transparent. But as yet, you're the only suspect we have. And you're the common link in all the killings except Iyad's."

"If there's another, will I be released?"

"Hard to say. Samadhi would certainly argue that you merely found a way to fool whoever is watching you, or that you have accomplices. For what it's worth, however, I'm going to do everything in my power to free you." Khaddam produced the warrant. "Do you want to look at this?"

Massoud shook his head. Suddenly his expression grew haunted. "There hasn't been any talk of torture, has there?"

"Samadhi brought it up, in passing. Ahwaz would have none of it, thank God."

"Samadhi," Massoud said, as though the name were a vile taste in his mouth.

"Look at it his way, for one moment," Khaddam said. "He's terrified of you. I don't think he's acting out of malice. I'd like to kill him myself, sometimes, but if I allowed myself to be infuriated, I'd only be playing the murderer's game. There's something diabolical at work here, insidious. It goes far beyond the killings. We're under assault, all of us, on a very fundamental level.

"Which is why I must make a request of you. I want you to summon your followers, and order them to keep the peace."

"I already have . . ."

"You weren't about to be arrested. Make them swear an oath."

"What about Samadhi's men?"

"He'll put them under the same oath."

Massoud's eyes narrowed. "You want me to announce my own arrest, I take it?"

"After you extract the promise, yes."

"You want me to humiliate myself in front of my followers?"

"It was the Grand Master's idea, not mine," Khaddam said.

"Where am I going to be held? Are you actually going to put me in a cell?"

"No. But Samadhi and Ahwaz decided we couldn't allow you to stay in your own quarters."

"Why not?"

"They felt you should be separated from your books. You'll be taken to chambers on the south side of the compound. They're comfortable enough."

"Are the windows barred?" Massoud demanded sarcastically.

"It's being seen to now. And Samadhi's working spells to interfere with any magic you might attempt—"

"What if *I'm* attacked?" Massoud cried.

"There will also be spells to protect you. Not to mention four guards at any given time."

"Four? How many do you need to watch me?"

"It's for your own good. I insisted. Protection aside, if someone else is attacked, Samadhi will have a much harder time arguing that you fooled so many men. He was willing to settle for two."

"I won't have any privacy at all," Massoud said numbly. "It just gets worse and worse. Is there no end to it?"

Khaddam took his hand, squeezed it powerfully between both palms. "Don't despair. I'm going to reveal the real culprit. Annihilating me doesn't seem to be within his powers. I have a guardian angel, it seems, and my angel and I will prevail. God help those who stand against us."

"God help them?" Massoud asked.

"Just a figure of speech," Khaddam said. "He won't lift a finger, I suspect. Indeed, I suspect it very strongly."

Soon after the oaths were sworn—over considerable grumbling—*Sibi* Ghazal went to see Khaddam, who was overseeing a practice duel between two Fifth-Level Adepts. As it happened, one was a member of Massoud's faction, the other of Samadhi's.

"Is this wise?" Ghazal asked as the two assumed their stances.

"Hmmm?" said Khaddam.

"Pitting them against each other?"

"Spoken like a true diplomat," Khaddam observed. "But it *is* their turn. Besides, I want to see if they'll respect the oath. An object lesson might be in order."

Indeed, the two seemed reluctant to begin; their first strikes proved quite tentative. Khaddam shouted several times before they began to put any real force into their bolts. As the beams started to fly in earnest, partisans of Massoud and Samadhi began to cheer from the sidelines; the flashing exchanges grew steadily fiercer.

At length Massoud's man was blasted to the floor. Samadhi's maintained his stance; for a moment it appeared as though he was going to lash out at his fallen opponent. His comrades roared approval, egging him on.

He stole a glance at Khaddam. The Sorcery Master folded his arms on his chest. The victor's friends fell suddenly silent.

"Help him up," Khaddam told him.

Dropping his stance, the man crossed to his antagonist and lifted him to his feet.

"Very good," said Khaddam. He signalled Raschid Zekowi, a member of the Knot of Serpents. "I wish to talk to *Sibi* Ghazal."

Raschid took over the proceedings. Khaddam and Ghazal went off some distance.

"I thought you'd be gone already," Khaddam said. The time had come for the diplomat's yearly visit to the Mirkut encampment south of Thangura, to pay tribute and various fees.

"A message arrived from the Emperor," Ghazal answered.

"Batu himself?" Khaddam asked.

"Yes," Ghazal said, handing him the scroll.

Khaddam examined the *Khakhan*'s seal and grunted, impressed. Breaking it with his fingernail, he unrolled the parchment.

"Well?" Ghazal asked presently.

"He wants me to come with you."

"Why?"

"He doesn't say." Khaddam allowed the parchment to roll back up, swearing under his breath.

"What's wrong?"

"This couldn't have come at a worse time. What if there's another sending?"

"You have no choice," Ghazal replied. "You can't risk offending the Khan."

"No, I can't," Khaddam agreed.

"Try to make the best of it," Ghazal said. "Bring Sigrun."

"That's not a bad idea," Khaddam answered. "She'd be fascinated." He paused. "It'll take us a few hours to make our preparations, but you could leave now—we'll catch up to you on the road."

Ghazal nodded.

* * *

Late that night, long after the departure of both Ghazal and Khaddam, Ahwaz lay dreaming of turtles and riverbanks; he was hip-deep in muddy red water, wading towards a particularly splendid specimen sunning itself on a log when he noticed Grand Master Ghaznavi sitting beside it. Ahwaz had no idea of how he had missed him before, but he did not let that trouble him.

"Did you give Erim my message?" Ghaznavi asked, rubbing the turtle's outstretched head with one finger.

Ahwaz halted. "About the reptiles? Yes."

"And the other message?" Ghaznavi asked, more urgently.

Ahwaz put a hand to his brow. " 'He cannot die?' "

"No," Ghaznavi said. " 'Death cannot conquer him.' "

Without warning, he rolled backwards from the log, head over heels. The turtle stared intently at Ahwaz with shiny black eyes as water splashed over it.

Not the least puzzled by Ghaznavi's peculiar departure, Ahwaz continued towards the reptile. But presently Ghaznavi's head lifted from the water in front of him. One side of his face sagged, seemingly paralyzed; he had been killed piecemeal by a series of strokes, Ahwaz recalled.

"Did they hurt?" Ahwaz asked.

"You know what it's like," Ghaznavi answered, brushing wet hair out of his eyes with a limp hand.

"Will I die from one?"

"Soon."

It came as no surprise.

"But not to worry," Ghaznavi continued. "As I said, death cannot conquer him."

"How does that help me?"

Ghaznavi began to submerge again. "You might be surprised."

"Wait," Ahwaz said.

But Ghaznavi had already vanished.

Ahwaz and the turtle stared at each other once more.

"Well," said Ahwaz.

The turtle dived off the log.

"Sorry," the Grand Master said.

A cold breeze swept over him. His sodden garments felt icy against his skin. He turned.

As far as he could see, north and south, the riverbank was heaped with human bones; raised like a fist against the heavens, a shadowy tower loomed in the distance. The sky had grown leaden; snow gusted on the wind.

Ahwaz felt a touch on his shoulder. He looked to the side.

There stood a man clad all in black, riddled with arrows and the stumps of arrows; the river's clay-red had gone blood-scarlet behind him, a vast ruby pennon spreading downstream. His countenance was hooded—even without the sun, the shadow was very dark—but Ahwaz could make out some details. The face had been slashed to tatters, a single grey eye glinting amid the glistening dark rags.

"I wouldn't believe what Ghaznavi told you just now," said the riddled man. "Death can't conquer *me*. But the other—*he* can die. And it won't help you at all. Precisely the opposite, in fact. Let me show you something."

Ahwaz found himself floating in midair above a great slab; on it lay a muscular naked man, skin webbed with small cuts. Iron spikes had been driven through his knees and elbows, fastening him to the stone.

"Behold," said the riddled man, hovering beside Ahwaz. "The Lamb of God."

Dressed as Sharajnaghi Masters, a half-dozen men approached the slab. From above, Ahwaz could recognize none of them.

"What are they going to do?" he demanded.

"Quiet now," said the riddled man. "Do you want them to know we're here?"

Of course Ahwaz wanted nothing of the sort. He watched in silence as one of the Masters unsheathed a long, beautifully honed knife. But when at last the blade rose above the victim, Ahwaz was driven to whisper:

"What has that poor man done to deserve this?" he asked.

"What *hasn't* he done?" the riddled man asked. "It's all his fault. Surely you've suspected as much."

Ahwaz was not quite sure who *he* was. Still, he had nurtured such suspicions from time to time.

"And he's agreed to pay," the riddled man went on.

The knife-wielding Master looked up. His face was in rags, just like the riddled man's; he too was imbedded with dozens of shafts.

"Now," said Ahwaz's companion.

With that, the Master simply rested the knife-edge across the victim's throat; so sharp was the blade that it sank in of its own weight, as though into soft butter. The victim's eyes fluttered. Then the life went out of them.

"Atonement," said the riddled man.

The victim's skin purpled. Dense black spots appeared and spread. Sweat shining against the darkness beneath, he took on a hollow, crystalline appearance. Then the reflections died, and nothing at all of him was visible; it was almost as though there was a man-shaped hole cut in the top of the slab.

The Masters howled in exultation before the blackness from the slab swept over them, completely obliterating them, billowing up towards Ahwaz.

"I've seen enough," the Grand Master said.

"Enough?" asked the riddled man. Ahwaz felt a slice across the wrist. "There's nothing to see! *This is the end!*"

The pain bit Ahwaz's flesh again. He whipped his wrist up before his eyes. His hand seemed half-severed, the blood almost orange against the gloom below.

The blackness boiled over his arm like lusterless tar, surged into his eyes, his nostrils, his mouth. His only feeling was a hideous strangling sensation, but it did not seem confined to his throat. It was as though his whole body was choking—as though nothing of it existed *except* the choking. . . .

The feeling intensified horribly. It was like hanging, like drowning, like being suffocated in sand. It was negation, his whole existence being annihilated. And it was excruciating, growing impossibly more terrible the nearer he approached to extinction. It was everything he had ever feared about death, the ultimate calamity, worse than Hell. . . .

He felt the pain again, stroke upon stroke, blissful distraction from the nothingness. He seized upon it, struggling to bend his whole attention on that sawing sensation. It no longer seemed as sharp as when the riddled man first slashed him; still, it was enough for Ahwaz to fill more and more of his mind with it, wrench himself out of the smothering sand.

There was a touch on his other wrist. Someone lifted his arm, very gently.

Ahwaz woke. Blood roared in his throat; his head ached furiously. Was he on the verge of another stroke?

He looked at the man holding his hand. It was Shoua.

"Thank God you're here," Ahwaz breathed.

Shoua pursed his lips as though to say, *Shhh,* although, strangely, no sound escaped him. He was holding Ahwaz's good hand up off the bed, feeling his pulse.

Ahwaz's other wrist throbbed. He wondered what could be causing his deadened nerves such discomfort—that arm had been virtually devoid of sensation since the stroke.

He turned. His arm was flung out to his side, hidden by his covers.

Something moved beneath them. It was about the size of a kitten, judging by the lump, its motions perfectly in time with the sawing pains. Taking his good hand from Shoua, he reached towards the lump—and pulled back at the last moment.

*Shoua?*

But Shoua was...

The Grand Master's head whipped back towards the doctor.

Shoua was gone. Across the room, Ahwaz's guard sat with his back to the wall, busily opening his belly with a shortsword, two tongues writhing in his mouth.

Ahwaz almost screamed; then it occurred to him that the pain in his crippled wrist had stopped. Somehow knowing that the cessation was more sinister than the pain itself, he turned once more, ripping the covers away from his arm.

The Chopper paused in its efforts, grinning at him. Ahwaz's wrist was all but parted.

"Almost done," it whispered, and began sawing away madly once more.

Another scream rose in Ahwaz's throat. But even as it burst forth, his second and final stroke tore through his skull. The last thing he saw was the Chopper leaping from the bed with its cleaver over one diminutive shoulder, the severed hand under a twig-thin arm.

# ✤

# Chapter 17

South of Thangura, in the strip of grassland between the Gura and the river Dawasir, stood the mighty fortress of Dhamar upon an isolated granite dome; built in the days of the Urguz Khanate to blunt a possible Numalian assault on Thangura, the stronghold served now as the Mirkut headquarters in the Kadjafi lands, with five regiments of the Silver Horde bivouacked at any given time about its walls. Batu visited the fortress every year, accompanied by his *Keshik,* or bodyguard regiment.

"So much dust," said Sigrun, shading her eyes against the midmorning glare, watching vast red clouds rising behind the fortress.

"Cavalry maneuvers," Ghazal said, riding beside her.

"How many horsemen does he *have*?" Sigrun asked, astonished. Some distance to the east, she could see an enormous herd of grazing horses; off to the west, the landscape was white with sheep.

"About fifty thousand are stationed here permanently," Khaddam said. "If we add the Khan's bodyguard, which is twice as large as a normal regiment—seventy thousand."

"Don't the horses run out of grass?" Sigrun asked.

"Near midyear. That's why the Mirkuts levy so much feed." Khaddam laughed. "Aren't you pleased that our taxes are spent so well?"

Sigrun shrugged. "I've heard that a woman can walk alone and unmolested the whole length of the Empire."

"An exaggeration, I'm afraid," Ghazal said. "The Anarites still commit crimes with impunity. But the common criminals aren't nearly so bold anymore."

"Then I'm *glad* the Mirkuts levy the grain," Sigrun said. "How do they punish rapists? Something nasty and eastern?"

Ghazal answered: "Castration. Then they let them bleed to death."

"Ah, well," she said.

"Not nasty or eastern enough?" Khaddam asked.

"*Everyone* castrates rapists," Sigrun said, and sighed. "I suppose it's the same all over."

"Human nature, eh?" Khaddam said.

With them rode forty guards, Sixth-Level Adepts. Ghazal had departed with thirty-five; the rest were Khaddam's men, three of them members of the Knot. The company's size was not merely due to fear of demon-sendings; the pack animals were laden with a vast sum in gold, fully one-third of the Order's yearly revenue. The Mirkuts' draconian savagery might well have deterred most bandits; but the tribute in those chests was no common temptation.

A lone rider raced northward from the encampment.

"A messenger, probably," Khaddam told Sigrun. "They gallop all over the Empire, with fresh horses waiting for them at post-houses. One man can cross to the Eastern Sea in six days."

"Six?" Sigrun asked, hardly believing it, turning to watch the Mirkut speed by.

"To summon the rest of the Silver Horde, if need be," Ghazal said. "The Mirkuts have the system down to a fine art. Batu can dispatch a million horsemen to any spot in the Empire within a month."

"Without even calling on his garrison troops," Khaddam added. "Small wonder that he conquered us."

"There was no way to resist him?" Sigrun asked. "Couldn't sorcery defeat mere numbers?"

"Mere numbers," Khaddam laughed. "There's nothing *mere* about a million mounted archers. We made them pay dearly during the invasion, but we were overwhelmed nonetheless."

"Did you ever think of attacking Batu himself? With a sending?"

"Sharajnaghim are forbidden to use demons except in immediate self-defense," Ghazal pointed out.

"Of course, we considered it anyway," Khaddam said. "The old laws are no longer considered absolute."

At that, Ghazal shook his head; but he did not seem to be in the mood to argue.

Khaddam continued: "Still, we concluded it would only have enraged the Mirkuts further. They had huge numbers of hostages."

They neared the periphery of the camp. At the head of a small body of riders, an officer with a plumed helm met the Sharajnaghim.

"We are emissaries of the *Comahi Irakhoum*," Ghazal said, "bound to the Khan with our yearly tribute."

The Mirkut grunted and detailed a man to lead the Sharajnaghim through the bivouac. It was a virtual city of huts—made of gaily painted felt, each was flanked by a pair of huge carts. Some of the dwellings were fully thirty feet wide.

"The Mirkuts bring them wherever they go," Khaddam told Sigrun. "That's what the carts are for."

Each doorway faced south; Mirkut women wearing trousers and elaborate headdresses sat outside, milking cows, scraping hides and stitching boots. Sigrun noticed a group of Mirkut girls practicing archery, shooting with great accuracy into targets that had been placed against a wall of hay bales.

"They're all trained to use those damn bows," Khaddam said. "Even the women fight, from time to time, though they're nowhere near as effective as the men."

"No?" Sigrun asked, shuddering to think what the men must be capable of.

"It comes down to range," Khaddam continued. "Men are stronger—they shoot farther. And the farther the Mirkuts can stand off, the better they like it. They keep their distance and launch clouds of arrows that blot out the sun. If by some miracle you survive and try to come to grips with them, they just ride away, shooting at you as they retreat. They can put an arrow in your eye at a hundred yards, riding full tilt in the opposite direction all the while."

Sigrun saw very few grown men, and those were mostly old or infirm; she guessed that most of the warriors must be off on the maneuvers.

But at length the company entered an area of armorer's stalls; looking like dwarves out of Kragehul legend, scores of squat Mirkut smiths toiled over bellows and anvils, making curving swords, spearblades, and double axeheads. Water hissed as red metal was quenched, and the air was sharp with a hot, acrid smell. Hammers clanged, beating hot blanks into helmet-skulls; bowyers and fletchers plied their trades. Khaddam pointed out the two types of Mirkut bow: single-curved for hunting, double-curved for war. Bundles of arrows were stacked by the hundreds.

Artisans labored beyond; slave-collars on their necks, there were some Kadjafim among them, fashioning objects of gold and silver. They looked up contemptuously at the Sharajnaghim. Sigrun read their expressions clearly—*What good are you, wizards? What can you do against our masters?*

The company reached another belt of dwellings. Little boys ran up with toy bows, pretending to launch arrows at the Sharajnaghim; several others were roasting something on a spit. Sigrun couldn't tell what the animal was.

"Cat, most likely," Khaddam said.

Sigrun winced.

"It's actually not bad," Khaddam went on. "We attacked some scouts early in the war—took their camp. We were very hungry, and there was the meat . . ."

"Enough," Sigrun said, feeling a twinge of nausea. "I like cats."

"As I said," Khaddam smirked, "so do I."

\* \* \*

It seemed to Sigrun that they crossed several miles of camp before reaching the foot of the great granite dome. Climbing the ramp that led to the fortress, they were confronted at the top by a line of pikemen.

"Part of the *Keshik*?" Sigrun asked.

Khaddam nodded.

The soldiers were sumptuously armored in coats of square steel plates, lacquered green; fringed by fine camails, golden helms rested on their heads, spires sprouting black plumes that nodded in the wind.

Evidently unimpressed by the Sharajnaghim, an officer gruffly demanded that they surrender their weapons; afterwards, the visitors were subjected to a careful search, although Sigrun was spared this at Ghazal's insistence.

Ghazal's men unlimbered the tribute-chests, and attendants led the horses away. A Kadjafi slave appeared; the officer instructed him to guide the Sharajnaghim to their quarters. With its whitewashed granite walls, the courtyard was a blaze of light. Crossing through the breathless heat, the company went up into the cool, almost damp air of the keep.

As they made their way along a spacious corridor, ten or so blackclad men emerged from an archway up ahead; the slave stopped in his tracks. Hand on Khaddam's arm, Sigrun felt his muscles clench—had he actually snarled?

"Anarites," he told her, and signalled the company to halt.

Sigrun eyed the black-robes with great interest, too curious to be disturbed by the sudden tension. She had never seen Anarites before.

The slave moved out from between the two groups, flattening himself against a wall. The Anarites too had halted.

"Khaddam Al-Ramnal," said the foremost, a mountainous man with broad muscular shoulders and huge but hard-looking paunch. He bowed, touching his scalplock in a gesture of mock respect.

Khaddam acknowledged the bow. "*Sibi* Mahayoun," he replied.

"*And* Ghazal Nafisi," Mahayoun continued. "How long has it been?"

"Since you were at our throats?" Khaddam asked.

"Oh," Mahayoun answered, "I'd like to think we're still there, wouldn't you? What would you do without us?" He chuckled. "I understand you've been having some trouble. The Khan informed me that you've lost several Masters."

"Did he?"

"Who could be responsible, do you think?"

Khaddam squinted at him.

"Surely you don't suspect us!" Mahayoun said, then looked at Khaddam sidelong. "Or *do* you? Is that why your men attacked mine on the Bishah road?"

"What are you talking about?" Khaddam said. Sigrun studied his face. He looked truly puzzled.

Mahayoun beckoned one of his men, a tall fellow with a blond topknot and a badly disfigured nose. His nostrils were flowing profusely, and his front teeth were missing. Yellowish remnants of bruises discolored his face. He wiped his upper lip with a heavily bandaged hand.

"This is one of my lieutenants, Torthas Al-Tarcha," Mahayoun said. "His party was attacked by Sharajnaghim at an inn. They pretended they were only protecting some women, but who would believe that? There were forty of them, led by Sharif Ben Shaqar—"

Khaddam laughed. "No, Mahayoun."

The Anarite Master eyed him quizzically.

"There were only three," Khaddam said. "And I expect Sharif did most of the work himself."

Mahayoun glared at Torthas. "Only *three*? Against twenty?"

Torthas did not answer immediately. "He's lying, *Sibi*."

"And for what it's worth," Khaddam added, "they probably *were* just protecting the women. We sent them to investigate Essaj Ben Yussef, not to quarrel with your men."

Mahayoun turned to another of his underlings, who had evidently been with Torthas.

"Who's telling the truth?" Mahayoun demanded.

"Torthas?" the man answered.

"Think, Mahayoun," Khaddam said. "You know Sharif's reputation. Would he have *needed* forty men to deal with this"—he gestured dismissively towards Torthas—"or twenty more like him? Furthermore: if your men had faced forty of ours, would there have been a fight at all?''

Mahayoun grimaced at the insult, but Sigrun could see that he recognized the merit in Khaddam's arguments. The black-robe Master bowed once more to the Sharajnaghim, then seized Torthas by the ear.

"Come, my boy,'' he said, leading his men back through the arch. "We have much to discuss.''

Slowly the slave peeled himself away from the wall.

"What are they doing here?'' Sigrun wondered.

"Presenting tribute, of course,'' Ghazal said. His look grew troubled. "I wonder what else the Khan told him?''

"Interesting question,'' Khaddam said, and motioned the slave to lead on.

They came at last to the third floor, where a series of inter-connecting apartments had been reserved for their use. Once Khaddam and Sigrun were behind closed doors, she asked:

"What did you make of Mahayoun's denial?''

"About the sendings?'' Khaddam replied. "He was just toying with us.''

"Strange,'' she said. "It seemed to me that he was telling the truth.''

"Mahayoun couldn't tell the truth if he knew it,'' Khaddam answered. "They're all liars. Their God is the Father of Lies. They can't even trust each other. You saw it, just now. Mahayoun believed *me* rather than his own man.''

"Maybe sometimes they tell the truth accidentally. They don't know it, they don't want to tell it, but it just shines through.''

"Maybe,'' Khaddam allowed.

Sigrun brushed dust off her sleeve. "Will you let me go to the audience?''

"It's not as though a concubine has any business there,'' he answered.

She bit her lip; she hated that word, which he used infrequently in her presence. *Mistress* was better, though she would have much preferred *wife*, which she practically was, as he had all but admitted several times.

"Will I ever get another chance to see the Great Khan's court?" she asked.

His expression softened. "If anyone asks, I'll say you're an interpreter."

In truth, she was fluent in several northern languages that he did not know; she had first come to his attention while the Order was negotiating a trade agreement with a group of northern barbarians. Often there were Tarchans and Kragehul at the Khan's audiences.

"But," he went on, "you must show the utmost deference to the Khan and his nobles."

"Will there be a feast?"

"I expect so, after the presentations."

Her first reaction was delight; then she frowned. "I hope I don't eat too much."

"Moo," he said.

At length the Sharajnaghim were summoned to the audience hall. Two rows of massive pillars upheld the great central nave; magnificent tapestries bedecked the lofty walls.

Mahayoun and his men arrived soon after. The chamber filled steadily with emissaries and their retinues. Strange perfumes drifted on the air, not all of them pleasant.

Sigrun plied Khaddam with question after question, captivated by the exotic costumes. She had never seen such a riot of color. Ambassadors from the lands of the Ch'in and the Sung shone resplendent in silks and cloth of gold; swarthy turbaned envoys out of Aryanastan blazed with jewels. Numalians stood out boldly in yellow and orange robes, scarlet caps upon their heads.

As far as Sigrun could tell, she was the only female among the various trains, although a score or so Mirkut women were seated to the left of the high golden throne at the end of the hall.

"Wives and relatives of the Khan," Khaddam explained. "The men on the left are his sons and brothers."

Sigrun pointed to a group of thin, bald men ranged below the dais, all wearing filthy-looking furs and elaborate bone necklaces.

"Who are they?" she asked.

"Shamans," Khaddam answered.

She had never heard the term before.

"Wizards," Khaddam said.

"Powerful ones?"

"They know some interesting techniques, ones we'd probably do well to study. But on the whole, they're too primitive to be much of a threat." He waited a few moments, then added: "Or so we've come to believe."

The striking of a huge gong announced the entrance of the Kahn.

"Prostrate yourself," Khaddam said.

But before pressing her forehead to the tessellated marble pave, Sigrun caught a brief glimpse of a small Mirkut, dressed in a simple tunic and trousers, making for the throne. Could that actually be the Emperor? She had begun to look up again when she heard Khaddam whisper:

"Don't."

As if to emphasize the warning, a Mirkut soldier strode up and kicked her powerfully in the thigh. Sigrun gasped, fighting back tears as he walked off.

The gong sounded again. With a great rustling of garments, the crowd rose. The little man was seated on the throne now, leaning forward, legs wide apart, a fist on one thigh, a forearm across the other.

"That soldier kicked me," Sigrun said.

"You're lucky he left it at that," Khaddam replied. "Five years ago one of Ghazal's men was *beheaded* for looking up."

Bearing a close resemblance to the Khan but considerably larger, a man had taken up position several steps below the throne.

"That's General Khassar, Batu's younger brother," Khaddam said. "He's Batu's Minister of State—and Intelligence."

Unlike the Emperor, Khassar evidently set some store by show, clad as he was in a magnificent suit of gilt plate mail; on his head was a huge horned helmet, with a flaring neckguard and strange winglike appendages warding the sides of the face. Looking out over the crowd, he announced:

"Batu, Khan of the Mirkuts, Prince of Conquerors and Scourge of God, will now receive the tribute of his subjects."

Slaves brought forward a huge set of scales. One by one the various embassies were summoned to present their gold. Working with great deliberation, speaking softly to himself, a Kadjafi scribe tallied the amounts in a great leatherbound book.

At length it was the turn of the Sharajnaghim. As their tribute was weighed, Khassar turned to Khaddam.

"Who is that?" Khassar asked, nodding towards Sigrun.

"An interpreter," Khaddam replied. "Her name is—"

"Sigrun, I think," Khassar said.

*How did he know that?* Sigrun wondered—then remembered that he was Batu's spymaster.

"Is she a good—interpreter?" Khassar asked.

"Excellent," Khaddam said.

The Mirkut smiled thinly.

"Khaddam," said Batu from his throne.

"My Lord?" Khaddam asked.

"I will speak with you after the ceremony."

"Of course, Great Prince."

Sigrun regarded the Khan. It was difficult to tell his age; he might have been anywhere from forty to sixty. His eyes were black slits, his features broad and flat. He had a long drooping moustache, and skin baked dark brown by a lifetime of exposure to the elements—it looked very hard. Sigrun wondered if it would yield to the touch.

Yet there was great wisdom in that face, despite its harshness. Somehow he reminded her of Ahwaz—and someone else, whom she couldn't quite place. . . .

He noticed her staring. Immediately her gaze fell.

Yet in that instant, she had remembered. He had not reminded her of some*one* else at all—she had been on a boat anchored in the Gura, looking into the muddy red water when a monstrous crocodile rose directly in front of her, staring ravenously into her face, ancient eyes brimming with wicked experience. . . .

Two thoughts followed hard upon that flash of recollection.

The first was that it no longer mattered to her if a woman *could* walk alone and unmolested across the Empire.

The second was that if any man were truly the Scourge of God, it was Batu Khan.

# Chapter 18

At length the presentations ended. The Khan nodded satisfaction and departed.

As the hall emptied, a member of the *Keshik* informed Khaddam that he would bring the Sharajnaghi to his meeting with Batu. But just at that moment, a messenger from Qanar-Sharaj appeared, grimy with dust and sweat.

"Ill tidings," he told Khaddam and Ghazal.

The Mirkut jerked Khaddam's arm. "My Lord is waiting."

"He may need to hear this news," Khaddam said, pulling free. The Mirkut subsided for the moment.

"What happened?" Ghazal asked.

"The Grand Master is dead," the messenger replied.

"Oh, God," Ghazal breathed.

"Murdered?" Khaddam asked.

"A stroke," the messenger said. "But there *had* been a sending. His right hand was missing . . ."

Khaddam swore.

"And there's been more fighting," the adept continued. "A mob of Samadhi's men tried to reach Massoud's chamber.

There were at least ten dead when I left. I thought I'd catch up to you on the road, but my horse went lame. . . ."

"We have to go back," Khaddam announced.

"*You* will come with *me*," the Mirkut told him, this time summoning other members of the *Keshik*.

"Khaddam, you can't—" Ghazal began.

Khaddam nodded. "Risk offending the Khan. I'll rejoin you as soon as I can."

The guard led him from the hall.


The tower was Dhamar's loftiest, its top open to the swiftly darkening sky; it commanded a magnificent view of the surrounding grassland, on which the Khan's regiments were still at maneuvers.

Batu watched with some satisfaction, Khassar at his side. When he had arrived at Dhamar, he had observed a certain laxness among the troops; but two weeks of dawn-to-dusk edification under his sternest drillmasters seemed to be taking the slack out of them.

He kept Khaddam waiting for some moments before turning from the spectacle.

"You appear agitated, Sharajnaghi," he said.

"I just received a horrible shock, *Khakhan*."

"Indeed?"

Khaddam told him of Ahwaz's death.

"Ah," said Batu. "I am saddened by this. I respected him."

"Furthermore, Khan of Khans, there has been some turmoil at Qanar-Sharaj. My men and I should . . ."

"I will not require your presence at the feast," Batu said.

"I am thankful, My Lord."

"Perhaps I can even help you set your affairs in order."

"How so, Emperor?"

Batu nodded to his brother.

"Recently I received a letter from an unknown source," Khassar said. "It advised me that a Black Anarite had penetrated Qanar-Sharaj. Naturally, I had no intention of passing on such information unless it proved trustworthy."

"Naturally," Khaddam said.

"Therefore, I opened my own inquiry. As I'm sure you're

aware, I have men inside Khaur-Al-Jaffar, and instructed them to look into this matter. One was killed, but not before sending a dispatch. There *is* an Anarite in your camp, Khaddam.''

Batu scrutinized Khaddam. ''You don't seem surprised, Sharajnaghi.''

''I suspected it all along, My Lord,'' Khaddam said. ''The murders have all the earmarks of Anarite attacks.''

''My man did not learn the spy's identity,'' Khassar resumed, ''but he did discover this much: that the Anarite entered your Order as a young man, and has risen to high rank.''

Khaddam mused on this for a few moments. ''But *I* entered the Order relatively late in life—''

''Hence we summoned you to this meeting, and not Ghazal.''

''Or Samadhi, even though he's Chief of Intelligence,'' Khaddam said.

''You and Ahwaz were the only Masters we could be sure of,'' Khassar said. ''And Ahwaz could not travel. We felt the information too important to be entrusted to a messenger.''

''When did the spy enter the Order, General?''

''We don't know,'' Khassar said.

Khaddam rubbed his chin. ''Once I uncover him, it will mean war, of course.''

''Of course,'' Batu said.

''But if indeed war breaks out, how will the Scourge of Heaven respond?''

''This is a matter between you and the Anarites,'' Batu said.

''Will we be allowed disposition of their lands and possessions, My Lord?'' Khaddam asked.

''Some of them,'' the Khan answered.

''I am delighted by your generosity, Emperor.''

''But heed me well, Master Khaddam,'' Batu said. ''To those whom much has been given, much will be expected.''

''I have always argued for closer ties between the Order and the Khanate,'' Khaddam answered.

''You will become Grand Master, will you not?''

''So I expect, *Khakhan*. But I also anticipate a challenge from Samadhi. He is very ambitious; regarding the attacks, he succeeded in pressing his opinions on Ahwaz, over my objections. *Sibi* Massoud was imprisoned as a result. But the information you've given me will strengthen my hand in the Council.''

"You intend to reveal it, then?''

"For any number of reasons, Great Prince. At the very least, I'll be partially vindicated—although Samadhi will probably argue that *Massoud* is the Anarite agent. Massoud's always been vague about the interval between his departure from Numalia and his entry into the Order. But many of us Masters spent some time sowing wild oats. Mine were very wild indeed.

"In any case, Emperor, I am badly needed—''

"Your house is burning,'' Batu acknowledged. "Go now, wizard.''

Khaddam bowed low. "My Lord,'' he said, and took his leave.

As the Sharajnaghim prepared to depart, Ghazal and Khaddam withdrew into the latter's chamber.

"So?'' Ghazal asked. "What did Batu tell you?''

Khaddam gave him a brief summary.

"And you trust me with this information?'' Ghazal asked. "Even after the Khan would not?''

"Ahwaz died in your absence,'' Khaddam answered. "We were already camped, south of Thangura. Even if you'd used a triggering-spell, you'd still have to have been within a certain radius.''

Ghazal smiled grimly. "It's good to know I'm not under suspicion.''

"Besides,'' Khaddam went on, "I intend to make no secret of the facts.''

"The better to press for your attack on the Anarites?''

"We're *already* at war with them, or haven't you noticed? What if you're next on their list?''

"Forgive me, Khaddam,'' Ghazal replied. "But I'm a diplomat. I have no enthusiasm for slaughter.''

"You do me a grievous disservice,'' Khaddam answered.

"Surely, if I'm convinced we're under assault, I have an obligation to argue for a response."

"But what if the Anarites *aren't* involved?" Ghazal asked.

"And the Khan is trying to fool us?" Khaddam replied.

"There *is* the matter of his conversation with Mahayoun," Ghazal went on. "He might be trying to set us off against each other, hoping to destroy both sides."

"Which would mean that he was behind the sendings."

"Yes."

"But his wizards aren't capable of such attacks," Khaddam objected.

"Unless we've underestimated them. It's also possible that someone else has entered his service."

"Someone else? From what Order? Who besides Sharajnaghim or Anarites have such power?"

"A renegade Anarite, perhaps," Ghazal suggested. "Or several."

Khaddam laughed. "You can imagine them in the Khan's service, involved in this wonderfully convoluted plot, but you *can't* imagine one penetrating our Order. Well, perhaps you're right. But my explanation is simpler than yours, and fits all the facts. Faschim's Razor: don't multiply entities beyond necessity."

"I don't need a lecture on logic," Ghazal replied.

"No," Khaddam said. "Of course you don't. Forgive me."

The road to Thangura was a pale ribbon in the night as the Sharajnaghim rode north from the Mirkut camp; the moon had just risen, half full but very bright. Galloping along at Khaddam's side, Sigrun could see quite clearly.

Karaz Al-Kara, a member of the Knot, came up on Khaddam's far side. Above the sound of the hooves, Sigrun caught only one word:

*Followed.*

Khaddam blew a small horn. The company slowed and stopped. Khaddam and Karaz rode to the rear.

"Anarites?" Sigrun heard a man ask.

"Could be anyone," another replied.

"No," said a third. "It's Mahayoun. I can feel it."

"Then he's badly outnumbered," the second man pointed out.

"What if they conjure a sending?" the first countered.

"Quiet, all of you," Ghazal broke in. "No point working yourselves into a panic."

It was some time before Khaddam returned.

"We saw them," he told Ghazal. "Ten at least. But they turned aside."

"There was another road back there," Sigrun put in. "Maybe they weren't following us at all."

"Maybe," Khaddam replied. "Let's just hope they're not coming up on our flank." He signalled the column forward once more.

The moon climbed towards its zenith. Presently Karaz reported another sighting, this time off to the right. The company halted once more.

"They're shadowing us," Khaddam pronounced.

"We should strike first, *Sibi*," Karaz said. "Dispatch a sending of our own."

"Madness," Ghazal answered. "We don't even know who they are. And we're forbidden to use sendings."

"We wouldn't think of asking you to violate your conscience," Khaddam said. "Also, you're quite right: we don't know who they are. What a blunder if we killed some of the Khan's men, eh?"

"Why would the Khan's men be shadowing us, *Sibi*?" Karaz asked. "They must be Anarites!"

"Even if they are," Ghazal replied, "does it follow that they plan to attack? Perhaps, being outnumbered four to one, they simply wished to go around us."

"Enough of this," Khaddam said. "Let's be off."

As the company approached the Gura, the ground rose in a series of gentle hills. When at last the Sharajnaghim sighted the ford from the last crest, Khaddam, Karaz, and the other two members of the Knot halted to watch for the phantom escort, sending their horses on with the others, so that the animals might be watered.

Leading her mount to the bank, Sigrun gazed across the river to Thangura. Still several miles away, the city was a vast shadow against the horizon, its domes and towers all but lightless; here and there lamps glowed in distant casements, yellow pinpricks. Swift but shallow over a stony bed, the river itself was speckled with deep blue reflections from the moonlit sky.

"Your man's very difficult sometimes," Ghazal said, coming up beside Sigrun with his steed.

"Are you asking for my opinion of him, *Sibi*?" Sigrun replied.

"Perhaps."

"He *is* difficult, My Lord," Sigrun admitted. "But he's usually right. He told me what he learned. The Anarites *are* responsible. He was right all along."

"I'm still not sure," Ghazal answered. "I don't trust Batu. And I know the old crocodile better than anyone in the Order."

"He reminds *you* of a crocodile too—?"

From the hill came a furious crackling.

"Force-bolts," Ghazal said.

They turned. Up on the summit, Sigrun saw a chaos of flashing hues, four black figures limned in the midst. They appeared to be discharging strikes directly into the ground, scores within seconds.

The display ended, even though a fading image persisted, burned into her eyes. A few seconds of silence were followed by repeated blasts from Khaddam's horn. Sigrun could barely make out the top of the hill; she was not sure, but Khaddam and the others no longer appeared to be there. The horn-blasts grew louder—were the four racing down the hill?

The earth rumbled, vibrating beneath Sigrun's feet. The horses nickered and squealed.

Just below the crest of the hill, a glowing red spot appeared, then another and another, lengthening and branching out, forming a garish network of cracks.

A tremendous section of the crest bulged upwards. The hill groaned, the sound horribly suggestive of a woman in labor. What monstrous offspring was about to be born?

Khaddam and his men ran up.

"We must go into the river!" Ghazal cried.

Sigrun guessed why: hadn't someone told her that demons couldn't abide running water?

"We don't know what we're up against," Khaddam said. "What if it can fly? What if it can *withstand* running water? Some demons can. But *our* powers will disappear."

Without replying, Ghazal assumed a stance and began draining off power.

Up on the hillcrest, the bulge was breaking, square sections of earth falling backwards from the glow. A luminous curve rose into view, covered with veins like lines of fire; not until two bulging, demented eyes appeared did Sigrun realize it was a gigantic forehead. As though to free itself from the imprisoning hill, the head rocked back and forth, at last bursting loose in a shower of dirt, twin tongues dangling from its mouth.

"Morkulg," Ghazal said. "We're finished."

"He can be beaten," Khaddam answered.

"Morkulg the Mask?"

"Zorachus stopped him."

"Of course!" Ghazal cried. "The hornets!"

Swiftly they conjured, an effulgent humming cloud appearing above them.

Spears of energy leaped from Morkulg's eyes. The insects scattered. Khaddam and Ghazal raised shields an instant before the beams struck.

There was a crack and a blinding flash. Hot air gusted over Sigrun, peppering her face with dust and small stones. Dazzled by the glare, she thought for a panicked instant that her lover must have been obliterated.

But no, there he was, still on his feet, Ghazal beside him. Sigrun looked up towards Morkulg. The hornet-swarm had knit back together, and was almost upon the demon.

As it approached, the Mask's tongues withdrew into his mouth. Booming forth a spell, Morkulg began to rotate, revealing not the back of his head, but a second, identical face before the twin countenances dissolved into a red-glowing blur. The demon ripped back into the earth like a whirling drill, flying soil scattering the hornets once more.

"It's not over," Khaddam said.

The rumbling began anew. Webbed with red fissures, another

bulge appeared below the crest, speeding down the hill towards the Sharajnaghim, the ground collapsing behind it, raising a great moon-silvered cloud of dust.

The hornets clustered yet again, racing along above the bulge, waiting for a chance to strike.

By then, most of the other Sharajnaghim had gathered near the two Masters, waiting breathlessly for orders. Only a few were mounted; Sigrun looked for her own mount. It was gone, as were most of the horses.

*Halfway across the river by now,* she thought, turning once more.

"What shall we do, My Lords?" the men asked the Masters desperately.

"The river's our only hope," Ghazal said.

"If we'd tried that, we'd be dead by now," Khaddam replied. "He'll have to break the surface. And then the hornets will take him . . ."

The bulge rumbled close. The Sharajnaghim dodged left and right.

Dashing after Khaddam, Sigrun found herself rising on an upthrust shoulder of earth. But her feet went out from under her, and she rolled back to level ground.

The rumbling stopped. She looked back breathlessly. The bulge had halted just at the water's edge. It pulsed slowly, as if breathing; small avalanches of dirt tumbled around her feet.

Suddenly rough hands were on her.

"Get up!" Khaddam cried.

The top of the bulge split open. A tongue stabbed heavenward in a red-lit explosion, then lashed down at Khaddam and Sigrun like a cracking whip.

Khaddam hurled himself flat, pulling her with him. The tongue snapped in the air, just shy of their faces; Sigrun heard a sharp report.

Already enveloped in a swarm of hornets, the tongue lengthened, rising once more. Sigrun and Khaddam rolled apart as the appendage slammed the ground where they had lain. Sigrun felt her whole body rise from the earth at the impact.

"Is it after you?" she cried to Khaddam.

He seemed not to hear. Swollen with sting-welts, the tongue

withdrew, leaving the hornets buzzing about the top of the mound.

Slowly the bulge began to move again, picking up speed as it rumbled away, parallel to the riverbank, the dust of its passage wafting out over the river on the south wind. Sigrun saw two riders lifted on the red-fissured crest; as the Mask moved out from under them, beasts and men vanished, sucked into the earth crumbling in the demon's wake.

The bulge circled to the south, the hornets keeping pace as it plowed back towards Sigrun and her consort. Khaddam *was* the target, she was certain. . . .

Then she saw a group of men running before the bulge. Several broke to the right; the Mask followed.

"Ghazal," Khaddam cried. "It's after Ghazal now."

The little band of fugitives split once more. A single figure reeled towards Khaddam. Just as Khaddam had guessed, it was the diplomat. And Morkulg was hard behind.

At last Ghazal paused and turned. He struck a defiant stance, but toppled as the earth heaved under him. Up he rode to the top, like a chip on a rolling wave, the swell stopping beneath. For an instant, he stood swaying on the bulge, lit from beneath by the cracks in the soil. Rushing to his aid, the hornets dived at the fissures, planting sting after sting.

There was a muffled roar, as though the demon was enraged by the pain. A tongue whipped out of the earth, hurling Ghazal high into the air. He seemed to hang for an instant against the pale night sky; then the tongue snatched him like a huge tentacle, throwing a loop about his waist.

The hornets blazed about the appendage in a golden fury. Another roar, and Morkulg whirled Ghazal around twice, then dashed him headfirst against the ground not five feet from Sigrun. Something splashed onto her shoes.

The tongue raised Ghazal on high once more. His head was split wide, hideously mushroomed. The demon squeezed tighter; blood fountained from the corpse's head, separated into a fine drizzle before it rained over Sigrun.

The tongue jerked back into the bulge, which immediately began to plow a circle around Khaddam and Sigrun, the ground caving behind it. They rushed to the brink of the sagging trough, tried to start across, but the churned earth was a morass, barely passable; with Morkulg returning, they had no choice but to slog back to the firm ground.

The demon spiralled inward, drawing the circle ever tighter. They retreated steadily into the center.

"Are we going to die?" Sigrun asked.

Khaddam clapped his hands to the sides of his head. Sigrun read pure desperation in the gesture.

"Are we going to die?" she cried.

"Silence!" Khaddam thundered.

*Let him think,* she scolded herself.

The bulge was bearing straight in on them now. She reached reflexively for Khaddam's hand, then twitched hers back before she could distract him.

Morkulg halted once more, barely twenty feet from them.

Khaddam assumed a stance.

The bulge shattered in a spray of crimson light. Out snaked a tongue, the hornets converging upon it.

Khaddam uttered a spell. Sigrun thought she heard Mahayoun's name. To her horror, the hornets vanished. Had Khaddam done it deliberately? Or had he simply exhausted his power? The tongue arched back like a great cobra, lunged towards him—

And vanished as well.

The red light died inside the bulge, which collapsed with a great rush of air. Dust billowed into the night.

Khaddam eased out of his stance.

"Is it over *now*?" Sigrun breathed.

He turned and nodded, his face grey in the moonlight. She flung herself into his arms.

"I conjured a demon," he answered. "Sent it after Mahayoun. It seems he was out there after all." He swore. "Such an obvious solution. I'm ashamed of myself."

"You were magnificent," Sigrun said.

Khaddam shook his head. "Oh, Ghazal. How I failed you."

✛

# Chapter 19

"What?" Nawhar demanded, trembling with shock and rage. "You married her?" He had expected some dalliance between Erim and Khalima, but had never expected it to go so far.

Erim raised his hands. "I know it will be hard for you to adjust to the idea. . . ."

"Why aren't you off rogering the slut?" Nawhar cried.

"That's low," Erim answered. "And stupid, if it comes to that."

"Have you gone insane?" Nawhar continued. "I can understand how Sharif would stumble into such a situation. But you? Didn't your experience with that Rusaifa creature teach you anything?"

"It taught me I should marry when I fall in love."

"Do your vows mean nothing to you?" Nawhar answered, practically screaming.

"Would you keep your voice down?" Erim replied. "We're guests in this house." The two stood in Nawhar's room, which was on the second floor of Terzif's mansion. "As for my vows, they no longer mean anything to the Order."

"That doesn't answer my question."

"I'm weak, Nawhar," Erim replied. "I like flesh—"

Nawhar hissed in disdain.

"But if I can't live up to the Canons of the Order," Erim continued, "I can at least obey God's Law."

"This is treason, and you know it," Nawhar answered. "Oathbreaking. Even if I'm the only one who cares, the last Sharajnaghi, it's still treason. Remember what Horde said? That you'd betray the Order?"

Erim's expression clouded. Nawhar was astonished. Could Erim have actually forgotten the demon's prophecy?

"Driven it from your mind, have you?" Nawhar jeered.

"I suppose I had," Erim conceded. "But I seem to remember him saying that *all three of us* would betray the Order."

Nawhar blinked.

"Perhaps you shouldn't put so much faith in evil spirits," Erim said. "Unless you'd rather think that you'll become every bit as much of a 'traitor' as I am."

Nawhar scrambled for a new line of attack. "You're simply being used," he said. "Those women found themselves without a protector, and you and Sharif came along at the right time. They don't care about the two of you. . . ."

"You couldn't be more wrong," Erim said in a simmering voice.

"Worse yet," Nawhar pressed, "you've compromised yourself completely. Your wife is a follower of the very man we've been sent to investigate."

The stroke seemed to tell.

"What do you think our superiors will say when you return to Qanar-Sharaj with her?" Nawhar asked. "How do you think they'll react to your report on Essaj?"

But Erim was quick to recover. "Why are you taking it for granted that Khalima's going to convert me?" he demanded. "What makes you think it won't be the other way round? If Essaj is a fraud or a heretic, we'll discover it. I'll recommend his indictment. And if I do that, who will suggest that I've been swayed by my wife?"

"But what if she *does* sway you, Erim? She's already seduced you."

"What is that to you?" Erim asked. "If I *were* converted, do you think I could successfully argue my case?"

"Never."

"*You've* already decided he's guilty, haven't you?"

"Let's just say that I'm unimpressed with what I've seen."

Yet hardly were the words out of Nawhar's lips when he remembered the incident at the wedding, his whole skull illuminated by Essaj's stare; even if Nawhar had found nothing in the experience to convince him that Essaj was the Expected One, he *had* been impressed, to say the least.

Then there were the miracles, of course. False or no, he had no explanation for them. . . .

He wondered if he should qualify his words, perhaps even retract them. He had not been lying, exactly; but if he said nothing, he would be acquiescing in the falsehood.

It struck him that he did not really care. Somehow that disturbed him more than the lying itself; he had an uneasy sense that he had crossed some sort of vague but dangerous threshold.

Yet how *could* he tell the truth? How could he afford to show the least trace of irresolution? He was the Last Sharajnaghi. The full weight of the Order was on his shoulders. He had to bring Essaj down, with or without Erim's help.

"Can it actually be that *you* can't see through him?" he went on, scrubbing at his scalp with his nails.

"Are we talking about the same man?" Erim asked. "Everything I've witnessed has only deepened the mystery. His powers far exceed those of any healer we've ever heard of. He casts out demons, *fallen angels,* without even raising his voice. If he's using magic, we've detected no sign of it. But if the miracles are genuine, then what do we make of this claim to divinity?"

"We use it to demonstrate the *falsity* of the miracles," Nawhar replied. "If indeed he makes such a claim, he's a heretic, pure and simple. There is one God. 'Hear, my people, the Lord is One.' And He is transcendent. *Completely* transcendent. The idea that he could become human is sheer absurdity. It is a spear pointed straight at the heart of our religion, a backsliding into paganism and God knows what else. . . ." He paused, studying Erim's face.

"Go on," Erim said, and laughed. "When you say something I disagree with, I'll stop you."

Nawhar almost laughed too. Of course Erim agreed with him. He was too intelligent to fall into any serious kind of error. If only he weren't so carnal.

So human.

"Put her aside, Erim," Nawhar said quietly. "For all our sakes, get rid of her."

The smile left Erim's face. "For the sake of our friendship," he said, "don't try to come between me and my wife."

He left the room.

Nawhar's scalp began to itch in earnest; rapidly the prickling spread to his chest and back.

"Deny the flesh," he whispered, scratching himself carefully, fighting the urge to rip his skin to shreds. "Deny the rot. . . ."

Furious, Erim thought of going back to his own chamber. But Khalima was making up for her lack of sleep, and he had no wish to wake her, particularly to subject her to a tirade about Nawhar. Guessing Sharif might still be watching the gate, he sought the outer courtyard instead.

Someone was sitting in the arch leading to the yard; as Erim drew closer, and his eyes adjusted to the glare through the opening, he saw that it was Essaj. Resting with his back against the righthand wall, he was carving something.

"Excuse me, Master," Erim said, as he neared the threshold.

"Certainly," said Essaj, withdrawing his long legs.

As Erim passed, he looked down into Essaj's lap. Essaj was fashioning some sort of animal. The wood was black; it could only be Numalian ebony. But for someone carving such hard material, Essaj was working very quickly, clasp-knife flying.

Erim stepped out into the courtyard. Mahir and Moussa were back at the gate; nearby, Sharif was lying flat on his back along the inside of the wall.

Closer to hand, Essaj's disciples were disputing heatedly about something; they seemed to be in exactly the same spot they had occupied when Erim first saw them yesterday.

"They spend more time arguing with each other than they do listening to me," Essaj said, behind him.

Erim did not quite know how to respond to this; he laughed politely, then crossed the yard. Sharif was fast asleep.

"Just sat down and went out like a light," Mahir said over his shoulder.

"We dragged him into the shade," Moussa added. "Must have had quite a night."

*Indeed,* Erim thought. He himself was totally exhausted. Given how energetic Khalima had been, he wondered if Zehowah was truly the more sensual of the two. Sharif gave every indication of having been put through the more difficult course; yet the sisters were evidently more similar than they seemed at first glance.

Yawning, looking at Sharif, Erim decided his friend had the right idea, and considered stretching out beside him; but he decided he'd much rather lie down with Khalima, whether or not she was asleep, and started back across the courtyard.

Essaj held up his carving as he approached. "What do you think?" he asked. "Catch."

Erim bobbled it out of the air and examined it.

*Surely you can't be this tired,* he told himself, amazed.

The figure was not merely done; it had been had brought to an incredible state of finish. The surface appeared to be polished, even though, as far as Erim knew, Essaj had only a knife. The surface was beautifully, even gratuitously, detailed.

Moreover, it was a scrupulously accurate representation of Ghaznavi's three-horned reptile.

"It's for you," Essaj said. "Wedding present."

"Thank you, Master," Erim said, feeling slightly dizzy. How had the man known that the horned beast was his favorite among the ancient creatures? Indeed, why did Essaj know anything about such creatures at all? Erim remembered the present at the wedding last night—the sailbacked carnivore, Ghaznavi's most outrageous fantasy. What game was Essaj playing with him?

"You know, Master," Erim said, "this figure bears a striking resemblance to a kind of creature—one that no longer exists—whose bones we Sharajnaghim have been study-ing. . . ."

"I invent animals," Essaj said. "It's a habit I acquired from my father."

Erim found the coincidence hard to accept. "You made up this creature?"

"Yes."

"You have no education in such matters? Ancient life, pet-rified bones, things like that?"

"I just do what I see my father doing."

"He's still alive?"

"Of course."

"I was under the impression that he was dead."

Essaj laughed. "You shouldn't believe everything you hear."

At that moment, the disputation between the disciples grew much more heated.

"*I'm* going to be first," a voice cried. "Everyone knows I'm going to be first!"

"Master!" several others called.

"I'd better attend to this," Essaj said, rising.

Erim wanted to follow, but knew he was far too tired to do a proper job of listening for heretical statements. His eyelids felt hot and scratchy.

Dragging off towards his room, he encountered Essaj's mother on the stairs.

"I see that my son made you a wedding present," Yasmin said, indicating the figure.

Erim had no desire to make conversation; still, he thought it best to indulge her in a few pleasantries.

"He has a marvellous talent," he said. "And as luck would have it, this carving's very much like a creature that's always fascinated me."

Yasmin nodded. "Essaj is very thoughtful."

An odd answer: was she saying that her son had settled on the horned reptile *deliberately*? Erim almost pressed her on the matter, but found himself distracted by the woman's unearthly loveliness. How was it possible that this youthful beauty was Essaj's mother?

"Is something wrong?" Yasmin asked.

"No," Erim answered, wondering what he had intended to ask her. "You know, I had a very interesting conversation with your son just now. Is it true that his father's still alive?"

Yasmin nodded.

"But I was told you're a widow."

"I am."

"But how—"

"Oh, I wasn't married to Essaj's father."

She admitted this without the least visible trace of shame. Erim was deeply embarrassed for her nonetheless. He cleared his throat.

"No?" he asked.

"I was married to a man named Yussef, as you might have heard. That is, I was betrothed to him before Essaj was conceived." She paused. "It's really quite a story."

"Did Yussef know he was not the father?" Erim asked, profoundly uncomfortable now.

"Of course he knew. I told him."

Erim tried not to wince. "And what did he make of that?"

"He didn't take it very well," Yasmin said.

"Understandable," Erim said.

"He considered exposing me to the law. But then the angel appeared to him."

"The angel."

"The same one who appeared to me."

"Ah," Erim said. "He appeared to you too?"

"Yes, but earlier. Before I conceived Essaj. It was late at night. A great light woke me, and there was the angel."

"I see," Erim said, nodding. "What did he . . . er . . . look like?"

"Very strange at first. Like wheels."

"Wheels?"

"Wheels and eyes. I don't know how to describe it better than that. But then he changed into a very handsome young man. 'Don't be afraid,' he said. 'You have found favor with God, and He has blessed you exceedingly. You will become pregnant and give birth to a son, and you will name him Essaj. He will be great and be called the Son of the Most High God.'

"Needless to say, I didn't know how to take this, exactly. 'I am a virgin,' I pointed out. 'How can this be?'

"'The Holy spirit will overshadow you,' the angel answered. 'God's power will rest upon you. And this is why the child will be called the Son of God.'"

"You're right," Erim said. "This *is* quite a story."

"I still wasn't sure I wasn't dreaming, but I decided not to question him. 'I am the Lord's servant,' I said, and the angel left me. I dropped straight back to sleep, and when I woke the next day, I told myself that none of it could possibly have happened.

"But I was pregnant all right, as I soon found out. And that's how I conceived Essaj."

"Remarkable," Erim said, thunderstruck, looking down at his feet.

"I know it's hard to believe," Yasmin said. "Yussef didn't believe it either. But when the angel told him I wasn't lying, he decided to marry me anyway. To protect me from the law."

"Let me see if I've been understanding you correctly," Erim said. "You're claiming that Essaj was conceived by God Himself."

"Yes," Yasmin said.

"That Yussef was only Essaj's stepfather, and that Essaj is *literally* the Son of God."

"Yes."

"Not the son of God the way all men are sons of God, but God's *actual* offspring."

"You're really quite clever," Yasmin said approvingly.

Erim began to wonder if that otherworldliness which so informed her beauty was merely a manifestation of some deep-seated madness.

*What devilish nonsense,* he thought, recalling the demoniac's father using precisely the same language.

"Oh, there's Terzif," Yasmin said. "It's been very pleasant talking to you, young man."

She started past the Sharajnaghi.

He looked round slowly, watching her descend the stairs.

Did she have any idea that she had just thrust her son several steps toward execution? True, Erim had not heard such heterodox dementia from Essaj. But it would never have occurred to Erim to ask Essaj if his father was a human being. A whole new—and potentially devastating—line of inquiry had just been revealed.

*Perhaps you're right after all, Nawhar,* Erim thought. But he was not going to pursue his questions now. Step by leaden step, he continued upstairs to bed.

✝

# Chapter 20

Awakened by a persistent nudging, Sharif opened his eyes to see Zehowah standing over him.

"If you sleep any longer, you'll miss supper," she said.

"Supper?" he said, sitting up. The courtyard was completely in shadow, though the sky above was still light. He ran his hands down his face. "I'd better wash up."

She accompanied him to their room. The window was open, a single strong beam of sunlight pouring through; splashing on the bleached cedar wall, it cast a mellow ochre glow over everything.

Sharif took off his tunic, wetting a cloth in the basin and wiping off his face and arms. But as he began washing his chest, he grew intensely aware of Zehowah's eyes upon him.

"You're embarrassing me," he said.

"After last night?" she said, leaning back against the door.

"It was dark," he said.

He heard a lock snick; then Zehowah crossed swiftly to the window and closed the shutters.

"What about supper?" Sharif asked, as she advanced upon him.

"We've an hour at least," she replied.

"Then why did you wake me up?"

"I thought you might have to wash," she answered, and slid her arms about his neck.

On their way down to the mansion's great hall, they met Erim and Khalima.

"Where's Nawhar?" Sharif asked Erim.

"Still in his room, I suppose."

"Did you tell him?"

"That we're married? Yes."

"How did he take it?"

"How do you think?"

Sharif laughed. "That badly, eh?"

They proceeded to the hall. Several of the disciples were gathered by the archway, among them two fellows named Anwar and Jalloud; as far as Sharif had been able to make out, they were Essaj's chief lieutenants, and vigorous, if not unfriendly, rivals. Anwar was stocky and balding, with a dense black beard; reminding Sharif of an older, taller version of Nawhar, Jalloud was thin and serious-looking, with greying hair and a fierce hooked nose.

"So, wizards," Jalloud said, "when does the questioning begin?"

"I was thinking tonight, perhaps," Erim replied. "If Master Essaj will allow me."

"Just don't make a nuisance of yourself over dinner," Anwar warned. "Yasmin hates discord at suppertime. It upsets her digestion."

"I understand you already interrogated her," Jalloud told Erim.

"That's hardly the word," Erim answered. "She was quite happy to speak to me."

"Did you learn anything?" Anwar asked.

"I did indeed."

"What did she tell you?"

"Why don't you ask *her*?" Erim replied. "In the meanwhile, could you please let us through?"

The disciples stepped aside.

"Enjoy your meal," Anwar said.

He sounded anything but sincere; nonetheless dinner, when it came, proved excellent—rice, tender chicken, beef in brown sesame sauce, and superb wine. Sharif thought Essaj was very fortunate to have an uncle as wealthy as Terzif, especially one who took such obvious pleasure in playing the good host.

Afterwards Terzif toasted the newlyweds, and called upon Essaj to bless them. Essaj rose, lifted his chalice, and said simply:

"My blessings upon them."

That was the kind of benediction Sharif preferred. *Short and sweet,* he thought. In spite of everything, he rather liked Essaj; a heretic and blasphemer the man might have been, but he certainly did have a way about him.

*Pity if we wind up sending him to the block.*

But Sharif had no intention of allowing himself to grow too fond of the man. The entire foundation of Sharif's conscience lay in his devotion to the Order. He believed in God because the Order taught that God existed; he believed heresy and blasphemy were sins because the Order held them so. And if the Order found against Essaj, that would be good enough for Sharif.

Of course, such a verdict would mean difficulties with Zehowah. If she refused to see reason, he would have to put her aside. She would not come between him and his duty.

Nevertheless, he fully expected her to come round. He was not sure he had the ability to convince her on his own, but there was always Erim. And Khalima, whom Erim would certainly be able to convince.

Zehowah's foot wandered casually against his—and casually onto it. She wanted to retire, plainly. But Sharif wished to hear Erim's conversation with Essaj; also to give him moral support. They were badly outnumbered. Nawhar had not appeared, though that was perhaps just as well. Nawhar was not known for his tact, and the situation was likely to get fairly ticklish as it was.

At length Yasmin excused herself.

"Please, son," she said, kissing Essaj on the cheek, "don't let things get too loud."

Most of the women left with her.

"Go on," Sharif told Zehowah. "I'll be up in a while."

She frowned but obeyed.

Khalima, however, remained at Erim's side. Some of the disciples looked askance at that, but if Essaj disapproved, he gave no sign. A hush fell over the hall; the disciples scowled at the Sharajnaghim, although Essaj and Terzif seemed perfectly at ease.

"So," said Essaj at last, addressing the wizards. "The time has come."

"You don't mind if I ask you a few questions, Master?" Erim inquired.

"Certainly not," Essaj replied.

Erim was silent for a few moments, apparently gathering his thoughts. Then he said:

"Yesterday my colleagues and I spoke with a man named Nihat. Do you know him?"

Essaj nodded. "Fatima's husband. There was a time when I counted him as a follower."

"Do you know why he turned away from you?"

"Yes."

"You recall the incident?"

"I was healing a paralytic. Nihat took exception to something I said."

"He told us you claimed the authority to forgive sins."

"So?"

"Did he accurately represent your words?"

Essaj answered without the slightest hesitation: "Yes."

"Are you aware of the implications of such words?"

Essaj smiled. "What implications are those?"

"Who can forgive sins but God alone?" Erim asked.

"You put that very well," Essaj answered, in a manner highly reminiscent of his mother's.

Erim pressed: "*Can* you forgive sins?"

"Which is easier," Essaj replied, "To say, 'Your sins are forgiven,' or to say, 'Get up and walk'?"

Erim nodded. "The same answer you gave the priests."

"Exactly," said Essaj.

"I think it is immediately obvious that it is far easier to heal than to forgive sins."

"Can you do either?" Essaj asked.

"No, but . . ."

"Then how would you know?"

Erim started a reply, then bit it back, staring at Essaj.

"There are many human healers," he said at last. "There is only one all-powerful redeemer God."

"Very true," Essaj answered. "But you betray your ignorance of Him. What power does it take to forgive a man's sins? It is a simple act of will. Any man can forgive a wrong done against him. But how many can heal?"

"But can *any* man forgive a wrong done against someone *else*?" Erim replied.

Essaj laughed. "Have you never heard of a judge showing mercy?"

"I never heard of a judge who could send a man to Hell."

"Men send themselves to Hell, Erim," Essaj replied. "Why do you doubt my doctrine? Do you doubt my works?"

"I doubt your works *because* I doubt your doctrine."

"But they are the proof. Do not be deceived. If they are from God, my doctrine is from God. If you cannot cast doubt on them, how can you cast doubt on me?"

Erim made no response.

Sharif had followed the exchange as closely as he could; he thought Erim had secured all the evidence necessary to indict Essaj. Essaj's arguments seemed quite lame, particularly that business about the judge and forgiving other men's sins.

Nonetheless, Erim's silence was thoroughly disquieting. Sharif knew that Erim was far wiser than he—what hidden truth had Erim perceived in Essaj's words? Sharif's suspicion that Erim had been dealt some kind of blow was soon confirmed as Erim switched to another line of inquiry:

"Your mother told me a fascinating story, Master," Erim resumed.

"She has many," Essaj answered.

"The essence of it was that you were conceived by God Himself," Erim said. "That the Almighty was your sire, the way my father was mine."

Essaj's smile broadened, his teeth beautifully straight and white; it was a very likeable smile, Sharif thought, but really rather foolish.

"Once again, it comes back to my works, Erim," Essaj said. "You know that I healed you. You've sampled my wine. You've seen that I can cast out demons like *that*—" He snapped his fingers. "And yet you cannot believe my mother. Are you calling her a liar? I assure you, her character is immaculate."

"To be honest, Master," Erim answered, "I don't know what to make of her."

"Then it's no surprise you don't know what to make of her son!" Khalima cried suddenly.

"Your wife has a point there, you know," Essaj told Erim.

"Are you God or God's son?" Erim demanded sarcastically.

"Does a child take after its parents?" Khalima shot back.

Erim turned with an exasperated expression. "Was I speaking to you?"

"Answer the question!" Khalima replied.

Essaj clapped his hands, laughing with delight.

"Of course a child is human because its parents are human," Erim answered.

*Ah*, Sharif thought. *So that's what she was driving at*.

"But if you follow that logic," Erim continued, "God's son would be a second God. And there is only one." He looked back at Essaj. "Only one!"

"Mind my works, Erim," Essaj said, taking an apple from a bowl on the table and biting into it with a loud crunch.

"Minding them is not my field," Erim replied.

"It's mine," came Nawhar's voice from the back of the hall.

Sharif turned; how long had he been standing there?

"And believe me, *Master*," Nawhar went on, "I will pay very close attention to your miracles. And I will discover the secrets behind them."

Essaj took another bite. "I have no doubt of it."

Anwar stood up angrily, pointing to Nawhar. "Must we tolerate the presence of these unbelievers, Master?"

"They have their parts to play, Anwar," Essaj answered. "Sit down, please."

Anwar complied. Another hush descended.

"If I might be excused—" Erim said, rising. "I think I should speak with my comrades—"

"Of course," said Essaj and Terzif, at once.

Sharif followed Erim, Khalima and Nawhar from the hall.

"I hate to say it," he began, "but I think he got the better of you, Erim."

"An embarrassing performance," Nawhar seconded.

"How so?" Erim demanded. "He proved his heresy beyond a shadow of a doubt. . . ."

"But what else did he prove to you, Erim?" Nawhar answered. "It seemed to me that you were wavering in there. As though he reached you with those absurd arguments of his."

"Absurd?" Khalima broke in. "*You're* the one who's absurd, insisting the Master's guilty even though you can't challenge his miracles."

Nawhar gritted his teeth. "Send her upstairs, Erim."

"Are you going to listen to him?" Khalima asked her husband.

"Come with me," Erim said, leading her towards the steps.

"Is yours better trained?" Nawhar asked Sharif.

"More than you'll ever know," Sharif replied.

Nawhar rolled his eyes in disgust. "Thank God."

"And Erim will bring Khalima around. You watch."

"What faith you have," Nawhar said.

# Chapter 21

Essaj and his followers spent the next morning preparing for their journey to Thangura. Terzif's household collected to see the company off; there were many embraces and farewells.

"The next time you come," Terzif told his nephew, "we'll be in the new house."

Overhearing that, Nawhar turned to Erim. "He's selling the mansion?"

"So it seems," Erim replied.

"No," Khalima said. "He's having it made into a hospital."

"A hospital?" Nawhar asked.

"For the poor."

Nawhar smirked. "And how big is his new house?"

"I'm told it's much more modest," Khalima answered.

"How very moving," Nawhar said, returning his attention to Essaj, who had come at last to Yasmin.

"You will be careful, won't you, son?" she asked.

Essaj's expression grew very sad; it seemed to Nawhar that there was something in it that went well beyond the sorrow of mere parting. Essaj was not a fool—he probably knew how dangerous Thangura would be for him. Had he resigned himself to martyrdom? How like a heretic!

"I'll try my best, mother," Essaj replied. "But I intend to do my father's will. We've already spoken about this, several times."

She began weeping furiously. Dropping to one knee, she kissed his hands. Nawhar was quite revolted—which was the parent after all? Face reddening, Essaj seemed to take exception as well.

"Mother," he said. "Please. Among other things, I am your child."

*What incredible cant,* Nawhar concluded, once he recovered from the initial shock. How could anyone reconcile such humility with Essaj's supposed Godhood? Everything about the man simply reeked. Nawhar found himself practically choking on the fumes.

Yasmin rose, wiping her eyes. "If there's trouble, you will send for me—"

"Of course, Mother," Essaj said. "Farewell."

They embraced; then he led the way through the gate.

Several disciples' spouses were along for the journey, and went mounted on donkeys; Essaj and his men were all on foot. Erim and Sharif helped their wives into the saddle, then led their own mounts.

"Why not ride?" Nawhar asked his comrades from horseback, much preferring to look down on Essaj's riff-raff. "Trying not to put on airs, is that it? Do you actually think you'll blend in?"

They did not seem to think the question worth answering. But Nawhar ultimately joined them on the pavement—it was simply much easier to listen.

He tried to work his way to the head of the company, but the lesser disciples were swarming about Essaj, asking questions. Falling back, he found himself closer to Anwar and Jalloud.

"Admit it, Jalloud," Anwar was saying. "You were wrong about Terzif. The Master prevailed upon him after all."

"About the hospital, yes," Jalloud said. "But I've seen the

little house Terzif bought. It may not be as great a mansion. But it's still a mansion.''

"His sons and their families live with him," Anwar answered. "Not to mention the Lord's mother. They have to have a roof over their heads.''

"Essaj told me I should sell everything I had and give it to the poor," Jalloud said. "*Everything*.''

"We're his disciples," Anwar answered. "The chosen few. Besides, Essaj seemed satisfied with Terzif's sacrifice. Who are we to complain?''

"Indeed," Jalloud said sourly. "What good would it do? Essaj doesn't listen to us.''

"That's right," Anwar said. "*We* listen to him. We're *his* disciples. And let me tell you, Jalloud. He who listens best will sit at the Lord's Right Hand when he comes into his kingdom.''

"I listen better than you do, Anwar," Jalloud replied. "Which is why I think Terzif was treated far too leniently—''

Without warning, he rounded upon Nawhar. The Sharajnaghi halted: Jalloud's eyes burned with hatred, and Nawhar wondered if the fellow was going to attack.

"Are you writing all this down, wizard?" Jalloud demanded.

"I have a good memory," Nawhar answered.

"Leave him alone, Jalloud," said Anwar.

Jalloud strode off with him.

Nawhar started forward again.

*The day is coming, heretics,* he thought. *For you and your devil-ridden Master.*

The company passed from the city, pausing at midday to eat beside a still blue lake; continuing on, they reached the outskirts of a village nestled among the cedars.

There a noisy crowd had gathered; before them, robes ripped open, breasts bare, a woman cowered against a low wall, both her eyes swollen and blacked.

"What's happening?" Nawhar asked a villager.

"Stoning," the fellow replied enthusiastically.

The woman tried to climb over the wall. At a nod from the local priest, a man with a club rushed forward and struck her on the head with it. She sank down whimpering.

"What did she do?" Essaj called to the priest.

"She was taken in adultery," the other answered.

Jaw outthrust, a man strutted up to Essaj, the very picture of righteous rage.

"I heard you preach forgiveness last week, on this very spot!" he cried, and pointed to the woman. "That's my wife. Should I forgive *her*? Forgive the whore who dishonored my bed?"

"Yes," Essaj replied.

"I have an infant son!" the husband shrieked. "I don't even know if he's *mine*!"

Tossing a stone into the air, he snatched it back—and hurled it at his wife. It struck her side with a loud slap. She moaned and coughed, curling up on the ground.

Nawhar watched her agonies with some satisfaction. He had no qualms about the law taking its course in such a case. Sins of the flesh he found particularly detestable. True, the Order taught that they were the least damnable of serious transgressions; but it was no more correct about that than it was about marriage.

He wondered when the crowd would follow the husband's example. What were the bumpkins waiting for? A signal from the priest, perhaps?

The holy man had placed himself in front of Essaj. "The Law is clear," he said. "She must die."

"Very well," Essaj replied. He looked silently at the husband.

The man had already picked up another stone, but under the pressure of Essaj's stare, made no further move.

"Let he who is without sin cast the next stone," Essaj said.

The priest's face went livid. "Would you overturn the Law itself?" he demanded.

"Are you without sin?" Essaj said.

The priest snarled and bent for a rock. Rising, he locked eyes with Essaj again.

"Are you?" Essaj asked.

There was a clack. Nawhar looked towards the husband. The man's stone had fallen from his hand, striking the rocks at his feet.

As though desperate to wrench his gaze from Essaj, the priest looked as well; seeing that the husband had given in, the priest seemed to lose his nerve too.

Nawhar was furious. *Cowards,* he thought. Were they actually going to let the whore go?

It crossed his mind that *he* should hurl the next stone. He would show Essaj what the Last Sharajnaghi was capable of—

Essaj turned slowly in his direction. Surely the man had read his thoughts—again Nawhar remembered the incident at the wedding, the light in his skull. He had no intention of putting himself through that again. He averted his eyes before Essaj could train his gaze full upon him.

Yet when Nawhar looked again, Essaj was striding towards the adultress; he was suddenly unsure if Essaj had been turning his way to begin with. Nawhar felt relieved, yet somehow slighted. Was breaking his will a task beneath the Son of God?

Essaj lifted the woman to her feet. Her legs were unsteady, and she was bleeding profusely from the head. Essaj covered her with his cloak, then passed a hand over her brow.

Immediately she straightened, her eyes no longer swollen. She searched her scalp with her fingers, as though examining herself for a wound that was no longer there.

Nawhar told himself that he should go forward and search for the gash himself; but his feet were rooted to the spot.

*You're a coward too,* he told himself. *Every bit as spineless as those yokels. . . .*

"How . . . how can I thank you, My Lord?" the woman asked Essaj.

"Just go," he answered. "And sin no more."

She reached out, trying to touch his face.

"Please, Master," she said. "Let me come with you."

Nawhar felt a spasm of revulsion at the spectacle. Her eyes were shining, her lips parted; it was disgustingly plain how she intended to thank him, tonight perhaps. . . .

Essaj slapped her hands away. Seizing her by the hair, he thrust that ruddy peasant face up next to hers.

"*And . . . sin . . . no more!*" he said.

His hands opened.

She staggered back, gaping.

"Go," he said, shooing her farther off.

She whirled and sprinted away into the woods.

But Essaj's show of self-restraint did not mitigate Nawhar's loathing for him in the slightest. How dare the man disappoint him?

Essaj stood silently, facing the crowd. Slowly it began to break up. Before long, only the husband remained.

"Forgive me, Lord," he said.

"Forgive *her*," Essaj replied.

*You abomination,* Nawhar thought.

The company left the valley long before nightfall; with no villages nearby, they made camp atop a hill. Long after the others were asleep, Sharif and Zehowah sat up talking, wrapped in a single great blanket. The night had grown quite chill, but Sharif found the effect rather pleasant so long as he was bundled up with his wife.

"I wonder what my father will think of you and Erim," Zehowah said.

"Your father," Sharif answered. She had not mentioned him for some time.

"You still don't believe, do you?" There was no edge to the question, only a certain weary amusement.

"That Essaj will raise him from his grave?" he replied. "No, I'm afraid I don't."

"The miracles you've witnessed haven't convinced you?"

He wanted to answer that she hadn't washed the corpse, seen just how far her father had gone in a mere matter of hours; but he restrained himself.

"I have no business being convinced of them," he answered at last. "Nawhar's the expert."

"But you know more about sorcery than he does," Zehowah said. "Wouldn't Essaj have to be a sorcerer to perform such tricks? And wouldn't you be better at detecting magic than Nawhar?"

"It's not as simple as that," Sharif replied. "Exposing false miracles is a field all by itself. There's a vast literature on sham prophets and their methods. More important still, Nawhar's very good at seeing the worst in people, and imagining new ways to be dishonest. I'm not like that.''

She laid her head on his shoulder. "No, you're not, are you?''

"He's also much more intelligent than I am, in a broad sort of way," Sharif said. "My talents are really rather narrow. For some reason, God decided to give me a head for spells, but very little else. Numbers, logic, philosophy—I can deal with them, but it's an effort. So far as I know, I can strike my enemies more powerfully than any sorcerer who's ever lived. But don't ask me about the history of the Order."

She nuzzled him. "You've some other talents."

"I'm glad you think so," he said. "They must truly be inborn. I certainly didn't have any experience."

"I think we're very well matched," Zehowah said. "*I* very nearly had some—experience. Several times, as a matter of fact. But something always stopped me." She was silent for a time. "I was so glad when the Master saved that woman. I could imagine myself doing something wrong."

"You can imagine yourself betraying me?" Sharif asked, wondering if he should be angry.

"No," she said. "Never. But you know how it is with young people, before they're married. How it was with us in the garden. We could have been flogged for that, you know."

"If we'd gone ahead with it," Sharif objected. "And if there had been someone to press charges."

"Even so," Zehowah said, "I like to think that I could be forgiven."

"What's the point of the Law if someone can break it and escape punishment?"

"I don't know," Zehowah replied. "But I think people aren't perfect. And that the Law must take account of that. I believe in mercy. I know that might not sound like much, but the thought of forgiveness moves me."

"Whatever moves you is good enough for me," Sharif said. He looked round at their slumbering companions. "Now let's go off a dozen more yards or so, and I'll show you what I believe in.''

They stood, walking awkwardly through the darkness in their blanket. Coming to a likely spot, behind some rocks, they lay down.

"I wonder if it's possible to get tired of this?" Zehowah asked.

"I don't know," Sharif said. "But I think we owe it to ourselves to try and find out."

As dawn broke, and Sharif was trying to decide whether to open his eyes, someone nudged him. At first he thought it must be Zehowah; then he realized she was lying next to him. He looked up, squinting.

"Wasting daylight," said Essaj. "Aren't you two a bit far from the fire?"

"We—er, had something to discuss," Sharif said.

"I see."

"You have no objections, do you, Master?"

"You're man and wife, aren't you?" Essaj replied. "Some *are* made eunuchs for the sake of God, but it seems you're not among them."

"I suppose not," Sharif replied.

"Yet what of your vows, Sharif?" Essaj asked.

Sharif raised himself on one elbow. "My vows?"

"You made a promise, did you not?"

Sharif began to feel uncomfortable. "Yes. But no one in the Order really cares anymore. . . ."

"It concerns *me*, Sharif," Essaj answered.

*And why should I trouble myself about that?* Sharif almost answered. But even though he had no idea why, Essaj's opinion did seem oddly important to him.

"Are you saying I should put Zehowah aside, Master?" Sharif asked.

With that, Zehowah rose from under the blanket, a horrified expression on her face.

"You *blessed* us, Master," she said. "You didn't condemn us."

"Nor do I condemn you now," Essaj answered. He smiled.

"After all, my wine *is* strong. You're one flesh, and I hate putting aside." He fixed Sharif with his stare. "But don't swear oaths you might not want to keep, Sharajnaghi."

He walked back towards the others.

Zehowah loosed a long trailing breath. "I was so worried for a moment there," she said.

Sharif barely heard her. For some reason, Essaj's advice had sent him back to the tomb at Bishah, the fight with Horde.

*I call you traitors because that is what you are,* the giant had said. Sharif had completely forgotten the demon's words; but now the prophecy reverberated through his mind.

*You don't know it yet, but the seeds are there. You will betray everything you love. Your friends, your Order . . . One of you will stand back as his love is slaughtered. Two will deliver the third up to be slain. One will kill another. And one of you will fight on* my *side when the final battle is joined. . . .*

"Final battle?" Sharif whispered. What had Horde meant?

"Sharif?" Zehowah asked.

He looked at her.

*One will stand back as his love is slaughtered. . . .*

Foreboding struck him like a physical blow.

The company continued south along the Bishah road, making good progress under an untroubled sky. Essaj was welcomed in the next village they came to, and preached a sermon to a small crowd; Erim found the message sound if unremarkable, although the audience seemed absolutely riveted.

*Just as well,* he thought. If indeed they had never heard of the Golden Rule, he hoped they took it to heart.

The next village was a different matter altogether. Essaj and his followers were reviled by practically everyone; they were not even offered a drink of water.

"Why is everyone so angry with Essaj?" Erim asked the one person who would speak to him, an old woman.

The crone spat in Essaj's direction. "The last time he was here," she said, "he said we could eat shellfish!"

Erim winced in disgust. Was she actually telling the truth? Surely such a pronouncement would disqualify Essaj from Godhead all by itself.

Erim also wondered why the question had arisen to begin with. The village was well up in the mountains after all.

The company spent the night beneath a huge overhang of rock, descending the following day from the cedar-clad uplands into the foothills.

"We're getting close," Khalima said. "Aren't we, Erim?"

Erim nodded.

"We're coming, Father!" Zehowah laughed. "And we bring the Lord!"

The sisters seemed less able to contain themselves with each passing mile. If they had the least doubt that Essaj would raise their father, they showed no sign of it.

Presently the company mounted the crest of the hill overlooking the inn. The sisters cried with joy. Erim saw Nawhar give them a quick cold stare; he felt a flare of wrath at his friend, if friend he still considered him. Surely the sisters were merely mistaken, and with good excuse—Essaj was such a brilliant fraud. Why did Nawhar insist on reading such wickedness into their pathetic hopes?

They started down the slope. When they reached the inn, Khalima practically leaped from her horse.

"Now you will see!" she told Erim.

He dismounted, shaking his head sadly.

Zehowah beckoned Essaj. "Over here, Master!" she cried, dashing with her sister to the grave. "Father's over here!" She sounded as though he had awakened already, and was only waiting.

"For a full week," Erim muttered. "Under three feet of earth."

He flinched inwardly to think of the disappointment she and his wife were about to suffer. Indeed, ever since they had journeyed from this place, the two had apparently staved off all grief with their astonishing faith. Now they would realize what they had lost. So long held in abeyance, the storm was about to break.

Or was it? Could it possibly be that their confidence was justified? Erim dismissed the possibility. It remained incon-

ceivable to him that Essaj could restore life to the thing that
had been laid in that grave. Erim had never seen anything that
evoked the permanence, the *omnipotence* of death as perfectly
as the gravel-imprinted face of Khaldun Al-Maari.

"At last," said Nawhar. "How I've waited for this! A *real*
challenge for God, eh?"

The Sharajnaghim approached the grave. Essaj was kneeling
by its side.

"Shouldn't we dig him up, Master?" Khalima asked.

"There would be a stench," Essaj replied.

"But, Master—" Zehowah began.

Motioning her to be silent, Essaj lowered his face, uttering
a low humming sound.

Nawhar laughed quietly. Erim had never heard Nawhar laugh
before; dry and bloodless, the sound was quite as strange in
its own way as that emanating from Essaj.

Essaj drew his right arm back, staring intently at the ground.
Then his hand drove straight into the grave with a noise like
a plunging spade.

The sisters gasped; Erim watched in amazement. Whatever
else happened, the sight of the man sinking his arm so effortlessly into the stony soil was wondrous enough.

The limb vanished instantly to the elbow. Another thrust,
and the dirt was almost to Essaj's shoulder; his sleeve bunched
against the surface.

"Khaldun," he whispered into the earth, face nearly touching it. "Wake, Khaldun."

Erim shook his head at the insanity of it.

Slowly Essaj pried himself back up, his sleeve uncrumpling
as his shoulder lifted.

*I refuse to believe,* Erim thought.

Essaj's limb was withdrawn to the elbow now.

*He's just a man,* Erim told himself.

Now to mid-forearm.

*Not God.*

Visible beneath the hanging fringe of the sleeve, Essaj's wrist
appeared, streaked with dirt.

*Not God's son—*

Erim glimpsed Essaj's knuckles. They were scraped raw, red and filthy. For a moment, Essaj paused; he drew a deep breath.

Erim became aware that his pulse was racing madly in his throat; he felt his heart would crack from the suspense.

*If my works are from God—*

Bones cracking audibly, Essaj resumed his effort.

Locked around his, another hand appeared.

*Then my doctrine is from—*

Essaj arched up from the ground with an explosive grunt. The grave erupted in dust and dirt.

Swiping grit from his astonished eyes, Erim saw a figure standing upright in the hole, shrouded in a blanket, one arm extended, protruding through a ragged hole in the fabric.

Essaj stepped back.

Khalima and Zehowah hurled themselves into the grave, ripping at the blanket. The covering fell away.

Khaldun's features were still printed with the gravel marks, but his eyes were open, blinking as though the light pained him after so much darkness. Plainly bewildered, he sat down on the side of his grave, rocking helplessly as his daughters kissed and embraced him.

"Enough of that, women," Essaj said, wiping his hand. "Give him something to eat."

Erim felt as though he had been struck by lightning.

Panting, he looked over at Nawhar. Grimacing, eyes bulging, Nawhar was scratching his cheeks furiously with both hands, dragging bloody furrows in his skin.

# Jack L. Chalker
## "A POWERFUL STORYTELLER"
—Orson Scott Card

## The Changewinds Trilogy

**Imagine winds like no other. Altering, transforming, and creating life wherever they travel . . .**

\_\_BOOK 1: WHEN THE CHANGEWINDS BLOW    0-441-88081-9/$3.95
\_\_BOOK 2: RIDERS OF THE WINDS    0-441-72351-9/$3.95
\_\_BOOK 3: WAR OF THE MAELSTROM    0-441-10268-9/$3.95

## The Quintara Marathon

**Three very different empires exist alongside one another, maintaining a delicate balance of power. Their only link: a strange, recurring legend of a horned demon...**

\_\_BOOK 1: THE DEMONS AT RAINBOW    0-441-69992-8/$3.95
          BRIDGE